MEGALODON
VS.
COLOSSAL SNAKE

A NOVEL BY MICHAEL COLE

SEVERED PRESS
HOBART TASMANIA

MEGALODON V COLOSSAL SNAKE

WWW.SEVEREDPRESS.COM

ISBN: 978-1-922323-56-9

CHAPTER 1

Eric Wesley twisted in his bunk. The damn spring was prodding his back again. It was sticking out right in the center of the mattress, forcing him to alternate sleeping in an odd angle or curve his body to avoid the annoying prick. Neither was suitable for a man who preferred sleeping on his back.

Seven million dollars to repurpose this damn boat, and they couldn't even install decent bunks.

Eric rolled to his left side and stared out into his tiny dark cabin. Silver moonlight streaked through the window, reflecting the vast ocean outside. He could hear the waves splashing against the hull. Any marine biologist never got tired of such a sound. However, for some, being at sea took a little getting used to, despite their love for the ocean. Eric was one of those, and he felt pathetic because of it, especially since this was only a thirty-hour voyage from Massachusetts to Florida. Comparatively speaking, he was barely at sea.

Then again, what did he expect? He stared at his Master's diploma, shuddering on his little countertop table with the ship's vibrations. Written in black bold italics were the words *University of Ohio*. Aside from a handful of personally funded trips to the coast, he had barely seen the ocean until a couple of months ago. Luckily, Gundrum Industries wasn't concerned with his seafaring skills. They just wanted someone knowledgeable with the behaviors of sea life, and who could handle the role of a caretaker for various organisms. It wasn't the grandest of career choices for someone of his background, but the pay matched that of the highest institutions for researchers with multiple years of experience. Plus, he needed to pay for his doctorate somehow. Student loan debt had piled up to the point of being overwhelming. He found himself envying people who found decent careers with only two-year degrees and ten percent of the debt.

Of course, he didn't expect the magnitude of what he'd be responsible for. And, as if reminding him of its presence, it struck the bulkhead, sending a vibration up into his cabin. It wasn't unusual; the specimen often swam in circles in a relatively enclosed space. His supervisor, Dr. Gina Hutson, had anticipated this, and warned his employer of the risks of shipping it to the facility in Florida. Despite her warnings, Dr. Gundrum ordered Project 9 to be loaded onto the *Truth Seeker* and ordered it delivered to Gundrum Industries. Why he needed it there so badly, Eric didn't know. But Gundrum was nice enough to add a five-thousand dollar bonus to his paycheck for going along and caring for the specimen during the thousand mile trip.

Wide awake now, he checked his watch. 4:13 a.m.

"Roughly ninety miles to go by now. Maybe less," he said to himself. He straightened out on his back…and felt the sting of that freaking spring. "Son-of-a—" Eric nearly leapt out of his bunk. This time it got him good. He reached under his white t-shirt and felt the tiny hole in his skin. He retracted his hand and looked at the blood on his fingertips. "Great. Might have to put in for a tetanus shot," he muttered.

Well, if this is the worst of my troubles, I guess I can't really complain. Five-grand in a day, on top of a ninety-thousand dollar salary? I suppose I can handle a little prick. He smiled at the thought. Many of his classmates were struggling to find work that paid more than breadcrumbs. Even for people with doctorates, it was growing more difficult to find steady placement in this field, and here he was just shy of making five figures.

Life could be worse. Right?

A tremendous boom rocked the ship to port. The room suddenly shifted, the floor now a forty-five degree incline. Eric fell against the bulkhead, absorbing the blow with his shoulder. The ship shifted back, throwing him back into the center of the room.

Eric regained his balance, his mind racing.

The hell just hap—

Another impact rocked the ship again. Again, the room rotated, throwing Eric against the wall. Alarms were going off now. He could hear running feet moving down the passageways. Men were yelling, some in a panic, others barking instructions. He only made out a few words.

"The cargo hold!"

Eric caught his breath. The impacts had come from inside the ship. Only one thing was powerful enough to rock a five-hundred foot ship like that. He quickly threw on a pair of pants, then ran for the door. He stepped back into the passageway, only to nearly be run down by a group of crew members.

He saw another sailor following them. In his hand was a .243 Winchester Bolt-Action rifle. As the *Truth Seeker* wasn't an international merchant ship, it was able to get away with having firearms on board. Of course, it wasn't Gundrum that demanded a small armory on board, rather, it was the Captain. Traveling this close to the mainland, it wasn't pirates he was worried about.

"Hey!" He grabbed the crewmember by the shoulders, stopping him. "What the hell's going on?"

"It's your fish, doc! It's going nuts!"

They were always calling him 'Doc', which he always felt the need to correct them on. But this wasn't the time.

"Where's the Captain?" he said.

"On the bridge. He's ordering us to kill it!"

"With that?!" Eric pointed at the gun. "Good luck with that, sailor. Besides, the guy paying for this trip won't have it."

"He can kiss my ass, Doc," the crewmember said. A third impact rolled the ship again. Both men struck the bulkhead, then stumbled back as the ship righted itself. The crewmember, wide-eyed, shook his head. "I'm not getting killed for your playing with nature!" He turned on his heel and started running down the corridor.

"Damn it," Eric muttered, then ran after him. Deafening alarms continued ringing throughout the ship, making it hard to think. With all the chaos, Eric had practically lost all sense of direction. He simply followed the crewmember with the rifle down the series of passageways, eventually finding a stairwell. He followed the crewmember down the steps, while a couple of other sailors followed closely behind him. One held a .38 caliber revolver, the other a rifle similar to the other.

Gunfire echoed from within the ship. Surprisingly, their sounds were nearly drowned out by tremendous watery waves, followed by sounds of men screaming. Eric's heart leapt into his throat as a large crashing sound swept through the vessel. It wasn't an impact like before; this one sounded like a collapsing bridge.

He reached the bottom of the stairwell and followed the crewmember out the door. They stepped onto a catwalk overlooking the cargo hold. Thirty feet below was a giant pool of water, nearly three hundred feet in length, and half-that in width. It swirled as though caught in a huge vortex. Debris clanged against the bulkheads as they whipped around in a wide circle.

It was then that Eric's eyes registered that a portion of the starboard catwalk was missing. He stared across the pool at several meters of metal passageway sloped downward, the end of which was frayed where a connection section had broken off into the pool. And then, he remembered the gunfire he heard…and that there were no crewmembers present firing rifles. Except for the men he came with.

They spread out along the long metal footbridge, gazing in horror at the swirling debris below. Eric searched the raging water with his eyes. Then he saw it. Between two large metal fragments was a seven-foot fin, slicing the water. Under that fin was a torpedo-shaped mass, weighing eighty tons, going around-and-around at frightening speed.

Megalodon.

Eric didn't know what was happening. Was it acting out of hunger? He had fed it before retiring to his cabin. Then again, the creature proved to be hungry almost constantly. Dr. Hutson had warned about its high metabolism, and how violent it had proven to be when requiring sustenance.

Or perhaps, it just craved freedom. Many times, in its aquarium in the Massachusetts facility, did it strike the walls, as though intent on freeing itself. It probably sensed the ocean outside. A monster as powerful as the megalodon was never meant to be contained. It was meant to thrive in the open water, a king of its domain.

Or maybe—Eric looked at the broken catwalk, lacking the numerous souls it previously contained—it just wanted to kill.

It turned the arc at the forward side, then traveled the short distance to stern under what remained of the starboard catwalk. Suddenly, it turned to its left, and with a flick of its enormous caudal fin, it crashed hard into the bulkhead directly under Eric.

The impact shook the vessel—a vessel many times the creature's size and weight. The crewmembers fell to their knees, doing whatever they could to shift themselves away from the guardrail. Eric, on the other hand, grabbed the bar and leaned out as far as he could. The shark turned away, a large wave taking its place. It splashed high, soaking the caretaker. Ignoring the sting in his eyes, he looked at the large bulkhead underneath him. It was heavily dented outward. Several creases lined the steel. He looked around. There were no other points of impact that he could see. The megalodon was striking this same exact spot. It was trying to free itself.

"Jesus!" he said. More crewmembers arrived from other stairwells and took positions on the stern and forward stairwells. Some had rifles in hand, while others were there simply to observe. Before Eric could protest, his ears were struck by loud cracks. Bullets made tiny, but violent splashes in the water. Some of them struck the shark's thick skin, which, unbeknownst to the crewmembers, was tougher than Kevlar. The loud gunfire and repeated stings of the projectiles spurred the megalodon's violent frenzy further. The beast swiped its huge caudal fin. In that same moment, it crashed into the forward bulkhead. The ship pitched as though a bomb had detonated underneath, the sailors overhead falling about.

Eric watched in horror as many of them were flung over the railing. Their screams vanished in an instant, drowned out by the watery waves. Rolling water threw them about. One let out a cry as the current hurled him right into a section of catwalk. His head collided with its edge, cleaving his skull inward. The water turned bright red all around him.

The megalodon whipped around, immediately picking up the alluring scent. In the span of a heartbeat, it closed the distance and brought its jaws down on the dead crewmember. Teeth minced his upper torso, severing everything under the shoulders. Other crewmembers shouted in horror, witnessing their companion's head and shoulders free fall from the jaws, and then scoop up a moment later.

Other crewmembers swam for their lives. The megalodon felt their rapid heartbeats and struggling motions through its lateral line. Its grey snout broke the surface. Its jaw opened nine feet, lined with rows of seven-inch serrated teeth. One of the sailors disappeared into its gullet, though his screams continued as he entered its immense stomach. The shark jerked its head to the right, snatching another crewmember. The teeth came down on his abdomen and lower back simultaneously. Like garden scissors to a weed stem, they sliced the man in half, flinging his upper body several feet ahead, trailing intestines.

The megalodon snatched the remains and swallowed, then angled itself to the left. It swung its tail and slammed into the bulkhead.

Eric fell forward, barely keeping himself from falling over the guardrail. As he caught himself, his eyes found the cavity in the bulkhead. Some of the creases had split, revealing the ocean outside. It was breaking through! Even he had underestimated the meg's strength. The damn thing was smashing through a twenty-millimeter hull.

Those rifles and handguns had no chance of stopping it. Nor did he have any needles thick enough to penetrate its skin to inject tranquilizer. Escape was inevitable at this point. Project 9 would be out in the open sea, free to kill at its leisure. And if he learned anything from the last few minutes, it was that this beast was more destructive than even his research of the species had indicated. Fishing boats, yachts, even some of the smaller merchant ships would be in grave danger. Oceanic researchers tracking hammerheads and orca pods could possibly find themselves in its path.

The only one thing Eric Wesley could do at this point was track its movements. Luckily, there was a tag in the shark's dorsal fin, which would allow them to track its movements and recapture it…

The shark breached as it snatched another sailor. Eric's stomach churned. It wasn't the horrible carnage that disturbed him this time. He saw the megalodon's fin. The tag's bright orange color should've been easy to spot. But no, there was only dark grey, denticle-covered skin. The shark must've scrapped the tag off during its rampage.

"No! No!" he muttered. The shark struck again. The breaches widened. Streams of ocean water poured into the cargo hold. Eric held firm to the guardrail as the ship shuddered, then made a mad dash for the stairwell.

"Where are you going?!" one of the crewmembers shouted, as if Eric's presence had any influence on the shark's actions. He ignored the idiot and ascended up the stairwell. Now, alarms were going off everywhere. Men were running back and forth through the passageways. In the confusion, he had lost sense of direction.

He grabbed a sailor running by. "Hey! Take me to the armory!"

"I can't! We're taking on water! Captain's ordered us to abandon ship!" the sailor said. Eric slapped him across the face then pulled him close. The man looked him in the eye, his face red with shock.

"The Captain made me store my harpoon rifle in the armory," Eric said. "I need to get a tracking device on that shark! If I don't, we won't be able to track it. Thus, we won't be able to stop it from killing anyone it comes across. Now, take me to the goddamned armory!"

The sailor stammered. For a moment, it looked as though he would simply continue on his way to the main deck.

"This way," he said. They ran sternward, winding through a series of connecting passageways. Something rocked deep below, sounding like a distant boom of thunder. There was another sound of crashing metal and screaming men. Finally, they arrived at the armory. Its door had been left wide open. It wasn't any larger than his cabin. In fact, it *was* a cabin, refitted for storing a few rifles. He went to the cabinet in the rear and opened it. His harpoon case fell out, striking his forehead with one of its corners. Muttering various curse words, Eric steadied himself and opened the case, revealing the harpoon gun. He assembled the stock and receiver, then grabbed one of the twelve-inch harpoons.

"Shit! The tracker is in my quarters!" he said aloud. There was nobody there to hear. The crewmember had already departed. It didn't matter. He could find his way from there. Weapon in hand, he dashed out of the armory and ran to port, finding the passageway where his quarters was located. He yanked the door and immediately saw that his belongings were scattered on the deck. Among them was a black suitcase containing an additional tracker that, now more than ever, he was so happy he didn't neglect bringing along.

He opened the case and found the orange tag. He attached it to the harpoon and loaded it into the gun.

The ship rocked again. Crashing metal echoed through the ship, followed by a tidal wave of water. The boat shifted hard to port, throwing all hands against bulkheads and deck railings. Eric found himself near his window, having broken the fall with his arms. A scream caused him to look out. In that same moment, the stream of moonlight flashed as something fell off the deck. Eric looked down. In the thrashing water were at least six men swimming for dear life. Directly below, he could see something sticking out of the ship. It was a flap of hull, bent outward like a flower petal.

Eric darted into the passageway, initially going for the stairwell leading to the cargo hold. He stopped and turned around, realizing he wouldn't get there in time. He ran sternward until finding a small stairwell leading to the main deck. As he went, he could hear water splashing about. The interior had been breached, allowing water to surge through the bulkheads. The lower decks were flooding rapidly. With the boat listing to port, he found himself nearly walking on the edge of the stairs until reaching the platform at the bend, which was now a forty-degree ramp. With the second flight of stairs nearly going directly upward because of the shift, he had to climb them like a ladder until reaching the top.

He emerged on the main deck, which now resembled a humongous ramp. Equipment and crew slid to the portside guardrails. Men were struggling to unload lifeboats. Some of the cranes swung uncontrollably, causing a couple of boats to crash down into the water, with over a dozen crew in each one. Spotlights beamed their white rays into the water, bringing the chaos below into full view.

Eric was near the bridge castle, located near the stern of the boat. He ran ahead until he was halfway across the midship body, then peered over the guardrail to the waters below. He could hear large thumping movements below. The megalodon had not escaped yet, to his relief. That relief was short-lived when he remembered he had one shot at getting the tracker on it. And attaching it to the shark was not as easy of a task as one might think. The only place the harpoon could possibly penetrate would be near one of the fins, likely the dorsal fin. Despite its seven-foot length, it would be difficult to hit, considering it would be atop a creature capable of swimming thirty-knots…in the dark of night.

He leaned down on the guardrail and shouldered the harpoon gun. He took a breath and ignored the hundreds of distractions all around him. There was splashing all around, men struggling to stay afloat. Many with lifejackets swam to those without them, forming rings of people clinging to each other. He had to drown out their predicaments in favor of this one mission. He had to. The ramifications of failure were too great.

Metal crashed beneath him. Then, it was as though the whole side of the ship exploded outward. Fragments of hull bounced over the sea like skipping stones before plunging into the depths. Now, in the place where the fragments had been, was the head of the enormous megalodon.

The breach, though immense, was only barely enough for the creature's huge bulk. It wiggled back and forth, swinging its tail inside the ship, trying desperately to push itself out into the open ocean. Inch-by-inch, foot-by-foot, it made its way out, jaws snapping widely as though cursing at its captors. Unknowingly, it created the ideal scenario for Eric to place the tracking device…if he could only see the damn thing clearly. Spotlights panned all over the place. They seemed to be putting the entire ocean in view, except for the one damned spot he needed.

"Get a light on the bastard!" he yelled. Nobody seemed to hear him. "Get a light on the shark! Do it now! Now!" He repeated himself a dozen times until one of those white beams panned to stern and down. He could see the leviathan clearly now. There were tiny marks in its body resulting from scraping against the hull. Nothing significant that would slow it down. Its left pectoral was free, though the dorsal and right pectoral were still stuck in the opening. The shark turned, bringing its fin out of the water.

Perfect!

Eric adjusted his aim and squeezed the trigger. The harpoon zipped away, hardly making a sound. The barb was so small and insignificant, the shark never felt it pierce its skin. The light reflected the tiny orange tag.

"Yes!" Eric exclaimed. With the task completed, he tossed the useless harpoon gun away and started looking for a means of staying afloat. The shark shifted again, finally unwedging itself. An eighty-ton missile composed of muscle, cartilage, and blood, it shot into the ocean. It swam out for several hundred yards then slowed, allowing its body to cruise at restful pace. It swam in a circle, a habit formed in its years in captivity, gradually branching out with each pass.

Now, it had a new mission: to replenish the energy spent during its assault on the bulkhead. The canals making up its lateral line picked up the frantic motions of small prey struggling along the surface. The megalodon turned toward the signal and ascended. From the crewmember's point of view, a barrel-shaped segment of ocean appeared to rise. Its fin was the first to break the water's surface, then its tail and snout. Men screamed as the beast closed in. Its jaw hyperextended, its inner mouth a tunnel blacker than the night air.

It passed through the center of the ring of men, engulfing three of them in a single bite. It closed the jaws, swallowing them whole. It sensed a large object in its path. The shark turned, sideswiping the ship's hull. Though not dead-on, the impact was still tremendous, causing the tilting ship to swing to starboard with enough force to hurl Eric and many others over the guardrail.

He opened his mouth to gasp, but shut it immediately upon hitting the water. A swirling current tossed the young biologist around, spinning him head over heels like a wheel. He opened his eyes and saw darkness. For a moment, he wondered if he was already dead. Finally, that gasp escaped his throat. Through the sting of seawater, he watched the dozen air bubbles travel to his left. He paddled his arms and legs, following the bubbles up to the surface. He emerged with a tremendous splash. After taking in a mouthful of air, he looked around for the shark. For a moment, he couldn't see anything but splashing waves. The only thing he saw was a piece of floating debris roughly ten feet ahead. He paddled to it, quickly closing the distance. He threw his arms around it, feeling its rubbery texture. Its red color stood out; he was floating on a segment from one of the lifeboats.

There were no screams around him. He looked around but could not see any crewmembers. Nothing. The only sounds came from the ship and the sailors fortunate enough to stay on board. It was behind him. He turned to look and was shocked to see that he had drifted over a hundred feet away. The stern was dipping below the surface, the tip of the bow yawning several meters high.

The spotlights along the superstructure and along the deck continued waving back and forth. Eric noticed one of the white beams traveling across the water. Following the light, he found where it met the ocean, and the enormous dorsal fin the crewmember was tracing. The megalodon was maybe four or five hundred feet out, finally moving away from the boat.

Eric sucked in a deep breath and held still. If he tried swimming frantically, he'd just attract its attention. He inhaled slowly, then exhaled, successfully slowing his heart rate. He watched the fin cutting across the water, lit by the spotlight. The plan seemed to work. The shark was going right by him, totally unaware of his existence.

At least, that's what he thought.

A few more seconds passed and suddenly, the fin rotated to the left, stopping after it was perfectly aligned with him. Eric fought the urge to paddle and kick. It was probably just a coincidence. The thing was in the open sea for the first time and probably just exploring. He took in another deep breath and waited. The fin continued closing in.

The hell?

His mind raced. To the shark, he should've been nothing more than a block of wood floating in the water. He knew how sharks used their senses to detect prey. He wasn't making any sounds, especially no low-frequency sounds to attract it. He was not causing any water displacement for it to hone in on. His dark clothing wouldn't attract its eyesight. If anything, it should've been attracted to the lights emitted from the spotlights. And he was too far away for its *ampullae of Lorenzini* to detect any electrical fields he was emitting. All that left was the sense of smell, which mainly picked up the scent of blood…

Eric's brain registered a small sting in his back—the same stinging sensation of rubbing salt on a wound. The prick in his back.

That damn mattress spring!

The shark's caudal fin sprayed water, driving it close. Finally, Eric gave in to panic. He screamed and paddled as fast as he could. His actions only worked in the shark's favor. It pinpointed his position and accelerated, jaws wide open.

The moonlight was overtaken by a huge shadow. Eric felt a brief and devastating impact along his spine. Serrated teeth stabbed deep, impaling his lungs and stomach. The lower jaw closed, the teeth ripping his stomach wide open. Half out of the shark's mouth, he was carried for several yards until it bit again, sucking his entire body into its throat.

Eric saw darkness again. This time, it wasn't night.

The megalodon explored further. Its digestive system went to work breaking down its prey. They wouldn't last it for long. It needed more. The megalodon swam in a wide circle, unsure if it wanted to inspect the sinking giant that previously imprisoned it.

Its lateral line picked up new signals. Its inner ears detected low-frequency sounds, which instantly attracted its interest. There were new distortions. Whatever was coming, it was big. Curious, and hungry for more prey, the megalodon swam northwest to inspect the phenomenon.

CHAPTER 2

The smell of fresh coffee entered Captain Earl Hobbs' nose as he lifted his thermos from the ebony dashboard. He stood proud at the helm of the seventy-foot fishing trawler, *Volcanic Cloud.* He embraced the cool salt air and the sight of waves splashing against the bow. The moon above was perfectly round and bright, allowing him to see the ocean ahead.

He kept his eyes on the fish finder. He had come across an enormous school of Atlantic cod. Already, they were on their second pass. The first brought in two-thousand pounds of fish. The nets could hardly sustain the weight. As the fish hit the deck, he and his men saw dollar signs. They had no problem being pulled out of their bunks in the middle of the night for success. They were midway through their second pass now. He watched the cod on his screen. Having fished for thirty years, he knew every which way they would scatter and how to intercept. He rarely followed the same pass twice. Studying their movements on the screen, he predicted their next gathering with great success.

It was a perfect way to start a new voyage at sea. This is where he belonged, not stuck in some twelve-hundred square-foot home with a bickering woman and an annoying stepson who never came out of his room to begin with. At the end of each voyage, he would catch himself getting a little bit homesick, mistaking it for missing life on dry land. Then, immediately upon arriving at the front door, he'd realize that homesick feeling was for the sea that he was about to step off of.

His wife would pester him about finding a new career. As annoying as he found her to be, her in-laws were worse. Every visit turned into a topic about careers—specifically his career, retirement savings and Roth IRAs, parenthood, among a dozen other annoying lectures. Apparently, they thought of fishing as some menial labor job, despite the great payload he brought in after each trip.

Why did I marry her? he thought. The answer was obvious. First of all, she had an excellent body, and to her credit, a fun personality. At the time, at least. Most women who'd displayed interest toward Earl were not the most particularly attractive, and it was fun to notice the jealous glances from friends when they all went out. Also, her parents lived in Virginia at the time, so he didn't have to endure their exhausting visits often. That is, until her father moved his medical practice to Georgia and found a residence fifteen minutes away from theirs. Now, they were over all the time, and with each visit came a migraine. That, and the quickly fizzled romance, only motivated him to take longer voyages. Each time, he'd have to listen to his wife complain about the same damn thing, while his stepson only spoke to him if he needed money for an Xbox update—whatever the hell that was.

He was at his house, but not at home. His home was the open ocean, with nothing but the horizon in his way.

Why not divorce her? The answer was obvious. He thought of his old friend, Warren. His divorced aged him ten years, the resulting booze-fest twenty. Earl was still convinced his cancer was brought on by the stress. The guy had to pay for his lawyers, *her* lawyers, the court granted her the kids and sixty-percent of his income—including his retirement. To make ends meet, he worked extra jobs to bring in more money. As a result, she took him to court again after finding out he was reeling a few more bucks. Earl would rather endure the misery he currently lived. It was cheaper.

He heard the door open behind him. Earl glanced back and saw his first mate enter the wheelhouse. Louis Ray had the same love for the sea as Earl. He was a man ten years younger, twenty pounds leaner, and twenty years smarter…in the sense he had nothing and nobody bogging him down. Also, the guy had the looks of a Hollywood model, despite being around bait, tackle, and tuna all day.

"Hey, you haven't received any distress calls, have you?" he asked. Earl turned around completely.

"Beg your pardon?" he said.

"To the south," Louis continued. "Spotlights. A bunch of them, pointing right up at the sky. It's weird." Earl slowed the engines and moved to the starboard window. There they were, just under a mile out. Had he not been lost in his thoughts, he probably would've noticed it sooner. This far out, the only thing that could project such lights were Coast Guard Cutters, Navy ships, or cargo freighters. Pointing searchlights skyward like that was not a common practice. The only thing Earl could think of was that the crew was trying to attract the attention of a helicopter. But then…

He checked his radio. It was working just fine. There were no weather faxes or other warnings.

"Where's Gerry?"

"Main deck," Louis answered.

"Raise the nets," Earl said. "Something's not right. I wanna check it out."

"You want me to call the Coast Guard?" Louis asked.

"Let's get close enough to figure out what's going on first. I don't want to send the Coast Guard on a wild goose chase. And if something's going on and they're already working on it, they don't need an old fisherman like me taking up their radio frequency."

He began turning the ship thirty-degrees starboard while Louis proceeded to climb down to the main deck. On each side of the forty-foot long work deck was a high-powered winch. The nets they were attached to were deep beneath the waves, passing through schools of shrimp and cod. Gerry was standing near the transom, watching the lights in the distance. As the ship turned, the superstructure eventually blocked his view.

"I'm assuming this means the Captain wants to check it out," Gerry said.

"Yeah," Louis said. He stepped off the ladder and moved to the starboard winch. "Nothing from the radio. It's probably nothing. Maybe just be some Coast Guard training exercise."

"Hmm, that makes sense," Gerry said. He went to the port winch and began reeling in the net. Atlantic Cod flapped their bodies, their mouths gaping to oxygenate their gills.

Earl Hobbs increased the speed to twenty knots. In the following moments, he had also convinced himself that it was probably nothing. Listening to the fish flopping on deck, he felt a slight urge to go back and continue the trawl. They had found a large school of cod and already had two full nets for the day. He wanted to keep going. If he could fill the hold fast enough, they could make their landing, set the market, and immediately head right back out and hopefully do the same without even having to resupply. Or waste time at the house.

He watched the fish-finder. The screen was alive with little green blobs that represented anything swimming under the boat. He was tempted to have his crew lower the nets back into the water and not lose any time while also doing this good deed.

"No, Earl…we'll go faster with the nets up," he said to himself. As he moved further south, the lights appeared larger. No longer did they seem to stream aimlessly from the horizon. They had a clear starting point. After another minute, he began to make out the ship's outline. It was a freighter of some sort. A smaller one, five hundred feet or so in length. Still, it was nearly seven times the size of the *Volcanic Ash.* Something was off about what he was looking at, and it wasn't the spotlights. It was hard to tell in the dark, but from what he could see, it appeared to be listing heavily. He grabbed the portable radio. "Louis, head around to the forward deck and aim a spotlight dead ahead."

"On my way," the first mate answered.

Louis walked along the side deck until he was at the foredeck. As he went, he watched the cargo ship and noticed the same oddities as Earl. He positioned a spotlight straight ahead. A huge white beam struck the hull. He panned up along the guardrail then followed it left to the bow. As he did, he noticed he was angling the light up.

"Holy shit!" The boat was sinking. Its stern was almost completely submerged. There were a few hands still on deck, many of them clinging to the guardrail to keep from falling to the other side. Water filled the cargo hold and stern compartments and was now pulling the ship downward.

Earl opened a window so Louis could hear him.

"Lower the light. See if anyone's in the water!" he said. Louis searched the waves, seeing nothing but floating debris. He could hear shouting from the deck. He brought the light back up and saw several crewmembers waving and shouting frantically at them.

"Hang on!" he yelled back. "We'll pick as many of you up. The Captain's calling the Coast Guard and—" he stopped to listen to the men shouting. Their voices overlapped, making it difficult to understand what they were saying. After a few moments, one of their voices was amplified with the aid of a bullhorn.

"Get away!" he shouted, his voice carrying into the night sky. Louis stared dumbfounded, then looked back at his Captain, who wore the same confused stare. The crewmember yelled again, "Get away! There's a shark in the water! Go! Go! Go!" He continued repeating himself.

"Son of a bitch," Earl said. "I don't know what these guys were smuggling, but it probably wasn't legal. Or healthy. I don't think we have to worry about some shark eating our boat." He grabbed the radio and turned the knob to find the Coast Guard's channel. As he did, his eyes passed over the fish finder's black screen. The school was further back. Anything else in the area had probably been scared off by any vibrations caused by the sinking. Then, a large green shape appeared on the screen. Earl found himself staring at it. It wasn't a school of fish. It was one organism. It was larger than the boat!

The great fish circled underneath, taking in the sweet taste of bait that lingered under the object above. The trawling net had left particles of residue from the bait. The megalodon took it in, then angled itself at the thing whose movements had attracted it. It was a large thing. The engine pounded like a heartbeat. There were other distortions echoing from its thick belly. They were slight pounding sounds, like those made from the humans when they moved around its entrapment.

The megalodon circled one more time. The scent grew as it neared. Hunger dictated its actions. It fluttered its tail, rolled its eyes back into its head, and struck the keel.

There was a thundering crash of metal, and the stern of the *Volcanic Ash* suddenly shot upward like a catapult. Gerry was thrown up and smashed against the wheelhouse. Earl hit the floor, nearly banging his head on the helm. The bow plunged, the first mate flipping over the railing. The stern smashed back down, the hull underneath cracked and started taking in loads of seawater.

Louis broke the surface and took a breath. He wasn't even sure what had just happened. He turned around and started swimming for the ship, unaware of the huge mass that closed in behind him. Had it not been for his own frantic splashing, he would've heard the water crashing behind him, making way for a huge oncoming mass.

The megalodon closed in on its prey and took it in its jaws. Teeth came down on Louis' neck like a guillotine. It swallowed his body whole, while his severed head floated into the depths, only to be picked at by shrimp and other small fish. The megalodon did not slow. It ducked down, then angled upward suddenly, jetting itself toward the boat again. Its nose struck the hull dead center. Hull, railing, and decking exploded, making way for the monstrous force that plowed through the boat like a lance. The megalodon passed through the boat, breaching the water. Both halves flipped upward, spewing contents into the ocean around it.

Gerry was on the side deck when the impact occurred. By the time he tasted the blood in his mouth, he was launched again. Now, he was tasting saltwater. Instinctively, he gasped, then gagged as that very same saltwater flooded his lungs.

The megalodon swam in a tight loop, detecting the movements of struggling prey. Its sense of smell picked up traces of blood that leaked from Gerry's nose and mouth. Like a homing missile, it went in for the kill. It opened its mouth and took the human into its gullet in a single gulp.

Gerry felt a sudden rush, followed by a feeling of warmth. The water suddenly washed away, filtered through strange slits in the walls, while he continued down a black tunnel. That warmth turned to boiling hotness. The sensation was so intense, he vomited the seawater he inhaled. Hot fluid engulfed his entire body. He tried to swim, but it felt like each movement grew more excruciating. The pain grew more intense with each passing second. His flesh felt as though it was turning to goo. Panicking, he touched his face and shoulders, and felt a strange softness. The clothes were breaking apart like wet tissue, and the skin and muscle underneath had turned soggy. His fingers found holes in his cheeks. He was melting!

The megalodon descended. There were all kinds of movements below the vessel. There were struggling fish everywhere, deprived of oxygen, fluttering their four-foot bodies in a last ditch effort to survive. The megalodon swooped in, taking several fish in a single bite. It moved like a bird, bringing itself back and forth through the school, filling its belly as it went. After four passes, it had consumed over a thousand pounds of food. The rest of the fish had scattered, seizing the advantage of a second chance at life. Some didn't make it past a few hundred feet before the leviathan chased them down.

The megalodon wasn't done. More struggling movements drew its attention toward the surface. There was at least one more human on board that vessel. It slowly closed in and tried to isolate the target with its various senses, hoping to avoid ingesting the inorganic material floating around it.

Water immediately flooded the wheelhouse as the bow crashed down. The front half of the boat had rolled to its side, the water causing bolts to crackle from the radio unit. The uneven distribution of weight caused the bow to roll, sending Earl bouncing off the overhead, deck, and walls. It was as though he was trapped on an enormous hamster wheel.

Both halves began to sink.

The water had completely filled the cabin. The spinning finally started to stop, allowing Earl to get his bearings. He held his breath and looked around. He realized the windshield was above him and the door was somewhere beneath his feet. At that moment, the glass clunked the top of his head. The *Volcanic Ash* was quickly sinking. Earl tried swimming down to make his way out the back, but could not swim faster than the ship was sinking. He was practically swimming in place.

His feet touched the glass. Earl looked back, realizing he could simply swim through the open window. He turned around and swam upward, nearly faceplanting into the windshield. He pulled himself to the right until he found the open window. He opened it the rest of the way and squeezed through. Next, he was shooting for the surface, swimming along the thick beam of light that streamed from the starboard bow searchlight. He kept his eyes on its white radiance, which seemed to guide him as he ascended.

The light went black suddenly, only to return a moment later. Earl kept swimming, thinking the mechanism was about to die. The light flickered again. There was a rushing current underneath him, pushing him upward. Earl looked down and saw the enormous white teeth lining the shark's mouth. The megalodon snapped its jaws shut, entombing its prey. After filtering the water through its gill slits, it swallowed.

Earl's screams went unheard by the outside world as he entered the same acidic bath that dissolved his friends.

The megalodon glided across the water, its dorsal fin appearing like a huge grey knife. Its hunger was satisfied for the time being. All it needed now was rest. It slowed its caudal fin to a gentle brushing, allowing its body to restore its lost energy as it continued east.

It dipped below the surface, leaving its captures to their excruciatingly slow demise.

CHAPTER 3

Marc Gundrum awoke in a jolting motion. His phone's beacon ringtone pierced through a lucid dream of his college graduation. He placed his glasses on and read the ID on the black screen. *Nathan Ellis*. He checked his watch. 4:54. If the Vice President of his company was calling him at this hour, it was definitely something important. He swiped the green *answer* key.

"This is Gundrum," he said, trying to pretend he was already awake.

"Marc, this is Nathan. Sorry to wake you but we have a major problem that needs to be brought to your attention." Gundrum was genuinely wide awake now. He sat up, feeling the beginning rush of anxiety in his veins.

"I'm listening," he said.

"The Truth Seeker, it sank."

"Sank?!" Gundrum's voice boomed through the Vice President's receiver.

"The Captain made a distress call. Their last reported position was ninety-one miles off of Gray's Reef."

"They couldn't have run aground that far out. How the hell did they sink?"

"Project Eleven, sir," Nathan Ellis said. Marc Gundrum took a minute to absorb what Nathan was telling him. *"Project Eleven breached the hull. Caused massive interior damage in the process, which led to flooding. Before losing contact, he stated that it was eating the crew."*

Gundrum swallowed before asking the next question. "Was the Coast Guard notified?"

"Not to my knowledge," Ellis answered. Gundrum breathed a sigh of relief.

"You're sure?"

"We've monitored their transmissions as you requested. The Captain followed the appropriate procedures that we provided. We've dispatched

our private contractors to rescue the survivors. So far, there is no public knowledge of the specimen's existence."

"For now," Gundrum said. "Do we have a status on the specimen? You stated it was eating the crew. Is it still alive?"

"The reports confirm that the megalodon is alive," Ellis said. *"But sir, we never anticipated this situation. The shark has proven to be highly aggressive. Take that into account along with its size and weight, and...well, it's going to be extremely difficult to capture. And we have to consider the potential loss of life it could cause if it proceeds to move toward the coastline."*

"What are you implying?" Gundrum asked.

"Sir, we might not have any choice but to destroy it. I don't see any other possibility other than that."

"Bull-fucking-shit, Nathan!" Gundrum's voice was sharp enough to make his lifelong friend shudder on the other end of the line. "I've invested fifty million dollars into this asset alone. My dollars. Not yours. Remember, I hired you to help me run this business. And running a good business does not involve losing your products before you sell them." Gundrum stood out of bed. The gravity of the situation was weighing heavily now. This couldn't have happened at a worse time. He had representatives arriving at his office in four days, followed by a meeting with Florida Senator Don O'Bannon. "Okay, Nathan..." he calmed his voice, "remember the Senator's very interested in buying this asset, along with Project Nine. We're looking at a billion dollars for each...minimum. They're expecting to see the shark, and we're going to deliver. As far as the world is concerned, this event never happened. Same with the Senator."

Ellis' response was delayed. It took several seconds for him to swallow his personal feelings on the matter. He knew arguing with Gundrum would be a losing battle in this case. He could debate budgets with him, staff issues, facility matters. But this? Arguing would accomplish nothing but take up time, which was more precious now than ever.

"Okay. We're going to need Captain Howard Seabolt and his ship to catch and secure it. I'm assuming you want me to contact Jason Nace?"

"Yes. Tell him to meet us in the office and have his team on standby," Gundrum said. "Did Dr. Hutson fly in yesterday?"

"Correct. We booked her at the Santorini Hotel."

"Good. Wake her up and send a car. We're gonna need her."

"Marc, how on earth are we going to capture this thing?"

"That's why we're having this emergency meeting, Nathan: to come up with a plan. Now, get it done. And I can't stress this enough: Keep it under the radar. If word gets out, Senator O'Bannon will back away from the deal."

"I'll get right on it."

"Be in Conference Room B in an hour." With nothing else to say, and no more time to waste, Gundrum hung up and went for his closet. He pulled out a white shirt, grey slacks and jacket, then went through his ties. He felt the sweat forming over his body. He needed to display confidence at this meeting, and the image of a sweaty, balding, forty-four-year-old didn't convey that.

He went into the bathroom and splashed water over his face. Dripping wet, he gazed at his reflection. The man looking back had the lines of someone who had harbored years of stress. His athletic figure was now a somewhat stocky one. There was a bald spot on the top of his head. All signs of his youth were gone. He thought, with money, such worries would go away. Instead, they only seemed to get worse.

His nametag was on the countertop. He gazed at the white letters. *Dr. Marc Gundrum – President of Gundrum Industries.* The 'doctor' part simply made him seem more eloquent. He studied genetics and biology, but focused more heavily on business. It turned out to be a smart move. He started off with a small retail business, then moved on to opening small hotels. Small hotels turned into larger ones. Next came the casino, where real money came in. His fascination with genetics never wore off though. With money pouring in from all his businesses, he opened Gundrum Industries. On the surface, it appeared to be a marine and reptile exhibit. On the inside, behind doors with red letters spelling *Restricted*, it was so much more. It was behind those doors that Marc Gundrum was poised to be one of the most powerful weapons contractors on earth. To do that, he needed to make this sale. If Senator O'Bannon liked what he saw, the funding would come rolling in. He had the scientists. He had the technology. He just needed more.

Who knows? The fact that the megalodon was capable of sinking a cargo ship was probably an excellent selling point. Maybe he could get the ship hauled up and display it for the Senator to see. Perhaps there was security footage that could be salvaged.

A wave of inspiration hit Marc Gundrum.

"We're going to capture this damn shark," he said to his reflection. In ten minutes, he was cleaned up and dressed. He pinned the nametag to his chest, grabbed his briefcase, and marched out the door.

CHAPTER 4

Dr. Gina Hutson was already awake and in the middle of her daily morning routine. Her feet pounded the conveyor belt. It took ten minutes of running before she even began to sweat. After thirty, she had run nearly four miles. The hotel she was booked at had an excellent gymnasium with the highest quality equipment. She joked to herself that she might simply reside here should she choose to take a permanent residence in Florida.

She increased the speed, forcing her to work harder. The exercise was the best way to relieve stress. She watched the clock and thought of Eric Wesley and Project Nine. They would be arriving in another couple of hours. With a little luck, they would not have a problem transferring the shark into the holding tank. Thinking about it only made her worry more. She had warned Gundrum against moving the fish. She didn't know why it was so important to ship it to the Florida lab, but whatever the reason was, it was enough for him to disregard her concerns.

Gina forced herself to think on other matters. She considered making a phone call to Massachusetts and checking the many smaller specimens that remained there. In a few hours, she would get to inspect the ones that arrived with her.

The achievements the genetics staff were able to pull off were amazing to say it mildly. Incredible was a better word. So incredible, she was shocked that Marc Gundrum wanted to keep it so secret. Upon hiring, she had to sign countless non-disclosure forms. The paperwork made her nervous, as though she was agreeing to something illegal. Despite her research, there was nothing about Gundrum Industries that made her suspicious. Maybe there was a rival company that was out to steal his research, staff, or resources. She felt her mind was going in circles speculating about this stuff. Gina focused on her running, while reminding herself to be grateful for this career. After all, she was given the opportunity of a lifetime. She was a marine biologist, with a specialty in paleobiology, who was able to work with real prehistoric creatures, while being paid a hefty sum in the meantime. Her career had never seemed better.

The door opened and a hotel staff member stepped inside. The young man looked like he was fresh out of high school. For a moment, he seemed to be gazing at Gina's athletic figure. Her brown hair swayed between muscular shoulders. Beads of sweat traveled down her neck, soaking the edges of her white tank top. He never would've guessed she was in her mid-thirties. Twenty-seven at best. The moment passed, and he remembered the portable phone he held in his hand, and the serious tone of the man on the other end of the line.

"Excuse me, Dr. Gina Hutson?" he said.

"That's me," she said.

"There's a call for you. It's urgent, apparently." He held the phone out to her. Gina shut the treadmill down and took it.

"This is Doctor Hutson," she said.

"Doctor, this is Nathan Ellis. I've been trying to reach your cell." Gina checked her watch. It was only ten after five.

"Uh, my apologies. I didn't expect a call so early—"

"No apology needed, but I need you to listen. I'm sending a car. It'll probably be there in ten minutes or so. It's going to bring you to our main building. An associate will escort you to Conference Room B," Nathan said. There was an urgency in his voice, which contrasted sharply with the very nice, calm man she met when she arrived yesterday. That, and he was calling her at five-freaking-ten. Something was wrong.

"What happened, Mr. Ellis? Are the specimens okay?"

"No, it's…uh…" Nathan Ellis realized he couldn't come up with a rational lie. His intent was honest; he simply didn't want to alarm her in the meantime. But, as Gina deduced, there was no other rationale for calling her this early. *"It's the megalodon, ma'am. It sank the cargo ship and escaped. We're having an emergency meeting to figure out what to do."*

Gina was suddenly sweating harder.

"It *sank*?!"

"Yes, ma'am. According to the distress call, it went on a rampage, killed many crewmembers. It breached the hull and escaped into the ocean."

"Jesus. What of Eric Wesley? Has he radioed in?" There was no immediate answer. She could hear Ellis take a breath—the kind someone made when trying to figure out how to word their answer. "Sir?"

"Captain's last transmission stated that Mr. Wesley was spotted on the bridge, but had fallen overboard. Rescue teams have been dispatched.

Right now, Dr. Hutson, we need you at our facility immediately to consult us in our next course of action."

"Jesus! I'm on the way." She handed the phone back to the attendant and bolted out the door. She ran down the hallway until she found the elevator. She pressed the button and waited. After several seconds, the thing was starting to move…from the top floor. Cursing under her breath, she abandoned the elevator and ascended the stairs. She took three steps with each stride until she was up in the third floor. She found her room and let herself in. She started the shower and stripped, not bothering to let the water warm up first. She jolted momentarily at the touch of the cold water, drenched her hair with shampoo, rinsed herself off, then stepped out. Wrapped in a towel, she hurried to her dresser and selected some clothes to wear. She decided to go with something business casual first. She placed on some black slacks, a dark green blouse, and her black velvet high-top boots. She found all of her paper files on the megalodon, stuffed them in a briefcase, then hurried out the door.

The car was waiting in front of the main entrance. There were bags under the driver's eyes. The poor guy was probably the first one to be called.

"Good morning, ma'am," he said, opening the door for her. She forced a smile, pretending there was no emergency.

"Thank you," she said.

"Don't know what's going on this early in the morning," the driver said. "Maybe the boss has a special breakfast party planned." He took his seat and steered the vehicle out of the hotel lot.

Gina couldn't even bring herself to respond. The thought of eating turned her stomach. She sat straight, trying to look as though this ride was planned from the get-go. She watched the streetlights passing by, then looked down at her briefcase.

She told them—she *implored* them to not ship the megalodon. She warned Gundrum of its aggression and strength. Despite her knowledge, even she was amazed to know it was capable of breaching the hull. Now, it was free to travel the ocean. With its elevated metabolism, it was inevitable that it would kill someone else.

Oh, God. How do we stop something like that? I don't see any other choice than to kill it. She despised the thought. The megalodon was a scientific marvel. Still, she had to consider the safety for mariners and people residing on the coast.

She took a deep breath and waited silently as the driver took her to Gundrum Industries.

CHAPTER 5

Gundrum Industries was an enormous building located on the coast just a few miles north of West Palm Beach. Gina rolled her window down and took in the salt air. She could see the ocean now. The sun was starting to come up, its glow forming a bright orange line along the horizon. The car followed a road that passed an enormous beach and picnic area, which was privately owned by Marc Gundrum as part of the facility's property. The road hooked to the right and took them to a large gate. The security guard inspected the driver's ID, then let him in.

They entered a vast lot. Yesterday afternoon, this parking lot was crammed full of vehicles from employees and visitors, with several moving cars going in and out. Seeing it so empty somehow made it seem so much bigger. She never realized there was another lot way off on the left side, equally as big. Both lots were as large as airports, and in her opinion, were more well-guarded. Security vehicles drove around the buildings, performing their rounds. At the door, two men in black uniforms stood at their posts. They wore semi-automatics on their belts.

All this for an aquarium? During the night shift, no less?

The driver cut across the lot and parked in front of the main entrance. The building towered above Gina as she stepped out. It was as large and complex as a university campus. The rising sun glinted off its silver panels and the enormous letters that spelled *Gundrum's World of Aquatic Life.*

"Dr. Hutson?" one of the guards asked.

"That's me," Gina replied.

"Come with us, please. We'll escort you to Dr. Gundrum's office." She followed the guard, while the other remained at the door. They passed an empty lobby and its check-in counter. Through the next door, they entered a large glass tunnel. On the other side were many different species of fish swimming about. The bio-illuminant species glowed blue and green, darting above her head, while some of the red ones swam under the walkway. Further down were several species of algae and coral harvested from the deepest points of the ocean. Additionally, there were volcanic vents, made from a combination of real-life samples taken from deep trenches and artificial dark lighting components to give the illusion they were letting off smoke. In this brief walk, Gina truly felt as though she was walking along the bottom of the Mariana Trench—minus the crushing pressure, of course.

At the end of the hundred-foot long tunnel came another doorway. The guard opened it for her, and she stepped into a world of glass walls, sheltering hundreds of species of aquatic life. She felt like she was in a maze of marine exhibits. There were sharks, turtles, rays, endangered species, all preserved. Directory signs were in place to guide visitors to the various other sections of the exhibit. Had Gina not been in such a hurry, she'd take a detour to the right where the fossilized specimens were being stored. But this morning, it didn't even cross her mind.

After passing several exhibits, the guard took her through the back doors. There, she saw the incomplete section of Gundrum's exhibit. There were vast aquarium tanks that had not yet been filled with water. Further along were the offices for the caretakers, along with storage rooms for food and medicine. Custodial staff were finishing up their duties, while the midnight caretaker completed reports in his office. All glanced at Gina and the guard escorting her, confused at what was going on.

There were three aquariums on her left. Two of them were six-by-nine feet, the third only twenty gallons. Power cables were hooked to the filtration units, allowing the water to circulate until the specimens could be transferred to their permanent holding tanks. Gina slowed to get a look at her specimens, making sure they were in good health and not suffering from stress.

In the first aquarium was *Gemuendina.* A placoderm of the order *Rhenanida*, this lime-green was a prehistoric species similar to modern-day rays. Its head was upturned, also known as a stargazer. The four-foot long creature had lived in the Early Devonian Period.

In the next large aquarium was a species called *Thelodus*, a genus from the class *Theolodent Agnathon.* This three-foot specimen was a jawless species that originally lived in the Silurian Period. Its white exoskeleton was composed of tooth-like scales that formed complex patterns along its body.

Its spiny appearance contrasted heavily from that of the much smaller jawless species, *Hemicyclaspis*, residing in the twenty-gallon tank beside it. Five-inches in length, this ancient species had a heavily armored, shovel-shaped headshield. Raising it in captivity, Gina discovered this Devonian Period creature fed off particles from the sea floor.

These specimens were only a small fraction of the miracles that Gundrum's genetic engineers were able to produce. There were many more species, including hybridizations of many modern day species back in the facility in Massachusetts. But, as amazing as each of these specimens were, none were nearly as grand as the megalodon shark. It was seen as the ultimate achievement, both in genetics, marine biology, and structural engineering. There were currently no Great Whites in captivity, much less their seventy-foot prehistoric cousin—and even a pure specimen would pale in spectacle compared to her ninety-three-foot specimen.

Now, that prize was lost at sea, and responsible for the deaths of numerous people. Her stomach tightened again, and she started to sweat. The moral gymnastics started playing out in her mind. Was she accountable for this travesty? Even partially? She did warn Gundrum that the megalodon was highly aggressive. Hell, she wasn't even confident they'd successfully get it into the cargo ship. Still, she had raised the thing since it was born out of its artificial womb. She watched it grow and become more vicious with each added foot. Despite being raised in captivity, as well as her many attempts to make it docile, the beast's aggressive nature was its driving force, and now, it was on the loose.

"This way, Dr. Hutson," the guard said. Gina followed him into an elevator. He hit the button to the tenth floor. Gina felt her ears were about to pop as she was lifted a hundred feet in a matter of seconds. The doors opened to a brightly lit hallway. She walked over fifty feet of expensive maroon-colored carpeting, then took a left turn. The guard unlocked an office pod exterior door and guided her to the back. Most of the offices were locked, save for one large one at the end. The guard knocked on the door.

A middle-aged man in a silver business suit opened it from the other side. Nathan Ellis. Gina immediately noticed his nervous expression and loose tie.

"Dr. Hutson. Thank you for arriving at such short notice," he said. He thanked the guard and let her in. The office looked like the living room of an expensive mansion. There were rocking chairs and furniture, surrounding a glass table. There was even a fireplace and ventilation for tobacco smoke. In the back, near a large mahogany desk, was a display of expensive wine and bourbon. Then she noticed the man behind that desk.

Marc Gundrum looked about as calm and collected as one could be in this situation. He had a cigar in his hand and a cutter in the other. It was his only vice at the moment. He snipped the end of the cigar and lit the other.

"Sorry to inconvenience you at this hour, ma'am," he said. He placed the cigar in his mouth and took a draw. "But, as you can imagine, this is a delicate situation to put it mildly. Please take a seat. There's coffee on the table behind you if you're interested."

"Thank you," she said, then sat down. Seated across from her was a woman with a sharp gaze and white hair, dressed in an equally white suit. It took a moment for Gina to realize she was taking a seat across from Dr. Trish Voltz, the lead genetic engineer. It was her miracles that had led to the creation of the megalodon and other specimens.

"Good to see you again," Gina said.

"You too," Voltz replied. "I wish it was under better circumstances."

"Me too," Gundrum said. He took another long draw. Several moments of silence followed, which surprised Gina, who assumed they'd get right to work discussing the scenario. She waited for one of the others to take the initiative, while taking a few glances around the office. On the bookshelf and walls were several glass frames displaying accolades, diplomas, and photos memorializing Marc Gundrum's past accomplishments. Gina couldn't help but notice a few familiar faces in those photos shaking hands with him. Senators, congressmen, a few other official looking individuals that she did not recognize.

Unable to contain her concern for her assistant, she looked over to Ellis.

"Has there been any new word from the ship? Did they find Eric?"

With a solemn expression, Ellis shook his head.

"Rescue crews are there right now. According to crew reports, anyone that ended up in the water, the megalodon would go right for them and—" his voice trailed off.

Gina rested her cheek against her palm. Her mind was a mix of bitterness, confusion, shock, with a tad of guilt swirling it all together. That mental argument ensued, with one side of her mind telling her she should've gone along to keep track of the shark herself. Meanwhile, the rational side argued back, reminding her that she had warned about the safety hazards.

Her thoughts were broken by the sound of footsteps outside, followed by the voice of one of the security guards.

"Okay I'll lead you down—"

"I know the way. Get back to your donuts and *YouTube*," another voice boomed.

Nathan Ellis went for the door. Before he could reach the handle, the door swung open and a largely built man decked in combat gear stepped in past him. At first glance, he looked like one of the security guards, until Gina realized his gear was much greyer and more…used, than those worn by the guards. His face displayed an equal amount of wear-and-tear. His huge forearms displayed various tattoos of bullets, knives, and other designs that Gina didn't recognize. The hair on the back of his head was standing on end, as though he had gotten out of bed minutes ago.

"Jason Nace," Gundrum said.

"Sorry I'm late to the party. I didn't get a private car like some people in this room," he said. He went for the coffee pot, then looked at the Styrofoam cups with disgust. "The hell—these things are practically shot glasses. Where's the—" He opened a couple of cabinets to the side.

"Excuse me, Mr. Nace," Ellis protested. "What are you doing?"

"Your pal Gundrum keeps real mugs up here somewhere and...A-HA! There they are!" Nace pulled a large ceramic mug from the cabinet and filled it with coffee. Gina, Dr. Voltz, and Ellis all cringed as he took several huge gulps, draining the freshly brewed coffee in seconds, then proceeded to refill the cup. "So? What's the job this time?"

Gina stammered. Was this person what she thought he was?

"Uh...Dr. Gundrum..." she paused to get the shakiness out of her voice, "I believe our first course of action should be to alert the Coast Guard immediately, if you haven't already. Second, we need—"

"Pardon me, Ms. Hutson, but that's not an option," Gundrum said. "If the military even takes that call seriously, their plan of action would be to destroy it the moment it presents itself to be a threat. I've invested more money in this asset than you'll make in two lifetimes, and I'm not going to let some chopper boys blow it out of the water."

"But sir..."

"Wait-wait-wait," Jason said, holding his hands up. Coffee splashed in his cup as he strolled up to Gundrum's desk. "What the hell is this asset? When you called me, you didn't tell me anything, except; 'Oh, Mr. Nace! We need your help...again! It's urgent. Please arrive in my office immediately.'"

Gundrum glared at the mercenary while bitterly shaking his head.

"I don't know which is more offensive: the fact that you used a girl-voice to imitate me, or the fact that it made you sound like a drag-queen."

"Hey, you're supposed to be accepting of that stuff nowadays, Mr. Gundrum. Or else you'll get a *Twitter* storm after you." Jason raised his coffee mug, "To the advancement of technology and progression of Mankind." He took a long swig of his coffee. "Ahhh! So, what is this asset and why is it so important?" Gundrum took a breath. Even to a man he'd used and trusted for years, it was difficult for him to let this secret out. That said, Nace was the only one with a likely shot of capturing the creature and keeping his mouth shut...for enough Benjamin Franklins, that is.

"Our asset is a shark," Gundrum said. Jason spat coffee in an attempt to suppress laughter.

"A shark?! This emergency meeting is for a shark? You have aquariums here full of them!"

"Not like this one."

"No?" Jason's grin widened. "Does it have two heads? And how did you lose it? Did a tornado come and sweep it away?" He chuckled at his own joke, then realized no one else was laughing.

"Have you ever heard of *Megalodon*?" Gundrum said.

"Megatron?"

Gina stood up. "Mega-lo-don!" Jason turned to look at her, then looked back at Gundrum.

"Megalodon. If the *Discovery Channel* wasn't lying to me, that's an extinct mega-shark."

"Close enough," Gundrum said. Jason's smile started to fade. He wondered if this was some sort of joke. Then again, a man like Marc Gundrum would not waste time on a joke.

"You're telling me that you have a sixty-foot dinosaur-shark swimming around out there?"

"Ninety-three feet," Gina said. Jason shot her a quick glance.

"Who's the hot chick?" he asked.

Gundrum replied, "Before we develop a plan to capture the shark, allow me to acquaint you with the target and the people who created it. And that story begins with 'that hot chick.' Her name is Dr. Gina Hutson. She's our leading Marine Biologist. She graduated from the University of Southern Mississippi, did a post-doctoral at Woods Hole Oceanographic Institution, with a sub-specialty in paleo-biology."

"Paleo, huh?" Jason said, unimpressed. He looked back at Gina. "So, what'd you do, doc? Go down the Marianas and find yourself a long-lost megalodon?"

"No. No living ones, that is," she said. "Before getting a job here with Gundrum Industries, the institution I worked for had me going all around the world, performing deep-sea submersible dives. I've made fossil discoveries in the Puerto Rico Trench, Java Trench, and Arctic Ocean's Eurasian Basin. In addition to these deep trenches, I studied habitats in reefs all over the world, extracting fossilized specimens from the crust. My most prized possession, however, was a group of megalodon teeth found along the coast of India. Carbon dating indicated that these specimens were only eight-thousand years old, setting a new record and igniting a fresh debate on when these prehistoric predators went extinct…or whether they went extinct at all."

Jason, still unimpressed, shrugged his shoulders.

"That still doesn't tell me why you have a ninety-three-foot fish swimming out there." Even as he said it, he still felt like he was in the middle of a bad joke.

"That's where Dr. Trish Voltz comes in," Gundrum said. "Dr. Voltz is the leading authority on genetic engineering."

"Genetic engineering. DNA reconstructing. Paleo-marine-biology. Fossils. Shark teeth. Submersibles. Trenches. I feel like I'm in a science class," Jason said.

"I'll save you the boring details that'll give you a headache," Trish Voltz said. "With the samples provided by Dr. Hutson, I've been able to carefully extract DNA strands from the bone fragments contained within the rock. Because of the depths many of them were found, the cold temperatures were able to preserve the integrity of the samples. Because of this, I was able to extract near-intact DNA sequences. To complete the sequence, I had to combine the DNA of each specimen with that of its modern day cousin. Technically, our megalodon isn't one-hundred percent Megalodon. It's part-Great White, its closest relative."

Gina opened her briefcase and pulled out all the files on the megalodon, including photos and discs. Nathan took one of the discs and switched on the big screen TV, then inserted the disc into the player.

Footage of the megalodon in its pool flashed across the screen. The camera went to an aerial view, displaying people standing near the pool edge. A crane lowered an orca carcass to the water. Before the cable could lower it completely, the shark breached, seizing the dead mammal, and dragging it down into the water.

Now, Jason was finally impressed.

"Holy shit."

"It was already dead," Gina said. She was always worried about people questioning the ethics of feeding the creature. Feeding regular sharks was expensive. But a meg? That was an experiment all in itself.

"Do you mean to tell me that shark broke out of that entrapment?" Jason asked.

"Not that one. We had it on board a freighter, which was taking it along the East Coast to the holding facility I spent the last year constructing. An hour ago, it breached the hull and escaped. That's why I need you, Mr. Nace. I need you to help us catch this thing, and keep it under the radar. I don't want anyone getting word that this creature exists, let alone the press."

"But the families of those who were killed…" Gina said.

"They will be well compensated," Gundrum said. "I cannot afford to lose this asset."

"Yeah, that's great and all, but uh, you do realize I run a small operation with a half-dozen guys, right?" Jason said. Gundrum nodded. "You want me to *catch* this motherfucking shark? Sure! I'll just get my fishing rod, a tub of worms, and get right to it. Oh! And don't let me forget the live-basket!"

"Mr. Nace…"

"How the hell do you expect me to catch that thing? Much less without killing it. Blowing it up, I can see how I'd be useful. But catching it? Bringing it back to you? What the hell's your plan?" Marc Gundrum stood silent. He went to puff on his cigar, but realized it had burnt out. Frustrated, he started to crush it into the ash tray, only for Jason to snatch it out of his hand. "Give me that. Not gonna let a good stogie go to waste." He used his own lighter and relit the cigar. "Alright, I get the idea. There is no plan. You said so yourself: this happened an hour ago. Odds are, nobody here contemplated the situation."

"Only me," Gina said. The words seemed to come out automatically, and she hated the lack of self-control. That regret was displayed in a cringing motion, which Jason noticed.

"Yeah, Dr. Hot-stuff…oh, excuse me, Hutson!" he said. "You knew this could happen and you did nothing about it?"

"I—" She felt stuck between telling the truth and outing her boss, and keeping quiet and appearing like a neglectful employee. What did it matter to a mercenary anyway? "I gave advice. It wasn't taken. End of that story."

"Okay. I presume you were called here because of your expertise on the runaway shark. So, what advice would you give me in catching it?"

"First, we need another cargo ship capable of holding the thing," she said.

"Already covered," Gundrum said.

"How the hell are we going to find it?" Jason asked. Gina pulled out her laptop and switched it on, revealing the satellite imaging. She pointed out the blinking red dot to him. "Tracking device. At least y'all did something right."

"We need to sedate the shark, get it on board the ship, hook up a large pump to keep water running over its gills, otherwise it'll die. While on the ship, it needs to be continuously sedated until we can get it into the new holding facility."

"That's gonna be near impossible," Dr. Voltz said. "Its skin is too thick. The only way to get a needle through is to get it in its mouth."

"What about the fins?" Jason asked.

"Sharks have extremely limited blood or nerve supply to their fins. It's almost pure cartilage," Gina said. "You could hit it with a hundred tranquilizer darts, and it wouldn't matter. Dr. Voltz is correct: the only way to penetrate deep enough is through its mouth."

Jason chuckled. "You know, Docs, I'm no scientist, but I get the impression that, to get the tranquilizer in its mouth, I'll have to…you know, get in front of the damn shark! Listen, I love a challenge. Hell, I'm considered something of a daredevil. That said, I'm not interested in getting swallowed. And we're talking about a fish that busted a twenty-two-millimeter hull. That tells me this thing is fast, strong, and mean. That's a bad combination, guys. Even for a mouth that big, it'll be impossible to pull off that kind of shot and live. And don't sharks sink? How the hell would we get it on board the boat?"

The room went silent.

"Maybe it'll swim out to the open ocean," Dr. Voltz suggested.

"No," Gina said. She rotated the laptop to show her the screen. "It's moving east. There are several harbors along the Georgia Coast. It's probably hearing vibrations from fishing ships. It's not going to be long before the megalodon encounters someone else."

Gundrum's fingers curled into fists.

"I hate to say it, but we might have to resort to killing it," Dr. Voltz admitted.

"We're NOT killing it," Gundrum snapped.

"We can create another one," Dr. Voltz said.

"And we will. But we are going to capture this one alive," Gundrum said, subduing his tone. "Okay, we agree that we need to sedate it. The ship we've hired has crane cables. Why don't we hook up a hook with some bait, lure the shark to the surface, have the bait laced with tranquilizer, and drug it that way?"

"The shark's stomach acid is very potent," Gina explained. "We'd need an enormous dose. And by the time it even makes the shark sluggish, it would break the crane off the ship. We need it to enter the bloodstream directly."

"Okay, why don't we draw the shark to the surface with bait. When it comes out, mouth open wide, we fire some darts as it tries to bite the bait."

"It's more likely to attack the boat," Gina said. "Besides, it prefers live prey. I can't be sure we'll be able to attract it with regular prey. We need to subdue the thing with a net or something—something strong enough to allow us to sedate the damn thing and allow us to pull it into the cargo hold. Then again, I don't know any net strong enough to hold it. We're talking about a shark that can bust through steel."

Gundrum and Voltz exchanged glances. Gina watched their facial expressions. They were exchanging ideas without words. They knew something she didn't.

"You think it'll work?" Gundrum asked.

Voltz nodded. "Dr. Lucero has demonstrated the broadcast emitter on the collar. It might work. We can use it in addition with this plan. It's risky, but I think it has the highest probability of success."

"If I may add," Nathan Ellis said, "it'd be an excellent opportunity to test Project Eleven."

Gundrum nodded. "That it would."

Gina could feel her hands trembling against the keyboard. She was not aware of any experiments outside of the Marine Biology division.

"What's Project Eleven?"

Gundrum bit his lip. Only a handful of people were aware of the existence of this specimen. Like the meg, it was something he wanted to keep close to his chest. But the situation at hand did not lend much room for secrecy. For the next twenty-four hours, the people in this room were his closest staff, closer than his board of directors.

"Nathan, get us a helicopter right now. And get Dr. Lucero on the horn," he said. He redirected his attention to Gina and Jason. "We have another facility, containing a separate asset. We call it the Colossal Snake."

CHAPTER 6

Dr. Miguel Lucero was in a peaceful sleep. Over the past year, the top of his desk had become more comfortable than memory foam. It was easier to sleep there. He would be at home for no more than four hours at a time before having to report back to the lab. Besides, he enjoyed being around his slithery friends. Their slithering movements against artificial canopies within their enclosures served as a white light for him. His unconscious mind took him back to his expeditions to the Amazon Rainforest, where he searched the riverbanks for hidden caves, with the goal of finding remnants of the almost-mythical Titanoboa. He could feel the burn of the malaria he contracted, as well as the fungal infections he picked up on his left calf. And that was when he knew it was a dream; the fungal infection was from Ecuador.

Suddenly the images were swept away by a blinding light, while a voice boomed through the sky.

"Dr. Lucero! Doctor! Hey, MIGUEL!"

Miguel threw his arms up defensively, then sat up. He looked around at his labs and the many aquariums containing his specimens. Snakes from all around the globe slithered about within their various climates. The door shut behind his assistant, Darryl Hugh, as he came into the room. The skinny thirty-three-year-old straightened his glasses and handed Miguel his.

"What's going on?" Miguel asked.

"Mr. Gundrum's coming here right now," Darryl said.

"Right now?"

"He said it's urgent," Darryl said. "He didn't give me specifics, but it's regarding Eleven." Miguel silently looked across the room at a set of double doors. Three hundred feet past the adjacent room was the containment unit for Project Eleven, as Marc Gundrum referred to it. He didn't form the attachments to the specimens as the staff had, particularly Miguel.

"How long until they get here?"

"Minutes," Darryl answered. "He called from the helicopter. He wants to see the specimen right away and…" his voice trailed off.

"And what, Darryl?" Miguel said, concerned.

"He mentioned the collar."

Miguel released a slow exhale. The moment he dreaded had finally come. When he was hired three years ago, he thought he had been granted the opportunity of a lifetime, thanks to Dr. Voltz' ingenious work on genetic splicing. In many ways, he had, but after a while, he began to realize it was under false pretenses. He saw the strings behind the paycheck, the miracles, the technology, and everything surrounding it. He was under the impression that Marc Gundrum was constructing an advanced zoo full of prehistoric/modern day hybrids. In a sense, that was true. The new reptile observatory was currently under construction and was well-known to the public. To his knowledge, there were experts being hired from across the globe for their knowledge on handling these creatures.

What initially struck Miguel as peculiar upon his hiring was Gundrum's interest in his paleo background, as well as the Titanoboa fossil discovery he had made in Peru a month prior to that. At the time he didn't think much of it: the guy probably just wanted an intact Titanoboa skeleton for his exhibit. Nothing too out of the ordinary, even for a zoo. Then he met Dr. Voltz and realized the true reason he wanted his fossil. Next came questions of genetic splicing and which species would be most likely for a successful crossover with that contracted from the bones. Miguel didn't think it could be done, but he was no geneticist. Besides, the primary reason he took the job was because Gundrum had promised to fund new expeditions into South America. The institution had lost funding, and nobody else wanted to step up to the plate, so Miguel accepted the offer.

Over the next several months, with top-of-the-line technology and millions of dollars, Dr. Voltz had done the impossible. He felt as though he was living in a science fiction world as Titanoboa birthed from its artificial womb. It was about a meter long at birth, but its growth was rapid, its appetite nearly insatiable. In less than a year, it reached the record length of fifty-five feet. Yet, it kept growing. That was the first sign that something was off. Then, he was asked questions on its ability to track prey. He had to provide exact details on how a snake typically seeks out its prey, though it varies within the species. The bizarre part was when he was asked to design a snake collar that would enable it to track specific targets. It was explained that it would be for spectating events to display to visitors what Joel was capable of doing.

Miguel could smell the bullshit, but forced himself to believe it. After all, his grant money was at stake, and also, he was given the opportunity of a lifetime to work on this project. Then he saw that the designer of the collar was a company that was notorious for designing weapons technology for the military, including black-ops projects that he could not mention. Such a meeting had to be orchestrated by a person in high power, and that was when Miguel discovered Gundrum's meetings with various government officials.

"Someone's going to get killed," he muttered to himself.

"Pardon me?" a shocked Darryl asked.

"Nothing. Gundrum's just a little overzealous concerning our snake. I'm just worried he'll want to…" he tried to come up with an explanation. He had never addressed his discoveries to his co-workers, as he felt there was no sense in burdening them with the truth behind Gundrum Industries. "He thinks Eleven's a circus animal, and I'm worried he's gonna request a demonstration or something."

"At this hour?" Darryl asked.

"Don't worry about it. Just go meet them out front," Miguel said. He walked into a bathroom and splashed water over his face. He glared at the unshaven man in the reflection. His beard was three days old. His muscular physique was still there, but slowly dissipating, as he had been sacrificing his exercise routine to keep up with the workload. He barely had time to shower in the last few days, not that it bothered him. He went weeks without a proper cleaning during his trips in the rainforest. However, in those cases, he was hundreds of miles away from the nearest hotel. Here, he was less than thirty minutes away, yet, he rarely found himself home long enough to flip on the TV, let alone maintain himself and the property. Hell, it had gotten so out of control, he ended up moving his personal pet snakes to the lab so he could care for them better.

He went back into his private office and pulled a fresh shirt from the closet. He knew he reeked of sweat, as the lab was kept fairly humid to accommodate the snakes. Only his office had air conditioning, but he was so used to the humidity, he never used it. After changing, he stepped out and began gathering his data-pad and paper files for Project Eleven. As he did, he heard a loud bang from deep within the compound.

"He's hungry again," he said to himself.

****

The helicopter sped across the morning sky, quickly closing in on Gundrum's facility in Brevard County. Gina could see the building to the north. The front of it was shaped similar to his aquarium exhibit, with large silver panels reflecting the morning sunlight. However, there was a dome-shaped structure behind it, nearly connecting to the artificial ledge that separated the facility from the Atlantic. Extending from that ledge was a huge steel tunnel going over three-hundred feet out into the water. Its top was comprised of retractable doors constructed with reinforced titanium. The basic design resembled the blueprints for Project Nine's exterior holding pen. However, this was not meant for megalodon, but rather the mysterious Project Eleven.

Gina almost fell into her seat when they explained the project to her. She hadn't even known that Gundrum Industries had built a reptile enclosure. And in that enclosure, Dr. Trish Voltz had conducted the same experiments. They were kind enough to let her look over the files of the Herpetologist in charge of the facility. She had read the files repeatedly over the short trip.

His name was Dr. Miguel Lucero. Age: Thirty-nine. Graduated from the University of Florida with Doctorate. Conducted post-doctoral studies in Marshall University. Specialty: Ophiology (study of snakes). What caught Gina's eye was his sub-specialty: Paleontology and geology, with a concentration on extinct species of snakes.

The next page went over his various trips to jungles in Colombia, Brazil, Peru, Ecuador, as well as various rainforests throughout Asia, including the Japanese Islands. In these expeditions, he discovered new venomous species, as well as record-sized anacondas near the Madeira River. But his ultimate achievement was his discovery of a near-completely intact skeleton belonging to the genus Titanoboa, believed to have gone extinct nearly sixty million years ago. The specimen measured a length of fifty-five feet, surpassing the theorized maximum growth of forty-two feet, with nearly three-hundred vertebrae.

Gina was amazed and appalled all in one. She was amazed that Voltz was able to conduct the gene splicing with other prehistoric species. But the secrecy of the project was somewhat unnerving. Even in a situation as monumental as their current predicament, Marc Gundrum was reluctant to inform her of the research being conducted in the reptile exhibit. Why? Secrecy? That didn't make sense, as she was in charge of the megalodon and was very well aware of the genetic engineering that created it. So, why keep Project Eleven a secret? Her non-disclosure agreement would prevent her from leaking it to the public anyway.

Jason Nace was squirming in his seat next to her.

"Damn, I shouldn't have had that third cup of coffee," he said. "Nature's calling, and she's angry."

"Thanks for that information," Gina muttered. Marc Gundrum, Trish Voltz, and Nathan Ellis were seated across from her. There wasn't much discussion during the flight other than a few phone calls made to a man named Captain Howard Seabolt and Jason's mercenary team.

"I'm eager to see this oversized snake," Jason said. "What the hell do you feed this thing? Cows? Alligators? Elephants?"

"Anything we can buy from farmers as well as fishing yachts. The specimen eats anything Dr. Lucero gives it," Voltz answered.

"Dr. Lucero knows more about this thing than anyone else," Gundrum said. "If this operation is going to be successful, we're going to need his help."

"You said something about a transmitter and a collar," Jason said. "It's a little vague, but I'm getting the impression that we're going to remote control this snake to go catch your fish. Am I wrong?"

"It's a little more complicated than that, but I'll just say you have the gist of it right," Gundrum answered. Gina kept quiet. She was still wrapping her mind around the existence of a resurrected Titanoboa. Despite the experiments she had seen, it still came as a shock to learn of these things. And Projects Nine and Eleven were the only two she was aware of. What else did Gundrum have Dr. Voltz working on? Giant crocodilians? Mammoths? The possibilities were endless.

"You sure this snake-guy can handle this thing? After all, wasn't it your shark people who lost your fish?" Jason said.

"His name was Eric," Gina growled. She resisted the urge to elbow him in the mouth.

"Well excuse me," he said.

"That transmitter on the shark, that's the secondary one," she said. "I can tell because of the code. The only person who could've accurately placed it there was Eric. He died so we could catch this thing and keep it from killing anyone else. So, you'll give him your respect."

Jason shrugged. "Don't mean to insult, Doc, but I'm not impressed by the notion of dying on the job. In my profession, it happens all the time. Eight years in the marines, another ten in my private business. I've been in over a hundred countries, and in each one, people died on the job. Many of them were buddies. It doesn't absolve them of their errors."

"That's a little different," Gina said. "Your profession centers around firefights and engaging hostile entities. No offense to your friends, but that kind of profession carries that risk."

"Yeah, right. Not like playing with giant genetically engineered sharks, right?" Jason's gaze went back to Gundrum. "I'll ask again: can we be sure this guy can handle this super-snake outside of captivity?"

"I'm confident he will," Gundrum said. "This snake has a superior intelligence than the shark. It and Dr. Lucero share a special bond. It trusts him."

"Aw, isn't that cute? He's got meal-immunity," Jason laughed.

The chopper set down on the empty lot. Gundrum opened the fuselage door and let everyone out. A salty breeze caught Gina's hair as she touched down on the pavement. The facility was a few hundred feet away from her, blocking the level stream of sunlight that stretched from the horizon. A man in his thirties, wearing a white lab coat, stepped out from the main entrance and approached them. He had a somewhat scrawny build and a nervous demeanor. Gina couldn't help but sense that Marc Gundrum had an intimidating presence to those who worked under him.

"Good morning," he said.

"Dr. Lucero?" Gina asked.

"No, sorry, my name's Darryl. I'm Dr. Lucero's assistant. One of them…there are many of us," he said. He looked back to his employer. "Well, you said it was urgent, so allow me to take you below."

"Please do," Gundrum said, his voice lacking emotion. They followed Darryl into the exhibit. The initial entry wasn't complete yet, but judging from its size and current setup, it was intended to be equally as elaborate as Gundrum's aquarium. Rather than mimic the Mariana Trench, it looked like it would contain virtual technology as well as live specimens to mimic the Amazon Rainforest.

The main exhibit was set up similarly, except this one began with a huge display structure of a giant snake skeleton. It was held up with a steel post, the specimen coiled around it repeatedly. In this coiled position, the specimen towered over twenty feet above them. The skull was perfectly intact, displaying rows of needle-like teeth. Like the anaconda, the species was a constrictor. It would wrap around its prey, squeeze it tight, crushing the bones and suffocating it, then feed at its leisure. As large as this creature was, Gina still considered it too small to go after a predator like the megalodon.

"That's just a partial reconstruction," Darryl said, noticing Gina's fascinated expression.

"This isn't the whole thing?" Jason asked. "What? Did you use plastic bones to put together a snake skeleton?" Darryl shot him an irritated look, which disappeared after he realized the hulking 6'3 man following him was an armed mercenary.

"Like most natural history museums, we used what we call conglomerates. We use 3D printing and casting to build a replica of what we know the creature looks like. It's all based on real discoveries, not something we've made up. The head's real, and most of the first half of the spine. The rest is made of casts that are properly measured, filled with resin, and painted to the exact color. These casts are an exact match of real bones that exist. We do this because fossils are fragile and can easily fall apart—plus it's very rare that a near entirety of any skeleton is ever found."

"I thought there was a complete skeleton?" Gina said.

"There is. It's downstairs, not too far from where we keep the specimen. You can say we—or rather, Dr. Voltz, brought it back to life."

They passed a large exhibit full of empty habitats. There were areas designed for alligators, crocodiles, snakes, frilled lizards, Komodo dragons, and various other species. Many of the billboards were constructed, but the specimens had not yet been brought in.

The exhibit seemed to go on forever. When they finally arrived at the back, Darryl escorted them into an elevator, which took them to one of the lower floors. They followed a maze of offices and laboratories. Here, Gina saw where Dr. Voltz had done her work. There were large machines containing artificial wombs that resembled glass tubes. In these labs were DNA extractors and supercomputers. The walls were lined with charts detailing DNA sequences with digital displays showing gaps in samples collected from bones.

They ascended a small flight of stairs and entered another lab. The humidity hit the group right away as they entered. They were now in a huge lab containing several different species of snakes. There were cobras, pythons, anacondas, sea snakes, king snakes, vipers. There were species from all over the globe.

To the right was a large desk. Standing near it, was a six-foot man with short black hair, wearing a white dress shirt and grey slacks. The cleanliness of the clothes did not match his face.

"Dr. Lucero," Gundrum said. Miguel turned around. He immediately noticed the mercenary and the short woman standing beside him. She was sweating rapidly. It was easy for him to determine that she did not frequently visit Florida.

Miguel cleared his throat and forced himself to be polite.

"Good morning, Dr. Gundrum," he said. "How can I help you today?" Inside, he was cringing. He sounded like a store clerk who was afraid of getting laid off.

"I'd like to get a look at the specimen," Gundrum said. Miguel looked over the small crowd again.

"Everyone?"

"Yes. It's important, Miguel." The herpetologist could tell his employer was in no mood for small talk. He turned and waved them to follow him.

"Right this way, please." He led them across the lab into the next room. Gina glanced at the various species as she crossed the lab. She was used to being around fish, whales, and crustaceans. Snakes, on the other hand, were not her forte. She passed one with a reddish-brown color. It appeared to be curled up asleep in an enclosure filled with vegetation and soil that mimicked some dry region of the planet. Probably Africa. In the blink of an eye, the snake snapped its head upward and sprayed venom across the glass. Gina yelped and jumped back, nearly dropping her briefcase and papers.

“Don’t mind him,” Miguel said, cavalierly. “He’s usually a little grumpy this time of the week. It’s almost feeding time.”

The next room was a large auditorium, mostly empty except for one enormous platform in its center. Resting on top of it was a complete Titanoboa specimen, discovered by Miguel during his expeditions in Ecuador.

“So, this is it?” Gina asked.

“Uh, I don’t think that’s the bad boy we’re here to see,” Jason said.

“No, I mean, that’s the specimen they retrieved the DNA from,” Gina said.

“That’s him. I’ve tried giving it a name, but kept going back to Eleven. I guess it grew on us,” Miguel said. Gina was amazed. The specimen was almost perfectly intact, which was rare for any fossil, let alone one of this size. Miguel must’ve taken great care to dig it up properly.

“It’s incredible,” she said.

“You like to meet him in the flesh?” Miguel asked. Gina shivered suddenly. Just looking at the dead jaw lined with spiky teeth was enough to make her heart jump. These things probably constricted and crushed creatures as large as Tyrannosaurus Rex, then swallowed them whole and digested them over the course of a year.

At the end of the auditorium was a hallway. It led them upstairs to another hallway. But the design of this one was different. The walls were made of reinforced steel. Jason Nace tapped a fist to the wall as they walked. It was like touching the hull of a battleship. He noticed little notches every twenty feet or so. He stopped under one of them and looked up. These were security doors, meant to lock something in.

The hallway ended in a small lab room. On the other end was a steel reinforced door resembling a bank vault. Miguel peered through a small porthole, then glanced back at the group.

“Just—don’t make any sudden movements. And stay in this little enclosure. It’ll block your body heat.”

Gundrum nodded. “Let’s get a look.” Miguel punched in a small code and the locks retracted. The door swung open and he stood aside to let them all in. Gina was surprised when she didn’t see the exhibit. Instead, she had stepped into a steel vestibule. She was no stranger to tight spaces, after all, she spent hours in a cramped submersible, miles under the ocean.

Miguel shut the door behind him. It locked automatically, then after a few moments, the other one opened outward.

Another wave of heat and humidity struck the group. Miguel was the first to step out, followed by Gundrum. They stepped into a small viewing room with thin orange glass walls overlooking the holding cell. Both Gina and Jason were hesitant in approaching the window.

"That doesn't look secure enough to keep out a giant snake," Jason said.

"Trust me, if it wanted to eat you, it'd find a way," Miguel said. Gina approached the glass and watched the exhibit. The ground was made up of real-life plants and trees harvested from the Amazon to give the thing its most suitable environment. In its center was an enormous pool, circulated from underneath to give it the feel of a river. There were rocks, trees, vines, all stretching from one end of the enormous enclosure to the other. Gina was also amazed by the size of this enclosure. She expected it to be big, but not as large as a football field. It was more than enough room for a fifty-five-foot snake.

Speaking of the snake...

"I don't see it," she said.

"I can," Miguel said.

"Where?" Gina asked.

"Hold on. Let me coax it out. Just don't make any sudden movements. He'll trace the vibrations," he said. He stepped to the right and exited out a door that led to a catwalk. Gina's eyes widened.

"What's he doing?" she said. Miguel walked seven meters out then rested his hand on the guardrail. He rattled the bars, generating vibration. The group waited, still unable to see the snake.

Suddenly, the canopy appeared to split open. Leaves and vines broke apart, and something enormous dropped into the pool. Tidal waves raced out into the exhibit, splashing the glass. Gina, Ellis, Voltz, and even Jason jumped back, while Gundrum stood in place, arms crossed, watching.

The creature rose from the pool like the arm of a kraken, slithering its way up to the catwalk. Its color was spotted green and lined with black rings. Its eyes were red, except for the catlike pupils. Gina watched its huge head rise until it was level with Miguel. It remained still, flicking its tongue, while watching him. Gina's chest ached. She trembled, feeling as though she had just completed a ten-mile marathon. For a moment, it seemed the snake would snatch its handler and swallow him whole. It didn't. It simply remained in place, watching him intensely. It bobbed its head slightly, studying him.

The adrenaline rush wore off, allowing Gina to study the creature scientifically, rather than as a potential man-eating beast. Judging by the way it studied Miguel, it seemed to recognize him. Behind its head was a black mechanical collar. The lower part was made from flexible components to allow the throat to expand when swallowing large prey. The section on the top of its head seemed to be stationary. From what she could see, the collar was either fused or bolted to the back of the snake's head. Either way, it was attached permanently. There was a small cone-shaped structure on the top left side emitting a green LED. She then remembered the discussion in the helicopter, and the mention of a transmitter. Was Miguel controlling this thing with an electronic device?

There was nothing in his hands. From where she stood, he was just like some pet owner interacting with a pet snake. An extraordinarily large pet snake! Then it hit her: Its tail was still coiled along the ground. Yet, its head was raised over forty feet high. She looked at the coiled body in the water. This thing was BIGGER than fifty-five feet.

"Holy Jesus," she said. She stumbled away instinctively. The snake tilted its head and tensed.

"Like I said, don't make any movements. He'll sense the vibrations," Miguel said. The snake eyed him carefully, cocking its head back as though about to strike. It flicked its tongue, then hissed. Miguel waved a finger at it as though disciplining a three-year-old. "Ah-ah-ah, don't give me any of that shit. You'll get fed when I'm good and ready." The snake waved its head back-and-forth, seeming impatient. Miguel chuckled. "Alright then." He pulled out his phone and punched Darryl's contact number.

"Our guests haven't been eaten, have they?"

"No, but they will be if this guy doesn't get something in his stomach," Miguel said.

"Alright. Give me a sec, and I'll get Randy over in his station. He should've clocked-in by now."

"I appreciate it," Miguel said. He hung up and continued to talk to the snake while they waited. It continued to flick its tongue, each time picking up his familiar senses that it imprinted on when it was born.

It whipped its head back to the sound of a mechanical door opening up across the enclosure. A fourteen-foot American alligator hissed as it wandered in, quickly turning back to bite at the mechanical crane that lowered it into the vestibule. The door shut and locked behind it. The alligator waited a moment, then decided it was safe. Hearing the flow of water, it dragged its five-hundred-pound body over to the pool.

By the time it saw the colossal snake, it had only enough time to take one last breath, which would be forced out of its lungs. The snake moved at lightning speed, plowing into the alligator and wrapping itself around its midsection. Because of the size difference, it only had to perform a single loop to constrict its prey. A quick squeeze snapped its spine and crushed its ribs and joints, killing it. The snake waited a moment until it was sure its prey was dead, then proceeded to bite on the small reptilian.

"Hot damn! That's awesome," Jason said. Miguel walked back into the viewing area and immediately looked at his employer.

"Satisfied?"

"Yes. It looks very healthy," Gundrum answered. His tone was less stern then it was few minutes ago. Jason watched like a little kid in a zoo as the snake finished swallowing the alligator.

"Don't know why he bothered with the coiling," he said. "He could've bitten that lizard and swallowed him while he was still kicking."

"Anything smaller, it probably would have. Otherwise, Eleven likes to constrict," Miguel said. "It's an instinct. These types of snakes constrict something until it's dead, or at least paralyzed. How would you like it if your cheeseburger was scraping and clawing in your belly after you've eaten it?" Jason winced at the thought.

"I would wonder what the hell was in that meat!"

"Would it eat something as large as…say, a human?" Gina said.

"You bet it would," Miguel said. "It wouldn't bother constricting you. It'd just bite you and let its fangs do the killing. Or if you really pissed it off, it'd lash you with its tail. I saw it take the head off an eight-point deer like *that.*" He snapped his fingers.

Gundrum smiled at the thought. Miguel opened the door and let everyone back into the vestibule.

"Come on. Show's over." They passed through the vestibule and let the security system do its work, finally letting them into the small lab on the other side.

"I must say," Gina said, "that was incredible. It really has a connection with you."

"Don't get too mushy. Eleven has no love for me. It just knows I provide the food," Miguel said.

"But, I didn't expect it to be that big! I mean…the specimen you found was only fifty-five feet, and that's considered to be the biggest one! The one in there has got to be a hundred feet long!"

"A hundred-and-fifty." Miguel gave a glance to Dr. Voltz. "You can say there were a few moderations made during the genetic engineering process," he said. His gaze returned to Gina. "So, are you the buyer?"

Gundrum stepped in, tilting his head as though trying to come off as intimidating. It didn't work. For a man who spent his life around twenty-foot snakes—and a hundred-fifty foot Colossal Snake that could take the life from him in an instant, a man in a suit, no matter how much money he possessed, did not frighten him. Especially in this moment when he was needed most.

Gina glanced at Gundrum. *Buyer?* He didn't pay attention to her, as his eyes were fixed on the herpetologist.

"No, Miguel. This is Dr. Hutson. She's here to help us. This is crucial. We have a critical situation and we think you can help us. You, and Project Eleven." Miguel's expression changed.

"A situation? What situation? And how would Eleven help you with that?"

"We have an asset out of containment," Nathan said. "We were transporting it by cargo ship and it got loose. Now, numerous people might be in danger. We need to catch this thing quietly and fast. And we need Project Eleven to do that for us."

"Another asset?" Miguel sounded surprised, but in reality, he wasn't. He figured there were other experiments going on that he didn't know about. "What is this asset? Another snake?"

"Not a snake. A shark," Gundrum said. Miguel took in a long, slow breath. He thought of the skeleton in the other room, and the life they were able to draw from its DNA. If this asset were any common shark, they wouldn't be so concerned with stopping it. And if it wasn't enormous and deadly, they wouldn't need something as large as Project Eleven to go after it. That begged the question: what the hell kind of shark was it?

"A shark?" He looked over at the unfamiliar woman. "Let me guess, you're a marine biologist."

"Yes," she said.

"I'm curious, Doctor, do you have any subspecialty in paleontology or paleobiology?"

"Yes," Gina answered.

"Let me guess, Dr. Voltz extracted DNA from a fossil and brought an extinct shark back from the dead. Am I wrong?"

"No, you're not wrong," Gina said.

"I thought so. Tell me Doctor, what prehistoric species of shark did Dr. Voltz resurrect?"

"Megalodon," Gina answered. Miguel's eyes widened for a moment. Now it made sense why there was a mercenary standing in this room, and not military officials. Right away, Miguel understood he was in a precarious situation.

He sighed.

"Megalodon, huh? Where is it?"

CHAPTER 7

Atlantic Ocean.
70 miles from Cumberland Island.

The huge shark glided through the Atlantic water with the grace of an eagle soaring high in the sky. Never in its life had it swum in a straight line for such a distance. The open ocean was its new home. Never again would it have walls enclosing it to a tiny pool.

For the past hour, it swam at a leisurely pace, while digesting its many victims from its recent encounter. It continued east, attracted to the many signals detected by its nostrils and lateral line. It could feel the presence of other large animals and the strange artificial surface craft that carried human prey. The bright light streaking overhead awoke it from its brief 'sleep-swim'. During most of its life, it had been under artificial light. This huge light, somehow, was different. It brought everything to view. The shark could see further than ever before. There were no walls or obstacles in the way. Its interest in the sunlight lasted a few short moments before its computer-like brain snapped into focus. There was only one interest that held its attention: survival. The number one key to survival was to feed. The shark was massive, and its metabolism was fast, thanks to the genetic engineering by its human creator. Already, it was feeling the drive to seek out new prey. Propelling its mass required tremendous energy. Its stomach had broken down most of the contents it had ingested, leaving nothing but the indigestible clothing, boots, and boat fragments it had swallowed along with the humans.

The megalodon slowed to a near stop, moving just enough to keep water passing through its gills. It tucked its head down, then back up, then down again, until finally, it regurgitated the unwanted segments. It passed through the cloud of muck and accelerated, escaping the scent so it wouldn't interfere with traces of fresh prey.

It glided twenty feet below the surface. Low frequency sounds filled its inner ears. Its lateral line detected water disruption coming within a thousand yards. After performing a slight left turn, the megalodon pursued to investigate. So far, its nostrils had not detected any scent of blood. The source of these signals was too far off. As it pursued, they gradually intensified. The shark quickly recognized the vibrations as something similar to the floating craft that contained a belly full of fish, as well as the human creatures that rode atop it like parasites. This memory spurred the shark forward, its interest piqued.

Within six-hundred yards, the pores that made up its lateral line detected many strong signals originating from one central location. After closing within four-hundred yards, the sense of smell detected a familiar scent: squid—something it had tasted regularly during its time in captivity. It could smell the blood and the oil.

At two hundred yards, the hunter was able to set its sights on the hunted. The 'creature' that created these low-frequency vibrations was a surface dweller. Another human craft. Here, the shark learned that the ocean was full of these things, and each of them contained sustenance. The smell of food intensified, and the megalodon moved in.

"For the love of God, where the hell did they all go?" Captain Heath Welch said. He stood in the wheelhouse of his sixty-foot trawler, his eyes fixed on the fish-finder. Minutes ago, his ship had come across a large school of tuna. The fish were flocking to his nets, drawn by the squid he and his mate had baited them with. It wasn't everyday he found such a large school of these tuna outside of their breeding grounds in the Gulf of Mexico. For a moment, it looked like he was going to have a grand catch for the day. The fact that they were considered endangered was of no concern. He knew of international buyers that occasionally flew in and out of the States that would pay top-dollar for these babies. He had read that in Japan, just one of these fish sold for a million-seven-five! Let the other fishermen keep their ethics. He wanted the money.

Then, in the blink of an eye, the school of fish dispersed. It was as though an air-raid siren had gone off under the water, warning them to stay away from the nets. Only a few were swept up by the pass.

Welch's face scrunched with irritation. He turned the boat to port, hoping he'd be able to locate the school again and salvage the opportunity. So far, the screen was practically blank, save for a few specks that indicated some stray mackerel in the area. But he didn't want them; he wanted the nine-hundred pound moneybags that were in the water.

"Hey, what's going on, Heath?!"

Welch groaned at the sound of his first mate's annoying voice. Seth was a good friend and a good fisherman, but the guy could occasionally be an impatient bastard. Especially when promised a good bounty. Welch had told Seth of the school of Atlantic Bluefin Tuna and how much they could get for it, as long as they kept quiet about it. It was illegal to trawl-fish this species due to their endangered status.

"I don't know. They scattered."

"You've got to be kidding me," Seth said. He stood on the deck, watching the net drag behind the boat. "Your engine must've scared them off."

"They don't frighten that easy," Welch said.

"Apparently they do," Seth said.

"Not from a boat engine." Welch was mumbling to himself this time while he focused on the fish-finder. He completed the pass, seeing only a few brief specks from a few tuna. He continued east. They had to be in this water somewhere.

The nets dragged behind, hauling a combined total of twenty-eight-hundred pounds from three tuna unlucky enough not to escape the binds. He thought about having Seth haul them onto the boat, but didn't want to risk not having the nets ready in case he found the school again.

A blob of green light formed on the top of the screen. Welch felt his blood rush. He almost called to his mate that he located the fish. Then he noticed the size of the object approaching. It was huge. Not just huge…ENORMOUS; larger than the boat. He thought he was seeing things. It closed within a few meters. He stared ahead and saw something that appeared to be a huge dagger slicing the water's surface, coming directly towards the bow. In a heartbeat, it dipped back under the surface.

The nets went taunt, and suddenly, the boat was racing backwards. The stern dipped low, water splashing over the transom. Seth hit the deck, caught completely off guard by whatever was happening. In the wheelhouse, Welch clung the helm. It was the only thing keeping him upright. He stared through the windshield, watching the tip of the bow lean further upward. He tried turning the wheel and accelerating. The propellers sprayed water, but did not move them forward. The boat was speeding backwards at twenty knots. Waves of seawater formed a small whirlpool on deck, tossing Seth back and forth in a mix of bait, netting, and equipment.

Finally, the net ripped violently, and the boat came loose from the invisible force that tugged it. The bow splashed down, sending large waves rolling to the sides. Welch throttled down then stood himself up. It was a struggle to catch his breath. He hurried out the back door and saw Seth drenched in water.

"What the hell was that?" Seth shouted.

"I…" Welch thought of the huge knife. It couldn't have been what he thought it was. A shark fin. It couldn't be; no shark could ever grow nearly that big. It had to be a whale or something.

But then, he saw it again. It was a hundred feet off the starboard quarter. Trailing behind it were tiny bits of meat mixed with blood and oil, as tuna were shredded to bits from enormous jaws.

The megalodon swallowed the huge fish. Its instinct had been proven correct yet again: these floating objects carried all kinds of prey. It shook its head, finishing off a tuna that was skewered in its teeth. Head, body, and tail came apart like leaves, and were wafted into its throat by the watery current. The megalodon swallowed, then focused its senses on the vibrations coming from the floating object. The faint distortions it detected matched those from the humans walking on top of the other floating objects it destroyed. The shark already learned it didn't have to fear these things, as it could destroy them easily. On top of that, this one was smaller than the last.

It turned and honed-in on the target. Its snout was now visible, as was its back and caudal fin. Water sprayed with each whipping motion. With a few quick flaps of its caudal fin, the shark made impact with its target.

Welch tried to go for the throttle, but it was too late. The shark struck the starboard midsection. A thunderous impact, rivaling the sound of a TNT explosion, pierced the sky. The hull cracked like an eggshell, and the boat violently split in two. The stern and bow shot away from each other as though jet propelled by opposing forces.

The megalodon passed through the wreckage, its enormous tail whipping the sea into a frenzy. It immediately circled back in search of new victims. The bow was taking in water from behind and quickly sinking, while the stern remained afloat at a perfect forty-five-degree angle.

Water surged into the wheelhouse, tossing Captain Welch to-and-fro. He was trapped in the structure, confused and disoriented. He took a last gasp of air near the ceiling before the water invaded its space, completely submerging the wheelhouse. He calmed himself and searched for a way out. The ship hadn't sunk far yet. All he needed to do was swim out the back door, which had been blown off its hinges.

Several yards back, Seth was clinging to the transom for dear life. An air pocket kept it afloat for the moment, but any shift in the structure would rupture it and allow the ocean to flood the interior. His boots scraped the deck as he tried to climb further up on to the ledge. His fingers were just barely over the edge. He looked back, seeing the sizzling ocean behind him. Groaning in desperation, he summoned all his strength and pulled. His arms slowly hauled his body up. His chin was over the coaming. Then his chest. He threw his arms over to the other side, got a better grasp, then hauled himself the rest of the way up.

Seth was now sitting on top of the transom as though it were a barn stable. He took in a deep breath and looked at the surrounding ocean. The churning water was starting to settle. Bits of floating wreckage bobbed around him, along with pieces of bait, netting, and a few buoys. Their life raft was nowhere to be seen, probably sinking along with the midsection of their boat.

Seth turned back and forth, looking for signs of the monster that broke through their vessel. So far, he didn't see anything. No fin, no body, nothing.

Maybe it went away.

He tried to fixate on that possibility. Maybe the shark caught some of the hull in its mouth and didn't like the taste. This frantic thinking didn't leave room for the question of how such an enormous shark could even exist. The water started smoothing out. He watched the tip of the bow slowly submerging. Suddenly, it registered that he didn't see Welch anywhere.

"Captain?" he called out. He was in the wheelhouse when the impact happened. Was he still in there? Seth watched the bow and waited. It was now completely submerged. Then, there was movement. Beneath the crystal clear water were the stroking movements of arms and legs. Welch broke the surface and took in a much needed gasp. "Captain!" Seth shouted triumphantly. Welch struggled to keep afloat. He grabbed a piece of decking, but it sank the moment he applied any weight to it. Seth glanced around him, hoping to spot a life jacket floating nearby. Or maybe a piece of netting he could toss to him and help pull him to the stern of the boat. He turned around and looked into the water.

Right by the propellers, he saw the lifeline and the donut, bobbing over tiny waves.

Perfect!

Seth reached down. His fingers fell short. Growing in frustration, he leaned further and reached, stretching his arm to the max. Still, the floating device was out of reach. He leaned further, nearly shouting in agony. Now he was grazing the water. He slapped it a few times. The rope drifted away, literally a few millimeters from his fingertips. Seth could feel himself starting to slip. He backed up momentarily, readying for another go for it. He kept his eyes on the line and the clear blue water around it.

His blood ran cold as a dark shape formed under that water. For a moment, it was as though a huge grey cloud had formed out of nowhere. In the following moment, the calm surface exploded in his face.

The megalodon breached, taking Seth and the entire transom in its jaws. Its body completed a full spiral in midair before splashing down.

Welch saw the beast landing down twenty feet beside him and screamed. A wall of water lifted him several feet upward. The shark turned to its right in a wide arch. Its tail swung across the surface. Welch saw the grey caudal fin coming right at him. It was the last thing he saw.

The tail struck the Captain. His body popped like a bug on a windshield, forming a huge red cloud. Mangled body parts were airborne, launched by the sweeping motion of the megalodon's caudal fin.

The shark circled the wreckage in search of other prey. There was nothing left here. Other small sharks rushed in, drawn by the scent of blood. The larger predator quickly snatched one in its jaws, the serrated teeth shredding the meat and cartilage. Detecting the threat, other sharks withdrew to the depths in search of easier prey.

Hungry for more sustenance, the megalodon continued its hunt. So far, its current trajectory had been a prosperous one. It resumed its journey west in search of more prey.

CHAPTER 8

"So, that's what happened," Gina said. She explained the megalodon's escape, the tracker, its current location, as well as its destructive capabilities and tendencies. "This shark is on the loose, and I guarantee it'll kill someone else if it hasn't already. Since killing it is not an option, we need to go about capturing it. At this rate, it might appear near Hamilton Bay by this afternoon. It won't stop for rest breaks. This shark will swim and eat indefinitely, until it is stopped."

"This is our fastest and most likely method of catching it," Gundrum said. "Nets will not contain it. We have a ship that can transport it, but we still have the problem of getting the specimen in the cargo hold."

"And you think my snake will do that for you?" Miguel said, restraining from chuckling. "He'll kill your shark. You put those two in the same location and you'll get a bloodbath."

"You told me yourself that you can use chemical signals with that collar to draw a snake to its target, and get it to withdraw when needed," Gundrum said.

"Once the snake attacks the megalodon, it'll constrict," Voltz said. "It'll hold the megalodon in place long enough for submersible units to attach cables to its mouth and apply tranquilizer. Once the shark is sedated, the cables will haul the creature into the cargo hold. You can use the device to call the snake off and lure it back into the ship."

Miguel closed his eyes and shook his head.

"*That's* your plan!" He chuckled. "I hope you have someone who's capable of piloting such a submersible."

"We do," Gina said. All eyes turned toward her. Gina considered her words. She had just volunteered herself to drive a submersible near a living megalodon's mouth. Even Gundrum looked surprised, but glad at the same time. He was going to ask her to perform this task eventually. It was better this way; they'd be hard pressed to get someone capable of getting the tranquilizer in the appropriate spot. Not to mention attach the cable.

Miguel shrugged his shoulders. "Your funeral. Just know; we've only conducted close-proximity testing. And I'm not convinced of the durability of that collar. A heavy impact could knock the receiver loose. With that gone, there's no controlling Eleven. Then you'll have two creatures on the loose. And no offense, I don't want to see my snake dead because of poor decision making."

"No offense taken, Dr. Lucero, because it's not *your* snake," Gundrum said coldly. "It's *my* snake."

"Yeah-yeah, I know you spent a bunch of money on it. But I'm the one who has been caring for it since day one. If the shark doesn't kill it, fishermen or the Coast Guard will. And frankly, I don't think you can guarantee its safety. Hell, are you even going on this trip?"

Gundrum ignored the question.

"Just go out and help me catch my shark. Do it, or I'll pull the funding for your institution. It's up to you."

All remaining sense of professionalism vanished from the herpetologist, and he marched forward, causing the mercenary to step between him and Gundrum.

"Listen, Gundrum, this idiotic behavior is gonna get people killed," he said. "And you're gonna DARE threaten me and my livelihood, and that of my colleagues, because I won't let you send a wild, prehistoric animal out into the open ocean?"

Gina heard a passion in his voice. Miguel spoke eloquently, but there was a demeanor behind it all that made her think of a child who was having a pet taken away to be put down. She remembered Gundrum stating that the snake had imprinted on him on the day of its birth. There was a connection there, unlike her and the megalodon. She felt honored to raise such a beast, but it would kill her without a second's hesitation. But the snake would not do that with Miguel, at least, that's what was implied from the interaction she witnessed. She would have to see more interactions to be fully convinced. Nevertheless, she understood Miguel's concern. However, it didn't change the situation at hand. The shark needed to be stopped and the most likely way to do that was to send the snake out after it. She listened to Gundrum and Miguel go back and forth, then finally, she stepped in.

"Listen! I don't want to see it dead either," she said. "This is a shitty situation that, yes, could've been avoided altogether. But it's happening, and we need to stop it. Please, help us."

Miguel stood silent. He felt the urge to argue back, but instead, he forced himself to think on what she said. He didn't want to bow to Gundrum's wishes and send his snake out into the open water. Unfortunately, he knew all too well that Marc Gundrum would not notify the Coast Guard. He had to handle this situation "quietly" after all. If he notified them himself, he probably wouldn't even be believed. Even so, any sort of effort would likely be undone by Gundrum or one of his aides. Lives were at stake, and his snake was now the only viable option to keep harm from coming to others. That left him and this marine biologist to handle the problem.

Time was running out.

"This is a bad idea," he said. He sighed, burning out the last of his resilience to this asinine plan. "When is your cargo ship arriving?"

"Within the hour," Gundrum said.

"Is it retrofitted to hold a ninety-something foot fish?"

"Yes," Gundrum said. "With designs given to us by Dr. Hutson, we've designed it to hold the megalodon firmly in place. We'll have restraints to keep it from thrashing about. Also, it'll be sedated."

"Okay, but how will it breath?"

"The cargo hold will have a pump," Gina said. "It'll be enough to keep water flowing over its gills until we get it into a proper holding cell. It was what I suggested we initially ship the specimen in, but…" she glanced at her employer, then away, "I guess, for one reason or another, we had to get the shark to Florida in a hurry."

"Yes, I admit I should've listened to you, Dr. Hutson," Gundrum said. Miguel resisted the urge to chime-in. Marc Gundrum was money hungry, for sure, but was also a patient man who took funded projects that took years to come to fruition. It wasn't in his character to make rash decisions, unless there was something significant he would gain from it. If he rushed the process of delivering the shark, it likely meant he had a strict deadline that came out of the blue. Somebody was interested in this shark, and Gundrum had promised them either a viewing, or a demonstration of some sort, or both. Whatever the case was, it didn't grant him the time to send a retrofitted cargo ship to Massachusetts and back.

"Hang on," Logan said. "I'm a little confused. So, the collar that snake is wearing is supposed to make it hone onto its target, right? For something to do that, it needs a signal to lock onto. How do you do that? Heat signature? Lock in on a satellite? How will the snake know to specifically target the shark?"

"For the snake to successfully trace it, the shark will have to have a special transmitter, called a chem-beacon, attached to it."

"And…" Jason was still confused, "that means the snake will lock-on and be like a homing missile?"

"No," Miguel chuckled. "When normal snakes hunt, they flick their tongues and pick up chemical signals around them. The signal is received by its vomeronasal organ, which allows it to know when prey is nearby.

The chem-beacon is placed on the target. Once secure it can be activated by remote. When that happens, it will send out a signal that is received by the collar. The collar sends chemical cues to implants in Eleven's vomeronasal organ, and increase as it gets closer to the target—in this case, the megalodon."

"Nice," Jason chuckled. "Sounds like an awesome way to take down an enemy ship." He noticed he was the only one chuckling, and that Miguel had sneaked another scathing glance at Marc Gundrum. "Alright, then. Next question: how the hell do we get a chem-beacon on the shark?"

Miguel looked over Jason's tactical attire. No doubt the man was a mercenary and not some private security professional.

"Well, I suppose that's where you play into this equation."

****

Miguel led the group into another laboratory full of various types of technical equipment, none of which Jason recognized. There were chemical display shelves, holding all kinds of fluid. All Jason knew was that he didn't want to be anywhere near them.

"To attach the transmitter, you'll need a harpoon," Miguel told him.

"Yeah, I figured that, Snake-Doctor," Jason said. He walked to one of the counters near the back of the room and glanced down at a black device. It looked like a big black pen. Curious, he picked it up and went to remove the cap.

"No, no, no! Don't do that!" Miguel said. Jason moved his hand away. Miguel snatched the dart away. "Freaking Darryl. What the hell was he thinking leaving this out?"

"Hey Doc, you're the lead scientist here," Jason said. Miguel nodded. The merc had a point. "What the hell is that, anyway?"

"It's an aerosol sedative, meant to knock Eleven out if he were to get loose or go on a rampage," Miguel said. "Because of his thick skin, we're unable to use a regular tranquilizer. So, we tried applying an aerosol version similar to chloroform that it would inhale through its nostrils. The problem is that it requires a high dose, which would be lethal for a human. Simply put, it could stop your heart. Contained in this room, it would've been lights out for all of us."

Jason laughed nervously, realizing he almost killed himself and everyone standing around him. Miguel locked the dart away in a steel box. He wasn't used to outsiders coming into this lab. Until now, it had only been himself and his assistants, all of which were trained to use these darts properly. It was a rare occasion where Jason found the silence to be awkward and uncomfortable.

"So, uh, does it work?" he asked.

"The sedative?" Miguel looked up from what he was doing. "Uh, sort of. Even at its high dose, it only puts the snake out for a couple of minutes at best. We don't know if it's the implants, or the creature's size, metabolic rate, or all the above, but we've struggled to find a long-lasting sedative that's effective on it. Maybe it's something in its Titanoboa DNA. I'm not sure yet." He moved to the back and opened a steel container, which held a black briefcase. He cleared some space on the center table and placed the case on top for Jason to see. He opened it, revealing a size-inch device attached to a tag that resembled a watch-strap.

Jason looked closer. The device resembled a smart phone. He looked back at Miguel.

"This is it?! This little thing? I feel like I should pick it up and play *Minecraft* on it."

"I figured you'd be more of a *Fortnite* guy," Miguel said.

"Ha! You're funny!" Jason fake-laughed. Miguel tried not to cringe as the mercenary slapped him behind the shoulder. His hand remained there for an awkward few moments, rocking him slightly as though they were old buddies.

Miguel cleared his throat and pulled away, then picked the chem-beacon out of its case.

"Get this on the shark. I can activate it electronically. 'This little thing' as you call it, can disperse enough signal to be detected by Eleven from a hundred miles away."

"Yeah? I'm not convinced. I'm almost tempted to switch it on now and see what happens."

"Then you'd hear a lot of crashing sounds—the last of which would be that door. Then you'd be crushed and eaten, along with everyone here. Except, maybe me," Miguel said. Jason appreciated the self-appreciating smugness.

"I'll take your word for it," he said. "So, all I got to do is shoot this into the shark and we'll be set up. Sounds easy enough."

"Not quite so easy," Gina said. "This shark has five-inch thick skin. It will not be easy to get a harpoon into it."

"Well, shit!" Jason said. "If a harpoon won't do the trick, then why the hell are you making me do this?!"

"I didn't say it wouldn't do the trick," Gina said. "I'm just saying you're gonna need a high-powered harpoon-gun to fire it into the shark. The skin near its fins, specifically where the fins connect to the body, is the thinnest and easiest area to puncture. It'll have no problem puncturing the cartilage underneath. And…you'll have to be at close range."

"Oh, beautiful," Jason said. "This was just what I was hoping to hear when I woke up to Gundrum's phone call: Hey, let's fight a shark with near impenetrable skin and a hyper appetite!"

"I'm paying you top dollar," Gundrum reminded him.

"Won't do me much good if I'm swallowed," Jason said. He took the chem-beacon. "So, Shark-Lady, you have something for me to track your fish with?"

"All I need is a tablet and I can install the data on it, that way you have a GPS on the megalodon at all times."

"We've got one handy for you," Nathan Ellis said.

"Alright then," Jason said. "So, I guess this is it. We have a plan. Go out, hook this little smart-device thingy to the fish, then you can go out with your pet snake and watch them fight, meanwhile the Shark Doctor will go down with a submersible and harpoon it with a sedative—while not getting eaten in the process. Then you guys will haul it into the cargo ship with steel cables and hook it up to a big-ass pump. All while hoping your snake doesn't go on a similar rampage—I need a beer."

"You and me both," Miguel said.

"I'm gonna need my choppers refueled," Jason said, looking at Gundrum.

"Already done. Your team should be arriving any minute."

"Good. Anything else you think I'll need?" Jason asked Gina.

"Chum. Lots of chum," she replied. "That's the only way you'll be able to bring the shark to the surface."

"Fantastic. Too bad there's no camera crews coming along. This'd be a hell of a *Shark Week* special."

CHAPTER 9

The sun was well into the sky when Jason Nace stepped out into the empty parking lot. Already, the temperature was over ninety-degrees and climbing. He listened to the calm waves rolling onto a nearby shore. He turned and looked at the big blue blanket stretching into the distance. It seemed so calm and tranquil. He allowed himself a brief gaze before imagining the violent sea he would witness.

"Freaking genetic research," he muttered to himself. He faced forward and saw the two Eurocopter HH-65 Dolphins. Their corrosion-resistant fuselages had been painted to a dull grey color, the exterior refitted to give them the appearance of News helicopters. The four-blade main rotor diameter was thirty-nine feet and one-inch.

Standing in front of them was his mercenary crew. There were five men, most of whom he had known since serving in the Marine Corps. The tallest member, Zielinski, stood in the center. He lived for the action rather than the cash. Had he not been booted out of the service for striking a superior officer, he would've stayed on for his full twenty years, denying promotion to stay on the front lines each time. Jason saw by the way he carried his M27, and that stupid-ass grin, that Zielinski thought he was going to shoot some pirates or some rival mercenary team.

"You won't need that," Jason said.

"The hell you talking about?" Zielinski's disappointment was clear in his tone.

"Is it cloak-and-dagger stuff?" Jason looked to the left and saw Saxon and Vaz. He wasn't sure which one had spoken, since both idiots sounded alike—and were equally as annoying. Good fighters, though. They had proven their worth during their first encounter in Yemen, even if they were Army. Standing beside them were Breton and Fox, the latter of which was already wearing his flight helmet.

"Not in these helicopters," Fox said. "Let me guess: we're performing another rescue." Jason noticed his tactical pants were still dripping wet from flying out to the *Truth Seeker,* while assisting Marc Gundrum's private security team in flying out and rescuing the surviving crew members.

"Nah! We're going spearfishing?" Breton said, pointing to Jason's harpoon rifle.

"I'm gonna break it to you guys as simply as I can," he said. "This is probably the most interesting assignment we've been given yet. And we'll probably not fire a single bullet." He braced himself for the inevitable laughter. "We're going after a shark."

Silence followed, and he was met with confused stares. The silence was broken by the snorts from suppressed laughter. The mercenaries exchanged glances; none were sure whether Jason was goofing around or being serious.

"A shark?" It was either Saxon or Vaz again. Jason was looking the other way. *Damn it, I have to actually see them talk to know who it was.*

"Not just any shark. A genetically enhanced, ninety-three-foot, megalodon shark. Like a Great White, but bigger and meaner. And prehistoric."

"You're shitting me?!" Fox said. Jason switched on the tablet and displayed the tracking signal.

"Nope. Not shitting you. Our job is to go out there, lure it to the surface with chum, and attach a tracking device so these idiots in that lab behind me can track it and catch it using—eh, another oversized genetic experiment."

"Are you jacking with us?" Breton said.

"I'm afraid not," Jason said. "Believe me, if I hadn't seen what they're holding inside that facility, I wouldn't have believed it myself. And I've seen a lot of crazy shit in my time. But the truth is that there's a giant shark swimming out there, genetically engineered by our employer Marc Gundrum, and he wants it back. Considering the rest of the plan, we've got the easy job."

"Wait, so we're just shooting a tracker into it?" This time, he saw that it was Vaz asking.

"We're not blowing it up?!" Saxon asked.

"No. The boss has too much money invested," Jason said. "We just need to get a tracker on the damn thing."

"Oh, what's the fun in that?!" Zielinski complained.

"The joy of not being eaten. I think when we see this thing, you'll understand," Jason said. The sound of engines drew their attention toward the gates. Two pickup trucks pulled into the lot and parked nearby. In the beds were several tubs of raw chum. The driver of the nearest truck stepped out and looked at the mercenaries.

"Hey *Gomer Pyle*," he called out. "You the one who ordered this chum?!" The exhibit doors opened up and Gina Hutson stepped out. A couple of the mercenaries whistled as they watched her approach the fishermen.

"Who's the babe?" Zielinski asked.

"Some paleontologist shark expert," Jason replied. Gina opened the lid of one of the tubs and gazed at the thick red mixture inside.

"Made of tuna and oil, just like you requested," the fisherman said.

"Excellent," she said. "Did you bring the harpoon?" The fisherman nodded and reached into the backseat of his truck and pulled out a stainless steel black Aquadyne Shark-XS Harpoon Gun. Gina did a check of the weapon and the harpoon it came with, making sure it would be sufficient to penetrate the meg's skin. "This'll work. Thank you."

"No problem." The fisherman and his associates carried the chum to the helicopters. The smell wafted straight into Breton's nostrils.

"What in the name of…shit!" he said. "You expect us to ride with that?!"

"Yes," Gina said.

"In a helicopter? That'll be fun," Vaz said. Or was it Saxon?

"Ladies, get a grip. They're sealed tight. They won't stain your precious outfits," Gina said. A few of the men chuckled at her brashness. The fisherman handed them some metal scoops.

"Have fun shark'n," he said.

"If only you knew the extent of it," Jason mumbled. The fishermen walked off. The mercenary leader looked at the harpoon rifle in the Doctor's hands. It was stainless steel black, roughly the size of an M4. The size caught him off guard; he thought it'd be twice as large.

"Tie the device firmly behind the tip. Obviously, make sure you leave enough space for the barb to embed itself," Gina said. Jason took the weapon and test-aimed it. It was heavier than it looked.

"What's the range?"

"For the shark, you'll want to be within thirty feet," Gina answered.

"Lovely," he said, lowering the harpoon rifle. He took the harpoon from Gina and glanced at its silver tip. "You sure this will be able to shoot straight with the device attached?"

"Yes. This model has enough power to pull standard cable," she said.

"I don't know about that," Jason said. He put the weapon into the chopper.

"So, this is it?" Zielinski said. "We just chuck this stuff out there and draw the shark to the surface."

"In a nutshell, yeah," she said. "Though, you'll want to try and make a stream. Try to scoop it into the same general spot and the tide will take it out. The megalodon will pick up the scent and follow it to you."

"I feel like I should be on the *Discovery Channel*," Fox said.

"Wouldn't it be easier to do this from a boat?" Zielinski asked.

"Trust me, you don't want to be anywhere near the water," Gina said.

"Besides, a boat will take too long to get out there," Jason said. "Speaking of which, Doc, I hope your boat's almost here. If that thing keeps heading west at this rate, it'll reach the coastline before you guys can catch it "quietly"."

"I'm aware," Gina said. "Trust me; this wasn't the way I thought my day would go when I woke up this morning."

"Same here," Jason said. He turned to face his men, and his voice boomed like a drill instructor. "Alright, men. Chitchat's over. Get these tubs on the choppers. According to the Doc's tracker, this thing is sixty-five miles off the Georgia coast. Roughly a hundred-and-fifty-four miles from our present location. At max speed, we can close in on it in thirty minutes."

The mercenaries hustled to get their supplies on board. Vaz and Saxon got in the cockpit of *Lavender*, with Fox strapping himself in the fuselage. Jason, Zielinski, and Brenton climbed aboard the second chopper, *Yeti*. Despite not intending to shoot the meg, Jason wasn't taking any chances. He did an inspection of the M240 machine gun. On Gas Setting 1, it would fire seven-hundred-and-fifty rounds-per-minute. An ammunition belt, containing fifty-one-millimeter rounds, was already inserted into the feed tray. The weapon was just waiting to be pointed out the door and fired.

He strapped himself into his flight seat, while Zielinski started rotation. The blades sliced the air above him, sending a slight vibration through his seat. A couple of moments passed and the mercenary team was airborne, going northeast at nearly two-hundred miles per hour.

CHAPTER 10

Miguel took a few minutes to enjoy the peace and quiet in his laboratory. When the mercenaries left, Dr. Hutson was transported to her hotel to change into a set of clothes more suitable for their upcoming expedition. He had done the same, changing into a set of Condor Tac-Ops pants that he used to wear during his trips to the Amazon. They were lightweight and durable, and wouldn't weigh him down if he found himself in the water. That, and he simply found them comfortable. The black t-shirt he had on would suffice for the trip. He took it off then went into the bathroom for a quick shave. The thick hairs on his face poked him, annoying the hell out of him. He was never a good beard-grower. Too many patches. Normally, it wasn't a huge deal, but considering the stress he was currently feeling, it was annoying him ten-times as much.

Since he practically lived here in the lab, he kept his toiletries here with him. He ran hot water and splashed his face, then proceeded to shave. The steam brought a mild level of comfort to him. Perhaps it was the desire for a hot shower. He ran the razor over his face, taking off patch after patch, until finally, the steel-wool feeling on his neck was gone.

He stared at himself again, watching the uncertainty in his own eyes. He questioned the morality of working for this company. He was doing it for a good reason. Right? That's how the thought process went each time. He wasn't just doing it for himself, but for other people. For science! Once again, his mind went over how working here was the opportunity of a lifetime.

Miguel had heard in his psychology classes in undergraduate school that doing the same thing over and over again was the definition of insanity. And here he was, having the same internal argument over and over again, going over the exact same beats. And it always ended the same way. He would stay with the company, despite a crushing feeling in his stomach that he was selling his soul to the devil.

He heard the lab door open behind him. Probably just Darryl or one of the other assistants. He dried his face, then turned around.

"Oh!" Gina exclaimed. She was surprised and embarrassed, feeling as though she was a guest in another person's house and walked in on them in the shower. Yet, she didn't look away. At first, she didn't realize it was Miguel Lucero. That man looked miserable, void of sleep, and generally filthy. This person still had the tired look in his eyes, but not nearly as grimy as the last.

Simultaneously, Miguel almost didn't recognize the marine biologist. She didn't look nearly as out of place as before. She wore tan belted shorts and an olive green tank top. For a moment, he was lost in her figure.

"Pardon me, Dr. Hutson," he said. He threw his shirt on and stepped out into the lab.

"Oh, no. Excuse *me*," Gina said. "I'm so sorry, I didn't think I'd find you like…" She held a hand toward the room, then let out a nervous chuckle. Inside, she was cringing. Her mind was screaming at her: *It's not like you've never seen a shirtless man before, you idiot.*

Miguel smiled. "Better than catching me with my pants down, right?" He heard himself talk and immediately realized what a stupid joke that was. *Gosh, I've been in this lab for way—WAY too long.* He walked to his desk and checked on his corn snake. It was only a foot long, red and orange in color. Miguel let the snake slither over his fingers. It coiled over his wrists, looking back and forth, flicking its tongue.

"That's a cute little corn snake," Gina said. "No offense, but I figured someone as knowledgeable as you would own more exotic species as pets." Miguel used his elbows to gesture at all the enclosures in the lab.

"You kidding? I'm surrounded by them every day. Besides…" he put his pet back in its aquarium, "it was a little ol' corn snake that sparked my interest in studying herpetology. I was an impressionable little kid. A school buddy brought home a snake from the pet store. His mom freaked out and said he couldn't keep it, so I took it." He laughed at the memory. "My mom just about had a heart attack, but luckily my dad was more laid back. I couldn't stay away from the damn thing. I started renting books from the library. I watched any documentary I could find. I guess it was an obsession."

"I prefer the word *passion*," Gina said. "I was the same way. I loved studying marine life, especially sharks. I didn't have a pet shark, mind you. But I loved reading and watching them. Got to go on a few tours and cage dives as a kid. The guy I was with let me hold this three-foot tuna out of the cage. A Great White swam by. I was only seventeen, I think. I remember it coming straight toward me, and despite my fascination, that instinct to flee was starting to kick in. But the tour guide had instructed me to remain still and just hold the fish out, so I did. I couldn't believe what happened next. It was like feeding a trained dog. It came up, took the fish out of my hand, turned and swam off. That experience really kicked off the desire to study sharks and learn more about them."

"Sounds like we had the same childhood. Just focused on different species," Miguel said.

"Very similar," Gina said. "I wasn't just focused on sharks living in present day, but I was equally as fascinated with extinct species as well. That's why I also studied paleobiology." She looked to the door at the end of the room and thought of the huge fossil on the other side. "Something you're fascinated in as well."

"Very much so," Miguel stated.

"Is that why you took this job?" Gina asked.

"It's a little more complicated," Miguel said. "During my studies, I took a unique fascination with the prehistoric Titanoboa. I became one of those conspiracy theorists that thought it might have been still alive somewhere. So, I arranged several expeditions to see if we could find clues, as well as search for new fossils. We found the fossils, but no titan snake."

"Gosh, I feel like I'm listening to myself talk. Only, substitute megalodon for Titanoboa," Gina said. "So, you found the fossil, and that's when Gundrum came to you?"

"Something like that," Miguel said. "The guy was very straight-forward in telling me what he wanted to do. Of course, I thought he was insane. But my institution had run out of money. Not only that, but it was on the verge of going bankrupt. He had agreed to fund further expeditions and helped to clear some of the institution's debts—on the basis that I work for him. But then the impossible happened: Dr. Voltz actually did it. It wasn't the way I planned to do it, but still, my dream came true in a way; I got to study a live Titanoboa, even if it was a genetically engineered one."

"What species did she mix the DNA with?" Gina asked.

"Anaconda and sea snake. That's why it has those rings," Miguel said. "Of course, I figured out why they were eager to add the sea snake into the sequence. They wanted to make sure the thing could swim in the open ocean."

"I'm not sure I understand," Gina said.

"You do realize why Gundrum wanted your shark here in such a hurry, right?" Miguel said. Gina shook her head. She had a few concerns, and the conversations she heard between Marc and Nathan made her feel a little nervous. But up until today, she had witnessed nothing that made her suspect the megalodon was bred for anything other than showcasing at the exhibit.

"What do you think they're for?" she asked, her voice shaky. Miguel hesitated to answer.

"I think they were developed as weapons to sell, either to the government, or some arms dealer," Miguel said. Gina cocked her head back. That couldn't be right. The government had nuclear weapons, for godsake. Why would they want a shark or a snake as a weapon?

The question came out verbally. "What good would wild animals be as weapons?"

"Good for attacking enemy ships," Miguel answered. "They'd be especially good at eliminating targets in countries we're not supposed to be in. Hence the secrecy. It'd be an easy denial if a snake slithered on board an Iranian battleship and killed the crew. The government could simply say, 'we didn't have anything to do with it.' Also, it'd be a good way of slowing supply shipments to nations we might not be getting along with. Either of these creatures could provide a great advantage in controlling the seas. And who'd believe the story of a giant sea monster?"

"I—" Gina stammered. "You really think that's what they're doing?"

"Why do you think both creatures have insatiable appetites? It's not just because they're so big," Miguel said. "Oh… and on that note, I'm sure you've noticed the size of the specimen. You've mentioned before that you didn't think they grew that large, and you were correct. How do you think that happened?"

"They were engineered that way." Gina was starting to sweat again.

"How big is your megalodon?"

"Ninety-three feet," she said.

"And they typically grew up to, what, sixty feet on average?"

"Yes," she said. His concern sounded a little too unbelievable. Then again, she thought the same thing when approached about the experiment. And those non-disclosure forms. She had given them a second look and recalled that there was no expiration on the agreement. She was instructed not to say anything to anyone…ever.

She still wasn't sure if she believed it, but it was clear that Miguel did.

"If you're convinced of this, then why do you continue to work for Gundrum Industries?" she asked. Miguel was silent. He took a few steps into his lab and looked at the snakes. His eyes then turned to a picture on the wall, which featured him and some of his colleagues at the dig site where the Titanoboa was found.

"I guess because I promised to help the institution…and…" he sighed, almost shamefully, "I can't seem to let go of my dream."

One of the lab assistants suddenly entered the lab.

"Doctors? Pardon me, but the ship has arrived."

CHAPTER 11

The *Armstrong* was six-hundred feet in length, with a beam of a hundred-and-seventy-five feet at its widest point. Its hull had been freshly painted grey. On its deck were crane arms, containing extension cables designed by NASA. It had two ramp doors, the largest of which was located on the stern, the other on the portside. The superstructure stood fifty feet high overlooking the main deck.

The ship aligned at the end of the transfer tunnel. Captain Vihaan Seabolt stepped out from the bridge and worked his way down to the port rail. He climbed down a ladder to the dock lining the back of the tunnel.

Gina and Miguel stepped out of the exhibit and saw Marc Gundrum crossing the dock to meet the Captain, then hurried out to catch up with him.

"Good morning, Captain Seabolt. I appreciate you arriving on short notice," Marc said.

"You ought to. It was not easy getting all my crew notified in the time I was given," Seabolt replied.

"Your payment has been sent electronically to your account," Marc said. "Once the task is complete, you will receive the full sum. With a little luck, this job will not take more than a day to complete."

"We'll need more than a little luck," Gina said. Seabolt grinned.

"Good morning, ma'am," he said. He removed his ball cap and extended a hand. As Gina shook it, she noticed the twin anchors tattoo. It looked like a military emblem, though not from the U.S. Armed Forces. His English was good, but there was a hint of an accent behind it. She couldn't place it, but it sounded East Asian. India, most likely.

"Good morning," she replied.

"May I assume you're the shark expert that will be tagging along on this voyage?"

"Not just tagging along. You won't be able to catch this thing without me," Gina said. Obviously, this man knew what they were after. It made sense of course. If the cargo holds were retrofitted correctly, it'd be difficult to hide from the ship's crew what they were doing.

"Ah! You plan on piloting the submersible near the mouth of a shark four times the size of a Great White?" he said. The way he spoke the question seemed like it was meant to invoke a reaction. The hesitation in Gina's answer gave away the anxiety she was feeling. It wasn't so much a test of her character, but a gauging of the dangers of this operation. "You see, Doctor, I might be a greedy ol' capitalist, but I'm not ruthless. I'm not going to put my crew in unnecessary danger. I know what it's like to inform loved ones of the demise of sailors. It's a part of my job I'd like to minimize as much as possible."

"Believe me, Captain," Gina said, "that shark will be sedated before it gets anywhere near the ship."

"Yeah? And what about this snake that I'm supposedly picking up from here?" Seabolt asked.

"Keep your crew out of sight," Miguel explained. "As long as there's no prey to distract it, I should have no problem luring it into the cargo hold. Speaking of which, how have the holds been refitted?"

"Would you care to take a look?" Seabolt asked. They followed him back to the ship and climbed a ladder up to the main deck. The deck was mirror-smooth, made from metal plating welded to the hull. "There are two holds, specifically detailed to accommodate each species."

"Which one will be used by Eleven?" Miguel asked.

"That'll be Hold Two. Follow me please," Seabolt said. They walked across the mid-deck to the cargo hold. It was covered by two steel doors. The Captain retrieved a radio from his pocket and looked to the structure. "Open hatch two." The doors yawned open, giving the scientists a view of the interior. It was set up similarly to the snake's exhibit. Artificial lights beamed down from the overhead, maintaining ninety-degree head inside the hold. There was a pool in the middle, though not nearly large enough for the snake to submerge in. There were catwalks along the top connected to access doors.

Miguel couldn't help but notice the relatively small size of the hold. The snake would have to curl up to its whole body to fit in, which made Miguel nervous. He wasn't sure how the creature would handle being trapped in such tight quarters.

"You couldn't give it any bigger of a space?" he said.

"Don't ask me. I just run the ship," Seabolt said. "Ask Mr. Gundrum's interior decorators. But if you want my opinion, I saw the pumps that they were installing for Hold One, and frankly, I don't see how they could make any more space if they tried." Miguel nodded.

"I'll have to go in there to place the receiver," he said.

"Do whatever you need to do. Just don't complain to me if your pet eats you," Seabolt said.

"It's not me I'm worried about it eating," he said.

"What about the megalodon's hold?" Gina asked.

"Back this way," Seabolt said. They approached the superstructure and stepped through the base entrance. They followed a set of stairs into the interior of the ship. They passed through a set of steel passageways, until Seabolt opened a door that led onto a narrow catwalk overlooking a huge pool. At the front end was a large pump as large as a train tunnel. The hold had already been filled with seawater, but the pump had not yet been activated. Above that pump was a separate winch containing a high-tension cable. Across from the scientists were huge metal restraints, designed like enormous handcuffs. There were three of them, one to come down over the shark's head, another to come down over its back, the third for its tail.

"Okay, it looks good," she said.

"Will this actually hold it?" Miguel asked.

"I'm confident they will," Gina said. "Once I drug the shark, we'll use the crane to guide it around the stern. The loading ramp will open and we'll use this winch here to attach a cable, which we'll use to pull the shark inside. Once the shark is in place, the restraints would come down over its back and latch to berths located underneath it. Once connected, the shark will be locked in place, unable to move. The pump will keep it from suffocating. One thing is for certain: the shark won't be able to rampage like it did in the *Truth Seeker.*"

"Okay, but how the hell would we get it out?" Miguel asked. "Last I checked, sharks don't swim backwards."

"Once we're in the pool, we'll detach the latches and open the ramp. Once that's done, we'll increase the pressure on the pump and literally push the shark out into the holding tank."

"I'd say you people are insane, but then again, I'm the idiot who chose to run this ship," Seabolt said. "Then again, I'm not the one planning on swimming close to the thing's mouth."

"Speaking of which, where's the sub?" Gina asked.

"Next hold over."

"I thought there were only two," Miguel said.

"I guess I should've elaborated," Seabolt said. "Two holds for the animals. The third is where we're storing the submarine." He led them back into the passageway into a juncture where they took a left-hand turn. After a short walk, they found a stairwell that led them down several meters, ending at a door that led into Hold Three.

Gina walked across the deck toward the one-man Triton submersible. The seven-foot sphere reflected her gaze back at her as she leaned near. The yellow body behind the glass sphere had a curved shape, almost resembling a recliner. Two mechanical arms jutted from the front side that arched under the sphere. On each side of the main body were two more mechanical arms, each curled up on the sides. On each side of the ballast were two steel harpoon guns with wire tubes connecting to the main controls. Each gun contained two barrels, equaling a total of four shots.

Gina climbed overtop and opened the hatch, then lowered herself into the control seat. Seabolt chuckled as he watched her examine the controls inside.

"You look like a guppy in a fishbowl," he said. "I'm afraid that's how your fish is going to view you as well."

"He'll be preoccupied by the time I'm in the water," she said.

"Yeah? That's if everything goes as planned," Seabolt said. "He'll swallow that thing whole."

"He'd choke before he'd do that," Gina said. "It's designed to withstand high pressures of deep-sea diving. And this thing is faster than it looks. Its modular construction allows for rapid re-configuration between tasks. He'll have to put extra work in just to catch me, and he'll have an even harder time trying to break through the glass."

"Believe me, he'll try," Miguel said.

"Then your snake collar better work," Gina said. She climbed out of the sphere. "Because I'm really not eager to test that theory."

"We're about to find out if it works," Miguel said. "Captain Seabolt, order your crew below deck. Have all of them avoid the cargo area. I'm about to initiate transfer of Eleven to its quarters, and believe me, if any of your men are in sight…they won't be for long."

"Understood," Seabolt said. "I'll have them armed with rifles just in case."

"It'd be a waste of time," Miguel said. "Its skin is strong enough to withstand a round from a Barret M82, much less a point-two-two-three rifle round. Everyone's best bet is to stay hidden." Seabolt's eyes narrowed. He looked over at Marc Gundrum. They would have words later; the bastard had said rifles would be sufficient protection should the mission go sideways. He handed Miguel a portable radio.

"I'll be in the bridge," he said. "I'll be watching through the monitors. Let me know when to open and shut the doors."

"You got it," Miguel said.

They followed the Captain back up onto the main deck. He continued on upstairs into the superstructure, leaving the scientists to prepare the cargo hold for the Colossal Snake. Miguel could feel the shakiness in his breath. Apprehension was wrapping him tight in its grip. He tilted his chin up to take in the cool ocean breeze. It didn't help.

"You alright?" Gina asked.

"Yes," Miguel lied. He continued to the ladder, hesitating before climbing down. He admitted the truth, "No. I don't want to get Eleven involved in this." He saw that Gina was about to climb down after him, which prompted him to continue down the ladder.

"Listen, I get it. You're worried about the snake. But keep in mind: there's no other way we're stopping that shark," she said. She climbed down to the walkway. "I'm actually really confident that even if the mission doesn't go as planned, your snake will come out of this just fine. If we can't tranquilize the megalodon, the snake will probably constrict it to death."

"I'm shocked you're so open to the idea of killing it," he said.

"Dr. Lucero, I don't want it dead, but this thing has already killed a number of people. Including my assistant, whom I've known for a couple of years now. And now it's out there in the open ocean, heading for the coast where it'll kill countless others unless we stop it."

"I won't argue against that," Miguel said.

"You said yourself that these things were secretly being designed as weapons," Gina said. "Then it's our responsibility to stop them before they cause any more damage."

"Eleven hasn't caused any damage...well, at least it hasn't taken human life. Came close a few times, but never killed anybody. It doesn't deserve to be put in this situation."

"Then why are you helping?" she asked.

"Because if I don't, Marc will just replace me with someone else. I figure I'm Eleven's best hope for survival."

"Miguel..." She stepped in front of him, stopping him. "I'm gonna tell you something that I think you already know, but don't want to acknowledge. We've both raised prehistoric creatures. Yeah, there was some genetic tampering in the process, but overall, they are as pure to their genus as can be. The truth is, these things are extinct for a reason, whether it's God's will, or just nature correcting itself. The Titanoboa and the megalodon are not meant to be in this world. I don't say that out of hate, or a desire to see them dead. I'm a scientist—studying the meg and seeing the Titanoboa has been an indescribable experience. But they're violent creatures that aren't meant to be contained. And if your concern about Marc's dealings are correct, then it's probably best that they both die in combat." An extended period of silence passed between them.

"Not going to happen," Miguel said. "And if you're so convinced with what you're saying, why are you volunteering to go down into that submersible? Or do you intend to, say, switch out the tranquilizer with a poison or something?" Gina didn't say anything. Miguel noticed her eyes turn away briefly—a telltale sign of dishonesty. He looked back to the ship to make sure nobody was around to hear them, then he put a hand on her shoulder and led her down the dock toward the shore.

"Are you insane?" he whispered sharply in her ear. "If Gundrum finds out, he'll kill you."

"He'll just fire me."

"That's if you're lucky. If he does, he'll go beyond having you blacklisted. Simply put, you'd be lucky to get a job making lattes."

"I can't go on knowing I raised something that's gonna be responsible for countless deaths."

"You're responding emotionally," Miguel said. "Besides, where are you gonna get the poison? They shipped you in from Massachusetts yesterday; I doubt you knew in advance to bring in a shitload of poison to kill your shark."

"No…but I know you have some here," she said. Miguel stopped. They stood outside the back door of the building.

"No," he said.

"Doctor, I know you have a supply of snake venom in this facility, as well as other poisons. We can collect it into some cannisters, and—"

"I already said no," Miguel said. Gina stood shocked. Here was the scientist who directly informed her what was going on; who openly showed distain towards Marc Gundrum, who knew that the snake would soon be taken away by some unnamed buyer. Yet, despite being probably the only person other than her to objectively understand what was going on, he chose inaction.

"Why?" Gina said.

"Why what?" Miguel replied.

"I get you're reasoning for not wanting Eleven destroyed. But the shark? Why won't you help me?"

"Because I'm the only one with access to the poison," he said. "If you acquire it, they'll know I was the one who helped you. Not happening. I give a damn about my future."

Gina felt herself on the verge of pleading. "As long as we're part of this, we're responsible. What good is our future if we allow this to happen?"

"It'll happen with or without us," Miguel said. They stood staring silently at each other. "I'm sorry. I gotta get Joel ready to transition to the vessel." He stepped passed her and disappeared behind the door.

Gina stood alone, angry. She felt her whole world had been turned upside down. Yesterday, she was just a simple biologist. Then, this morning, she became a shark hunter who learned her company was manufacturing monsters. Now, she was helpless, stuck with only one action: Tranquilize the shark as originally intended and help Gundrum Industries recapture it. At least she could get it out of the water for a few days. The rationale failed to bring her comfort.

She felt anger toward Dr. Lucero. He was a smart man, yet, he couldn't withdraw his emotions from the experiment. She knew that he knew that the snake's instinct would cost the lives of countless innocents, and that creatures of this magnitude could not be controlled.

Hopefully, he won't be proven wrong when transferring it to the ship.

CHAPTER 12

“Closing on target. Decreasing altitude to thirty meters,” Brenton spoke into his microphone. Jason could hear him plain from the fuselage, despite the drone of the rotators. His eyes went from the tablet to the crystal blue ocean. With the speed in which they flew, there was hardly a detail to be noted other than the ocean’s basic color and infinite reach.

“Decrease speed by fifty knots,” he said. “*Lavender,* confirm.”

“Confirm. Decreasing speed.” It was either Saxon of Vaz. Jason watched the tablet again.

“We’re within five-hundred meters of target,” he said. “Brenton, we’re gonna need to get lower. *Lavender*, move twenty degrees to port, then decrease altitude to twelve meters and initiate chumming procedure. I want you aligned with its trajectory.”

“Lovely. At least we’ll finally spare ourselves from the smell,” one of the pilots said.

“Actually, it’ll get worse when you open the lid,” Jason said. “Remember to do it gradually. We have to let the current form a trail. Brenton, wait for them to get into position, then bring us seven meters in front of them, then get us low so I can stick this harpoon when the bastard surfaces.”

“Do we really want to be that low?” Brenton asked.

“Do I *want* to? No. But I guess it’s necessary to stick this in just right,” Jason answered.

“Oh shit, they’ve hired YOU to attempt the sticking. Well, then we’re really fucked. Unless you pay the shark fifty bucks.” Laughter filled the radio waves. Brenton and Zielinski joined in, the former stepping back into the fuselage. He positioned his mic, the smile on his face indicative of his willingness to get in on the fun.

“I don’t know, guys. Fifty bucks only buys oral services.” More laughter filled Jason’s ears.

“Alright, knock it off. Let’s focus, please,” he said. The laughter subsided and the other chopper started getting into position. Several moments passed. "Shark doesn't have a big enough mouth anyway, if you know what I mean."

"Nice try on a comeback, boss. But now I can only imagine a cookie cutter shark hanging off your dick."

"The fact that my dick's in your mind to begin with is something I find very disturbing, Fox," Jason said. He waited a moment for the chuckles to wane, then watched the chopper's position. "Alright, enough about my dick and back to the job at hand. *Lavender,* stop there. Descend another five meters and open the fuselage door. Fox, get that scoop out and get to chumming. Brenton, bring us around to the front."

"Copy that. Turning eighteen degrees starboard," Brenton said. He brought the chopper in front of *Lavender* and rotated so the starboard fuselage door faced the bow. A rush of salt air hit Zielinski and Jason as they slid the door open. They saw the ocean below them, churning from the endless onslaught of air blasting its surface.

Jason grabbed the three-foot harpoon. The chem-beacon was secured through tiny loops located a few inches behind the barb. He glanced at the narrow tip. Just by looking at it, he could tell it could puncture an inch of steel and not lose its form. But what was an inch of steel compared to five-inches of megalodon skin? He didn't know.

"Go for the fin," he mimicked Dr. Hutson. He loaded the harpoon into the gun. Its tip extended nearly a foot over the weapon's barrel. He felt like a calvary soldier in medieval times wielding a spear.

He harnessed himself to a safety-line and knelt by the open door. The goggles protected his eyes from the constant onslaught of wind from the chopper blades. Twenty-one feet ahead of him, *Lavender* at equal elevation. The fuselage doors were open and brown red blobs of chum spilled into the water.

The operation had begun.

"Ugh!" Fox complained. *"You sure I can't just dump this shit all at once?"*

"No, Fox," Jason said. "We have to make a trail. Apply the chum gradually, or Dr. Hutson will smack you."

"Oh, I'm scared now," Saxon…or Vaz, replied. A few more scoopfuls of chum hit the water. Jason watched the surface gradually turn brown. If it wasn't for the wind gusts bombarding the surface, he'd be able to see the meaty cloud forming under the water, enticing anything lurking below.

"Zielinski, watch that tracker," Jason said. "How far off is the target?"

"Seven-hundred meters east," Zielinski answered. Closer.

"Moving towards us?"

"Affirmative."

"Keep chumming boys. It's working," Jason said. He watched as more chum was tossed into the sea. The mixture swished, gradually trailing a large brown line that went northeast.

"Looks like the shark's picking up the scent," Zielinski said. "It's at five-hundred meters."

"Yummy-yummy-yummy, I got chum in my tummy!" someone sang.

"Knock it off," Jason said, shaking his head. "For godsake, I'd rather attend an Amy Schumer concert than listen to you sing."

"That's low, boss." Once again, the airwaves flooded with laughter. Several more minutes passed. Fox continued flooding the ocean with chum.

"Damn! When's this shark gonna show up?"

"Gotta date, Fox?"

"What if I do?"

"I'd ask what his name is."

"That's insensitive, Saxon. Remember, love is love."

"Love, and a sore ass!" Brenton added.

Jason shook his head, enduring the banter through his headset.

"Boss," Zielinski said. "Target's increasing speed. Distance two-seventy." Jason perked up.

"Jesus, he's going twice as fast," he said. "Alright, boys and girls, we've got company coming. Let's set the table."

"Wait...who's the girl he's addressing?" Fox remarked.

"That'd be you, Fox, screaming like a little bitch if you don't listen," Jason said. "Saxon, I want you to ascend gradually. Fox, keep chumming. Brenton, move us closer. Keep it slow. I don't know how well this shark can see, but I don't want to risk scaring it off with any sudden movements." *For godsake, I'm talking about scaring a ninety-three-foot shark that sunk a cargo ship five times its size.*

Lavender ascended. Scoopfuls of mixture continued falling over the side. There was a pancake shaped blob of minced meat and oil floating about. Brenton gradually brought the *Yeti* to starboard, stopping as they were a few feet beneath the others.

"It's approaching," Zielinski said. "We should see it at any moment." Jason drew a breath, pressed the weapon to his shoulder, and took aim.

"Cease the chumming and pull away. Standby to provide cover fire."

Lavender pulled off another ten yards to create space, then rotated to aim its port machine gun at the target area. The sea beneath thrashed, mixing oil and ocean. There were a few fish picking at the bits, splashing the surface. Jason searched the few shapes, waiting for a giant one to engulf the feeding frenzy.

"It's right below us," Zielinski said. He stood on the other side of the door and watched the water. The airwaves went silent. All sense of humor vanished from the group. They waited, eager to see the mammoth shark in its full glory. After several seconds, Zielinski pointed to the right. "I see something. There!"

The water thrashed and they saw a tail. It was a crescent-shaped fin, splashing the water. They saw the open mouth breach the surface, taking in a tuna and several gallons of chum.

A series of *huhs* came through the airwaves.

"That's one scary fish. Looks a little shorter than ninety-three feet," Fox said. The mercenaries started laughing at the fourteen-foot tiger shark swimming along the surface. It thrashed about, shredding its prey. Saxon and Vaz laughed into their microphones as they witnessed its four-hundred-pound prey split in half.

"I think those science friends of yours need a measuring stick," Zielinski said.

"That's not the shark," Jason said.

"Hey fishy! Want a little dessert?!" Fox shouted. He took a scoopful of chum and tossed it into the water.

"Guys, knock it off," Jason said. "Zielinski, what are you looking at me like that for? Keep your eye on that monitor."

"Sorry, boss. But according to the feed here, the target is exactly where that tiger shark is." Jason's eyes went wide. He looked back to the water.

He saw it.

For the span of a heartbeat, it looked like a massive cloud lingering beneath the cloud of chum. Then it breached the surface like a surface-to-air missile, its massive jaws clamping shut on the tiger shark. Its momentum drove it completely out of the water, until its nose smashed into the *Yeti's* undercarriage.

"FUCK!" Jason yelled. The chopper bounced upward then spun wildly. Alarms began sounding off. Brenton fought for control. He tugged on the joystick, unable to steady the aircraft as it spun to starboard. A rush of wind invaded the fuselage.

Jason held tight to his rope, while keeping one hand on the harpoon gun. The ocean twirled around them outside. Brenton tugged on the joystick. The spiral slowed, but the chopper was still flying out of control. He looked up from his controls and realized he was speeding right towards *Lavender*.

"PULL UP!"

The *Lavender* ascended. Unfortunately, Brenton had done the same.

“Bank right!” he yelled in desperation. Both choppers dove in opposite directions, their rotators sawing within a yard of each other. The *Lavender* descended too rapidly; it was heading right into the ocean. The pilots slowed the descent, stopping it just a few feet above the water.

“Son of a bitch!”

“You see that thing?”

“Yes. That was too damn close!”

“No shit. Speaking of which, get us the hell away from—”

As though containing the power of a volcanic eruption, the ocean exploded upward. Thick sheets of chum-infested water engulfed the *Lavender*, blinding those inside to the huge mass shooting up at them from under the nose.

The megalodon shot up out of the ocean. Teeth, still containing thin strips of tiger shark flesh, struck the hull. The force of the impact flipped the chopper backwards. The shark was completely out of the ocean again, arching its head downward, driving the chopper down into the water like a bass with a dragonfly.

Brenton steadied the *Yeti*, then saw the fish crash back down into the ocean. Jason and Zielinski looked into the ocean and witnessed the explosion of metal fragments bursting from the chopper’s body. The tail broke off completely, the rotators still going. The main rotors exploded into two-foot projectiles. Some of them skipped several yards over the ocean’s surface, while others shot straight up into the air.

Brenton cursed as shrapnel struck the hull, forcing him to pull up again.

“Jeeeesus CHRIST!” Jason snarled. The ocean spun into a whirlpool. The megalodon swam along the surface, its dorsal and caudal fin making huge ripples as it went. In its mouth was the *Lavender*…what was left of it. “Vaz! Saxon! Fox!” It dipped before anyone could answer, carrying its prize under. By now, the radio equipment could be fried anyway, making the crew unable to respond if they were still alive. “Get us lower!”

“Are you insane?” Brenton argued.

“Fifteen meters,” Jason said. “We need to be ready if any of them surface.” Brenton gripped the joystick, then focused again. Jason was right: they didn’t leave any of their crew behind. He ascended a hundred feet then steadied the chopper. Jason hung his head out of the fuselage door. He could hear crashing sounds somewhere under the water, but couldn’t quite see anything yet. The chaos had spread the chum about, thinning the cloud until it was almost gone. He could see a few meters deep, but nothing beyond that.

"There! Portside," Zielinski said. Jason turned to look. In the water was a man, he instantly recognized the buzzcut. It was Fox. He saw their chopper and began swimming in their direction, seemingly uninjured.

A hundred meters beyond him, a huge mass creased the ocean's surface. The dorsal fin rode atop of the enormous grey body as the megalodon patrolled the waters. It turned, sensing Fox's movements. Jason watched the beast. It raised its head slightly, briefly revealing its teeth. There was a mash of body parts in its teeth with flakes of black clothing trailing behind it.

It was either Vaz or Saxon. Or both—Jason couldn't tell. All he did know was that there was no other movement.

"Bring us down there. Zielinski, prep a lifeline," he said. Moist air flooded the fuselage as the aircraft descended. The mercenaries opened the portside doors. They were a dozen feet above Fox now.

Huge swells rolled behind him. The meg approached, spurred by the vibrations caused by the rotor gusts.

"Shit, it's moving fast!" Brenton said. Jason tossed the line. Fox grabbed for it but missed. Gritting teeth, Jason positioned the port gun, aimed it out at the grey mass, then fired several bursts.

"Eat this, you fat bastard!"

The bullets splattered over the megalodon's nose, chipping away thin strips of flesh, but otherwise causing no injury.

"Fox, grab the damn rope!"

Fox grabbed again, feeling the damn rope bouncing off the tip of his gloves. Every time he swam towards it, it got pushed back just out of reach. It felt as though the ocean was just toying with him at this point. The mercenary looked back and saw the huge tidal waves cresting behind him, and the pointed snout pushing them along. He screamed and reached out again. Finally, his hand found the line.

"Pull up! Pull the fuck up!" he shouted. He felt the line go taut and his body lift from the surface, dripping water. His look of terror became one of relief as he saw the ocean below him instead of around him. He glanced back at the shark, which had dipped under the waves. "HA! Nice try, you dumb oversized—"

The ocean burst again, and the meg soared skyward. Its jaws closed over Fox and the lifeline. Gravity pulled the shark back to the ocean. The rope went taut, dragging the chopper down briefly before it snapped. The *Yeti* dipped to port. Jason fell forward, but was braced with the gun harness. Zielinski, however, had no such safety device attached. He threw his hands for anything he could grab, but found nothing but open air. He hit the water right after the meg, disappearing in the tremendous splash.

Once again, Brenton had to fight for control.

"Don't stall. Don't stall. Come on, baby," he said. He started the compensation process by incorporating a vertical flap.

Jason combed the waters with his eyes, watching for Zielinski. He saw the former marine breach the surface, and the huge cloud forming underneath him. The 'cloud' opened its mouth, lined with seven-inch teeth. Zielinski was caught up in the initial swell, then swept into the megalodon's throat. The shark continued along the surface, swimming along its side. Its right pectoral fin served as a dorsal for a few short moments, before the fish ducked under again.

Jason seethed, watching the water with unblinking eyes. In a span of a few short minutes, the shark had wiped out his entire team except himself and Brenton. A bloodlust boiled within him that he had to mentally subdue. He couldn't succumb to his emotions and blow the shark out of the water. If he did that, then his men died for nothing. No, he would tag the shark as planned.

He watched it slithering under the waves, waiting for them to come back within reach. Jason Nace eagerly awaited as well. He rested his finger on the machine gun's trigger, ready to go toe-to-toe with the beast.

I'm ready, you fat bastard.

The megalodon completed a circle, its nostrils still picking up traces of the chum mixture the mercenaries had dropped. It could see the helicopter high above, but it was far out of reach. There was no other sign of prey in the immediate area, and the flying thing carrying the land dwelling creatures showed no signs of drawing near.

Finally, its lateral line detected vibrations coming from the west. Something dull and large, like something struggling on the ocean floor. However, this wasn't coming from down below. It was way off in the distance, directly ahead of it, out of sight. The vibrations were accompanied by deep humming sounds, similar to that of the inedible creatures that traveled the surface. Where those things were, there was food. The hungry megalodon swung its mighty tail, zipping southwest toward the new sound.

Jason watched the shark swim out of sight, his racing blood causing his veins to bulge.

"Get after it!" he shouted to Brenton.

"You insane? That thing almost brought us down TWICE!" Brenton argued. "And it killed everyone else. Every time we get in range to sink that harpoon into it, it breaches!"

"Brenton..." Jason stomped his way into the cockpit. "You're speaking as though you have a choice in this matter." The pilot looked into Jason's blazing eyes. The unspoken threat was genuine. Jason would toss him overboard and resume the chase himself if need be. How he'd get the harpoon into the shark while piloting the chopper was beside the point—he wasn't thinking that far ahead. Nor would he in this state of rage.

"Not how I thought my day would go," the mercenary pilot muttered. He turned the ship southeast and began following the shark's trajectory.

****

Captain Richard Redway stood by the winch, soaked in a mixture of sweat and seawater. He kept his hand on the winch, ready to retract the net once the go-ahead was given. Along with being irritated, he was embarrassed. He had bottom-trawled for many years and should've known to avoid the shallow reefs. His three crewmates stood silently, not daring to say a word about the incident.

It was the fourth day of their trawl, which was their sixth of the summer. While other ships were bringing in hot loads of catch, Lady Luck was turning a cold shoulder to the Captain and crew of the seventy-foot *Great Reef*. Each trip brought back roughly a load of eighteen-thousand pounds. After the checks were cut, the expenses paid for, the crewmembers were left with a share of two-grand or less each time. Considering the time spent at sea and the cost of living on the coast, they needed a hell of a lot more than that.

Now, Redway was facing the consequences of his recent decision. With this voyage bringing in numbers comparable to the rest of the summer, rumors began to spread of crewmembers seeking work on other ships.

At 9:30, he finally got several blips on the sonar. Hundreds of them. Mackerel, cod, and flounders, just waiting to be scooped up. The problem was that they were gathering near a shallow reef. Trawling in this area with a net would likely result in a snagging; a fact that all of his crew, including his brother, reminded him of. Redway, however, succumbed to desperation and attempted the pass. At 9:47, he regretted that decision. On the first pass, he steered too close to a rock and snagged the net on something below. Attempts to reel it in strained the winch and bent the otter board. He tried reversing the ship to pull away, only managing to entangle it further.

The only option was for someone to dive and free the net manually. Cutting it away was not an option for Redway, as he couldn't afford the twelve-grand it would cost to replace it. His saving grace was his brother, Nathan, who was a certified diver. After gearing up with his scuba equipment, the thirty-two-year-old first mate splashed down and freed the ship.

Fifteen minutes felt like a lifetime. Thirty felt like an eternity. It was a quarter after ten now. Later. Redway could see the net twitching a few inches as his brother worked on it. His hand tapped the ledge, waiting for Nathan to appear and tell him to try reeling it in again.

There were whispers from his crew. Jacob and Ted were standing by the transom, arms crossed. They had just about had it with their Captain and his juvenile decisions. Even Pepper, the first-year rookie, had the good sense to speak up about avoiding the reef. When the rookie had better sense than a ten-year Captain, these crew knew it was time to move on.

"Almost done," Redway said.

"Uh-huh," Ted muttered. Redway's fingers squeezed the lever to the point, his veins bulging. He exhaled slowly through his nose. All he could do at this point was absorb the unspoken insults. The crew were right to be pissed at him anyway. He kept his eyes on the water. Air bubbles popped near the hull. A moment later, Nathan stuck his head up and removed his goggles.

"How's it looking?" Redway asked.

"Try bringing it back slowly," Nathan said. "Give me just a sec." He started paddling back to avoid getting caught up in the net. "Alright. Go ahead." Redway started the winch. The machine rattled loudly. Something had come loose during his previous attempts to bring the net in. But it still worked. The net came in, carrying shards of coral reef up along with it. Some of the netting had been ripped but it wasn't anything the crew couldn't mend.

"Oh, thank God," Redway said. A tremendous weight came off his shoulders. No longer was he looking at spending twelve thousand he didn't have. He gave a thumbs up to his brother. "Nathan, you're a lifesaver."

"That's what I'm told," Nathan retorted. He turned around and started swimming for the stern ladder. Ted and Jacob leaned over the transom to take his gear. Nathan handed up his flippers and scissors, then grasped the ladder bar. He climbed two steps then stopped, noticing the two crewmen staring out past him. Their mouths were agape, like they were staring at a ghost. Then he heard the swelling of water.

Nathan's first thought was a rogue wave. He tucked his head down and braced for impact. Then the men screamed. Nathan lifted his head and saw the huge tunnel-shaped shadow come over him. Suddenly, the world went dark. There was a searing pain in his wrist. He felt the gushing of his own blood and the mixture of sea water stinging his insides as he was whooshed around. Then, the black world turned boiling hot.

The boat pitched forward with the impact, throwing Richard Redway to the deck. In the instant prior, he and everyone else stood in stunned silence, simultaneously questioning their sanity when they saw the seven-foot dorsal fin sailing toward their ship. Then the torpedo-shaped head burst from the waves, its demonic mouth baring teeth as long and thick as soda bottles, and came down on Nathan Redway.

The impact sent the ship into a spiral. Redway rolled to his hands and knees, trying to grasp what had just happened. When he stood up, he saw that Ted and Jacob were gone. Only the rookie Pepper could be seen on the deck. He was on his back, looking as though he had been sucker-punched. Redway looked at the stern. The transom had been splintered. The ladder was bent inward, curving over the deck. Clenched on one of the bars was Nathan's severed hand, the fingers frozen in death.

"Oh God. Oh…oh my God, Captain!" Pepper said. He stood up and staggered. Redway could barely hear him. His eyes were fixed on the hand, his mind replaying the horrific event that had just unfolded. Pepper's voice was a distant echo.

"Captain! Captain! CAPTAIN!"

Redway shook as a pair of hands grabbed him by the shoulder. Pepper was in his face, his expression pale and wrinkled with fright. He jolted Redway twice before he came back into reality. Pepper pointed out beyond the port aft. Both men stared in horror, realizing it was not a figment of their imaginations. They were looking at a monster shark. It was impossible—such a thing couldn't exist. Yet, they were looking at the impossible.

It was over a hundred yards out, swimming in a straight line along the surface. A hundred feet ahead of it was Jacob. The crewman was staring directly at the beast, backstroking frantically, screaming for someone to wake him up from this nightmare. The jaws came down on him like a cigar cutter, splitting him in half instantly.

Pepper stumbled back, shaking.

"Oh, no…Cap…"

The fin was turning toward them now. Redway sucked in a breath, searched the ocean briefly for Ted, who was nowhere to be seen, then climbed the short distance into the wheelhouse. He started the engine again and looked back. The shark was closing in rapidly. Its head was out of the water again.

Redway cut the wheel to port and throttled, but there was not enough time to veer out of the shark's way. Its eyes rolled back into its head, and with a stroke of its tail, the fish propelled itself into the port quarter. The boat rocked to starboard, then went into a spin. Redway fell against the helm, using it to keep himself upright. He cut the wheel back, then applied throttle again. All he could think about now was getting to the harbor. At full steam, he'd reach port in three hours. But first, he needed to get his bearings, and figure out where the shark was.

He checked the compass. The ship was pointed northwest. As he started to cut the wheel to starboard, he noticed the fin emerging seventy meters off the starboard bow.

"Shit!" He cut the opposite direction.

"Cap!" Pepper yelled from the deck. Redway ignored him and kept going. Pepper's voice grew louder and more desperate. "Cap! CAP! REDWAY, STOP!" There was a scream, which ended with a dull thud against the hull under the bow. Redway paused long enough to poke his head out the window. In the water was Ted's limp body, his skull plastered against the hull.

"You fucking killed him!" Pepper shouted. Redway hyperventilated, realizing what he'd done. He glanced back to the approaching shark, then back to the red water below. He returned to the wheel and continued throttling, hoping to make some distance between himself and the body. Ted's broken body rippled like a noodle as it was pushed away by the swells. Redway gunned the engine, watching the shark. It had slowed its advance, its interest having shifted to the smell of blood. There was a brief splash behind the vessel as it snatched Ted's body.

Redway pushed the engines to the max, gunning the ship southwest to port. He watched the back window for the fish, then cursed when he saw it turning toward them. Ted's involuntary diversion had only granted them a few short seconds of flight.

The megalodon swallowed the bite-sized piece of meat, then resumed the chase. With each stroke of its tail, it accelerated its speed. It closed in and struck the port quarter. The hull cracked and the bow dipped forward, once again throwing all hands to the deck. The megalodon circled away, its senses dulled momentarily from the repeated impacts. It only took a moment for the throbbing to subside, and its inner ears to pick up the distressed movements of the damaged vessel. It circled back and prepared for another assault.

A gust of wind swept down over it, and a series of sharp projectiles struck its hide.

Both Redway and Pepper looked back and saw the helicopter descending like an angel. It traveled parallel to the fish, with a gunman firing a military-style machine gun from its starboard side. The shark jolted from the little bee stings, finally veering off course to combat the new threat.

"Come on, you little bitch," Jason muttered. He fired in short bursts, moving the barrel slowly as though trying to surgically open the shark from afar. It turned left to pursue him, though this time they were well beyond its reach. He focused the assault on its head to keep its attention on them. After several more bursts, he stepped away from the turret and grabbed the harpoon gun. He squatted and aimed. "We're too high. Get us lower."

"Jason, I don't think this is a good—"

"Don't make me tell you twice," Jason growled. Brenton shook his head, clenched his teeth, then brought the chopper down to thirty feet. Jason aimed for the meg's dorsal fin. But it was coming too fast. There was a splash of water, and the beast dipped. He could see it arching upward, jetting toward the surface for another jump.

"Pull up!"

Brenton was way ahead of him. He banked to port, ascending twenty yards. The shark blasted out of the water. Open jaws snapped at the chopper, coming close enough for Jason to see the strands of fishmen's clothing stuck between the teeth. It struck back down and disappeared under a giant splash.

Jason righted himself after falling back. As Brenton steadied the chopper, he looked back down.

The megalodon reversed course. Again, it had given up on the chopper, preferring to go after the fishing boat instead.

"It's no use, Nace," Brenton said. "We can't get into position long enough to pull off the shot." Jason didn't reply. He watched the shark as it raced. He estimated it was going at forty miles per hour on a collision course for its target. It knew it had to ram the boat to sink it. *Goddamn genetic engineering!* The dorsal fin broke the surface. It was now a thousand yards from the fishing boat and closing fast.

An idea sparked in Jason's mind.

"Let's try again," he said.

"Ugh! You're gonna get us killed!"

"No, I won't. Because its attention won't be on us," Jason said.

"Wait..." Brenton watched the shark, then traced its trajectory to the fishing boat. Suddenly, it all made sense. "You crazy? You're gonna use the boat as bait?"

"Just long enough to get the harpoon in," Jason said.

"What do you want me to do?"

"Travel parallel to the fish. Get low. If it comes at us, we'll get out of the way," Jason instructed.

"But what about the guys on that boat?" Brenton said.

"We tag the bastard first. If we don't, we'll see a hundred other boats sunk just like this one."

Brenton swallowed. Being a mercenary didn't erase his conscience. Innocents being in the crossfire was unfortunately a common hazard of the job, but never did he ever USE them to get the job done. However, he couldn't argue with Jason's reasoning. They not only needed bait to distract the beast…they needed *live* bait. Or else, it'd be a never-ending cat-and-mouse game of evading the shark as it jumped at them.

He steered the chopper toward the megalodon. In ten seconds, they were a hundred feet directly overhead. It was seven-hundred yards from the vessel now. He banked a few yards to the left and carefully lowered toward the water. The shark kept moving straight, gradually picking up speed with each swing of its tail.

"Closer," Jason said. Alarms rang in Brenton's mind, but he couldn't afford to hesitate. "Closer!" He nudged the aircraft to starboard until finally they were so close that Jason Nace could feel the mist spraying off the shark's body. The dorsal fin was directly in front of him, its tip an arm's length lower than the landing gear. He aimed down and to the left, lined up the shot, and fired.

The harpoon zipped away with a slicing sound, streaking through the air like a silver laser, embedding its barbed tip into the megalodon's skin. The shark didn't feel a thing. It kept going, now two hundred yards from its prize.

"Chem-beacon attached," Jason said, triumphantly.

"Nace! The boat!" Brenton immediately said. Jason tossed the weapon aside and got back onto the machine gun. Already, he realized they were too late. The shark closed the distance and smashed directly into the vessel. The keel splintered into a dozen pieces. The propellers imploded into countless shards of metal, as if they had been stung with grenades. The stern of the vessel dipped back, water surging up on to the deck.

The shark angled over to the portside and struck again, pitching the boat to the side. The crewman on deck was launched into the water. Sensing his vibrations, the shark passed under the ship. With the vessel in the way, Jason couldn't see the crewman…until the shark breached with him in its jaws. The mouth closed, the teeth scissoring him at the chest, sending arms, shoulders, and his head flopping into the waves.

"Oh shit." Jason winced. He completed the task, but at the expense of…whoever that was. He could feel Brenton's anger radiating from the cockpit. The pilot's silence was enough to convey his thoughts.

The vessel was starting to sink now. Jason knew there was at least one person in the wheelhouse. Jason debated mentally on what to do. The moral thing was to save the guy, but he knew that would invite unwanted questions. And he knew Gundrum wanted to keep as much of a low-profile on the shark as possible. Bringing a civilian on board a mercenary chopper, right after witnessing it shooting a giant, genetically engineered shark—

which had just sunk his boat and killed his crew, would possibly bring unwanted attention.

However, if he was saved by someone else, who didn't know of the shark's existence, anything the fisherman said would likely be chalked up simply as the rants of a distressed individual. It was the perfect middle ground, provided he was able to lure the shark away.

"Hold position. Wait for my signal, then pull away. We'll lure it off from the boat," he said to Brenton. Jason waited for the fish to circle around the stern, putting its head in view. He fired the machine gun. As planned, the shark started going after the chopper. "Keep low, turn five degrees to port. Okay…GO!" Brenton veered left, keeping a distance of fifty feet, just enough to keep the fish enticed.

"Come on. Come on," Brenton said. He watched the boat grow steadily smaller in the distance.

"What the—" Jason said. The shark dove under, barely within sight. It doubled its speed, passing under the chopper. Brenton lifted up on the control stick to pull out of reach. But the shark never breached. It kept going. Both men looked through their port windows, and saw white sails reaching fifty feet into the sky. Both men were silent, realizing they had accidentally led the fish to a sailing yacht. There were two people aboard that they could see, both standing on the main deck, watching their chopper. The rotors spared the mercenaries from hearing their screams as the shark launched itself from the water. The shark came out of the water like a rocket, twisting in mid-air, until it came down on the middeck face-first. The two halves of the boat blasted apart, the entire middle erupting into a series of debris.

The sailors floundered along the surface, dazed and confused. The megalodon's demonic face came up from underneath, scooping both of them into its jaws. Strands of red ejected from its gill slits. The beast swallowed, then continued swimming southwest.

Both mercenaries sat in silence.

"Well, that didn't pan out like I intended," Jason said.

"Nace, I'm done," Brenton said. "You can go fuck yourself."

"Hey, I didn't engineer the fucking thing. We had a job to do and we did it."

"Yeah, I know where you can take this job," Brenton said.

"Knock it off. The hard part's done. We'll have to monitor it for a while and slow its progression before it gets to the coast."

"What about that other guy?"

"Notify the Coast Guard," Jason said. "Give them the coordinates. Tell them we witnessed a boat crash."

"Yeah, that works out conveniently for you, doesn't it," Brenton said.

"Just doing what I'm paid for," Jason said. "You want to quit, you can feel free to take your morals somewhere else. Right now, I need to get on the horn with Gundrum. I hope those guys are ready for departure, because that fish is heading for Hamilton Bay."

CHAPTER 13

The radiance from the hot overheads drew a sweat from Miguel as he stood in the snake's holding tank. He felt like a cricket being served to some exotic house pet. His imagination went wild, 'seeing' a lizard or tarantula coming out from behind the big rock over on the front left side, or a frog stepping from the pool in the center.

"Damn. I'll never look at feeder mice the same way again when it's dinner time for the corn snake," he said to himself. He held the Chem-beacon in his hands, and searched for a place he could install that wouldn't block the signal, but offer protection from the snake's movements. He didn't want to risk the device getting damaged, or else he wouldn't be able to lure it back in after they'd captured the shark…

…*if* they captured the shark.

It would probably curl up around the rock, so Miguel knew not to install it there. There was an artificial tree near the back, he could probably set it there. He checked and saw the thing was barely installed into the flooring. The snake would rip it out with ease. His best bet would be to install it into the corner and cover it with some dirt.

Yeah, that'll work. Eleven will be drawn to the scent, but it won't recognize the device as food. Hell, it's so small compared to it, Eleven will have a hell of a time even seeing the damn thing.

He placed the chem-beacon into the corner, then started climbing the ladder up to the catwalk. He followed the passageway up to the main deck. As he reached for the door, it suddenly swung open, seemingly on its own.

"Whoops," Captain Seabolt muttered. Miguel saw the frustrated look on his face, then heard the commotion outside.

"What's going on?" he asked.

"Mr. Gundrum's mercenaries got your chem-thingy on the shark, and they reported that it's heading toward Hamilton Beach. If we're going to intercept it, we needed to leave twenty minutes ago, but those two idiots are too busy arguing." Miguel stepped outside and saw Gina and Marc middeck.

"Mr. Gundrum, this won't work. We HAVE to notify someone. Call the Coast Guard. Hell, call your mercenaries and have them hit the shark with missiles. Anything at this point."

"Dr. Hutson, I've just about had enough of this," Marc said. "I've got too much money invested in this thing to destroy it. And I'm not broadcasting to the world of this thing's existence. We're lucky nobody's discovered this thing yet."

"They have, it's just that those who have are dead!" Gina said.

"Dead?" Who's dead?" Miguel asked.

Gundrum let out a frustrated groan. "Don't concern yourself with this, Dr. Lucero." Miguel approached.

"Did that shark kill somebody?"

"Yes, a fishing crew and a sailing yacht," Gina said. Her eyes turned back to Marc. "And it won't be long before the entire east coast gets an up-close view of your shark, Mr. Gundrum. It's heading for Hamilton Bay. There are thousands of people on the beaches alone, much less all the sailing and fishing boats in the nearby area. The megalodon senses a damn smorgasbord and it's going right for it! We need to get some choppers out there with explosives and blow it out of the water. If not, more will die!"

"You want to save lives? Then proceed with the mission as planned," Gundrum said.

"Mr. Gundrum, we'll be cutting it close as it is," Miguel said. Gina's eyes turned toward him. The anger they expressed toward him was now replaced with a sense of gratitude. "Best case scenario, a hundred-and-fifty-foot snake will be doing battle with an oversized megalodon off a very populated beach. Both animals have violent tempers and big appetites. We're walking a very thin line here. If this goes wrong, it'll go WAY wrong."

Marc didn't even look at him. Miguel could see the tension in his jawline; he was going to say something, but for whatever reason, he held it back. The businessman was clearly under a lot of stress—and it wasn't stemming from concern from the collateral damage. Despite all of this knowledge, all of the death, and knowing the risks, he was not going to back down. Miguel suspected he received a couple of phone calls from potential buyers. And if Miguel was a betting man…and he occasionally was, he would bet that these buyers got wind of the situation and were threatening to back out. They didn't own the specimens yet, so it would be easy for them to deny any involvement. For Gundrum, there was too much money at stake.

"At least call Hamilton's mayor and have them clear the beaches," Gina said.

"With what justification?" Marc said. "You think they'd believe me if I told them a giant shark was swimming toward their beaches?"

"I hope you knuckleheads make up your minds, because if you want to get there in time, we need to be on our way now. Up to you," Captain Seabolt called out. He was standing on the upper deck of the superstructure, just outside the bridge. By the look on his face, he was more amused by the argument than alarmed, as if he was watching an *Oprah* rerun. Gina's initial thought was that he was being condescending with his seemingly nonchalant attitude, but it came to mind: that's how he kept a level head. And he was right—arguing was just taking more valuable time. Gundrum was not going to budge on his position.

"How soon can you get us to Hamilton Beach?" she called up to the Captain.

"At full speed, we can get there in under four hours," Seabolt said. "But we need to leave now if we plan to get there in time."

Gina sighed, then gave one last look at Marc.

"This is a bad idea," she said.

"I didn't ask for your advice, Doctor," he replied.

"Yeah, you'd ignore it anyway. Just like when I told you the *Truth Seeker* was not fit for transporting the shark."

Marc tensed. If she was any other employee, he'd have her fired and blacklisted. Unfortunately, she was essential, given the circumstances.

"Get the snake into the hold and get out there and catch my shark," he said, followed by a fast march to the side ladder. Miguel slapped his hands to his sides, frustrated, a feeling mirrored by Gina's clenched fists and wrinkled face.

"You'll want to get inside," he said. He turned around and looked up to Seabolt. "That goes for everyone. Get out of sight. If Eleven sees you, the last thing you'll see will be the inside of his throat."

Seabolt stepped into the bridge. A moment later, a loudspeaker boomed over the deck.

"All hands, drop what you're doing and get below deck immediately."

****

Miguel stood on a vacant deck, staring over the port deck railing at the steel tunnel. He held two radios, one to communicate with the bridge, another to communicate with his assistants in the lab. Derick was in the control room, standing by to flip the switches connected to the passageways between the exhibit and the tunnel.

"Lead it out of the exhibit into the interior passageway," he said. He could hear faint drumming sounds as reinforced steel doors shifted deep within the facility. "Let me know if it moves." There were monitors in the control room for Derick to monitor the snake's movements.

"Hang on. He's looking at the door, but he's not moving. It's probably too cold."

"Damn it," Miguel said. He wanted to move the snake gradually from section to section, and only activate the Chem-beacon when it reached the exterior tunnel. He waited, hoping to hear good news from the assistant.

"Still no movement. I've tried coaxing him with the lights, but it's no good."

"He needs bait." Miguel sighed. "Standby." He switched radios. "Lucero to Bridge, be ready to close the hatch." Without waiting for a reply, he hurried to the cargo hold, positioning himself so he could see the corner where he placed the device. He clipped his radios to his belt then grabbed the tablet from his pouch. He typed the code, wirelessly connecting the tablet to the Chem-beacon's receiver. An electronic button appeared on the screen: *Activate.* He pressed the button and then grabbed the lab radio. "Derick, open all doors right now."

"Okay. It's acting intrigued now. It's going right for the tunnel."

"The collar's activated, Derick. Open the doors now."

"Interior passageways are open."

"Open the overhead," Miguel said. He backed away from the hatch, holding his breath in anticipation. Silent prayers left his lips. *Please, follow the device. Pleeeease work."*

There was a heavy thud from under the pool. It wasn't a mechanical sound from the door sliding back…the snake was under that door and trying to break through.

"Derick? Why isn't that door open?"

"I was opening it, Doc, but it's jammed. Eleven hit it from underneath. It wouldn't wait. It's drawn to the signal."

"Ugh, he waited too long," he said to himself. There was another crashing sound. The overhead dented outward, forming a metal mountain over the pool. There was a high-pitched hiss. The snake was enraged. It struck again, enlarging the overhead doors.

"Dr. Lucero?! What's going on down there?" It was Captain Seabolt's voice.

"We had a malfunction in the door…" Miguel radioed back.

"Yeah, sure. The damn thing's going on a rampage. Your toy is making it crazy. If it can bust through that door, then it can smash through the bulkheads in my ship. Shut it off."

"No, I can handle it," Miguel said.

"I hope you're right, because I'm ordering my crew to arm themselves."

"They'd be wasting their time," Miguel said, though not into the radio. The snake hit again, cracking the tunnel roof. Another hit, and the tunnel erupted into several pieces. Jagged steel hit the deck, denting some of the plating. Miguel shrieked and dove back, right as a huge piece of tunnel crashed where he was standing.

Seabolt's voice blasted through the radio.

"All crew. Ready your weapons and set up firing positions. We're killing this thing!"

"NO!" Miguel shouted. "You do that, you might as well serve your crew up on a platter! Let me handle this."

"Miguel, if that thing continues to get riled up inside the cargo hold, it could cause major interior damage." It was Gina's voice.

"You might be eager to kill your fish, but I'm not killing Eleven." He immediately regretted that reply, realizing it made him sound more concerned about the reptile's well-being than the human lives on board. In that regard, it didn't help his case in convincing them he could control it. He got back on his feet, then panicked when he realized he didn't have his tablet. He saw it lying on the deck a few feet away. He scooped it up, mumbling "thank God" after confirming it was undamaged. "Just wait! I got it."

All he could do was hope the Captain would listen. He turned to face the tunnel. The snake's enormous head rose from the gap it created, tongue flicking several meters. Its upper body coiled into an "S" shape as it examined the ship. It held that position until it decided the ship was not a potential enemy. It saw the human standing on top, and swiftly moved in. Miguel's heart jumped into his throat. Never since the snake was a baby did it move at him so hastily. For a moment, he was genuinely concerned it would scoop him up, forgetting its imprint on him.

The first thirty feet of its length came over the guardrail, bending it down into the deck. Miguel held his breath. He forced himself to remain perfectly still. There'd be no outrunning this beast. At this point, fleeing would only reinforce the idea that he was prey.

The snake stopped within ten feet, then stared at him. It clicked its tongue, sensing familiarity in the human in the strange environment. It took every ounce of energy for Miguel not to flinch. For a full minute, they remained in place, not moving a muscle.

Every muscle in Gina's body went taut as she watched the snake and its caretaker. Deep down, she was cursing Miguel and his so-called special bond with the serpent in front of him.

Oh, you idiot. Yeah, you might have had a special bond with it in the past, but now it is stimulated with chemical cues, and right now you're the only piece of meat it sees.

He was a goner. She was sure of it.

Gina let out a small gasp as the snake drew back. It was ready to strike by the looks of it. There were murmurs of nervousness from other crew in the bridge, including Captain Seabolt, who stood at the helm with a radio in hand. There were crewmembers lined up in the passageways, armed with rifles. All he needed to do was give the order, and they would invade the main deck like an invading army and gun the snake down. Which, as Gina had warned, would only lead to more death. But Seabolt wouldn't have it.

"Standby," he warned his men. His voice was shaky, which somehow added to the tension. Seabolt struck Gina as a kind of guy that didn't get nervous easily.

The snake lifted its head, flicked that tongue again, then turned to its right…looking right at the bridge. Her chest tightened. The snake moved, bringing more of its huge body onto the ship. It came near the open hatch and peered inside, flicked its tongue repeatedly. In the blink of an eye, its entire body slipped into the cargo hold.

"Shut the hatch," Seabolt ordered. A crewmember hit a switch, and the hatch doors closed shut over the snake.

Miguel caught his breath, amazed by the swiftness of the giant. He could hear it thrashing about inside.

His mind screamed *shut the beacon down, you idiot!* He got on the tablet and deactivated the beacon, ceasing the signal that went to the collar's receiver. He heard the snake moving about, searching for the nonexistent prey. It took some time for the stimulation to cease, and as it did, the snake slowed.

He got on the radio to the bridge. "You've got cameras in there. How's it doing?"

"It's settling down," Gina replied.

"And it's damn lucky it is," Seabolt said.

"No, *we're* lucky," Miguel said to himself. He heard the Captain's voice over the speakers.

"All hands, back to your stations. Prep for departure."

CHAPTER 14

Reflective white sands soaked in ocean water squelched under the feet of thousands of beachgoers going in and out of the ocean. As afternoon crept in, the five-mile long beaches of Hamilton Bay were flooded with residents and tourists taking advantage of their summer. Swimmers and rafts extended out for hundreds of feet, while lifeguards patrolled the sands. It was the busy season. Hotels were booked and waiting lines for restaurants went around the buildings. Private vendors near the beach made their killing, selling oversized food and merchandise, and the hotels were completely booked. The salty air mixed with the scent of sunscreen and tropical flavored drinks. People of all ages splashed in the water, some attempting to achieve athletic feats by swimming as far out as possible, others sat in the shallow regions, chitchatting while enjoying the cool sensation of the water, while some sat on the beach, simply watching the waves.

Further out beyond the drop-off barrier, jet skis sprayed water as they banked left and right. Sailing boats passed along the horizon, their white sails appearing angelic from afar. Parasailers glided high overhead, tugged along by speedboats. Surfers rode the waves, performing great leaps and turns, and often failing.

For these residents, it was a typical summer day. For Richard Redway, it was a nightmare.

Coast Guard helicopters arrived within fifteen minutes of the call. By then, his vessel was almost entirely submerged under the waves. After successfully hoisting him out, and seeing no major injuries, they transferred him to Hamilton General to be evaluated. Terrified, exhausted, and confused, he warned the guardsmen of an enormous shark that had attacked his boat and was now lurking beneath the waves. Of course, that led to a meeting with a psych analyst.

For two more hours, Richard Redway endured questions and took drug tests, all of which came out clean. Apparently, because of the trauma of the 'crash' and the experience of losing his brother and crew, he was suffering from shock. That wasn't entirely untrue. Every time Redway closed his eyes, he saw that huge fin and gaping jaws. That severed hand kept reaching out to him, curled like spider legs, blood dripping from the bony stump.

"Mr. Redway, the Coast Guard has dive crews over there right now. There's no sign of any shark, other than the occasional blue swimming by," the Guardsman stated. He was like a cop taking information on a traffic incident, jotting notes from Redway's statements.

In the time answering what seemed to be an endless series of questions, Redway understood the path in front of him if he continued talking about a giant shark. The fisherman stared at that notebook in the guardsman's hands. The words he jotted down would be typed into a computer, and then permanentized into digital files. Then Redway would never be able to take them back. Apparently, whoever reported the 'crash' had stated they had witnessed a sailboat had rammed into the back of his fishing vessel. Redway knew that wasn't true, but other than his poor judgement on fishing, he wasn't a complete imbecile: he knew they weren't going to believe him. Thus, all he would achieve is a week-long stay in the psych ward at best. There were no charges pending against him, nor was there evidence of wrongdoing on his part. And he wanted it to stay that way, considering he didn't want to disclose the accident with running over Ted. Hopefully the ocean would wash away any evidence that might've gotten plastered to the hull. He forced the thought from his mind, as well as the guilt. It was the shark's fault, damn it! He didn't run over Ted maliciously. Hell, he thought he was already dead!

Since there was no chance of getting word out about the fish, all he had to focus on was his own well-being. To that, he had to play along by changing his story.

He had taken a long drink of water then asked for a break. He couldn't make a complete one-eighty turnaround in his deposition, as that would probably come off as odd. He would have to do it gradually. So, he did. He told them he remembered seeing a shark, but it was just an 'ordinary' Great White, sixteen feet in length. For the psychiatrists and investigators, that explanation combined with the trauma was enough to rationalize his rantings of a giant shark sinking his boat. Redway was a quick thinker, which either led to good or bad outcomes, such as the decision to trawl near a reef. Luckily, this was looking to be one of the better outcomes.

It was almost two in the afternoon when Redway checked himself out of the hospital. He walked for a mile before finally being able to hail a taxi, which was able to take him to the harbor. Normally, he'd complain how this simple drive cost him forty-five bucks. But all he could think of was his brother, and that damn shark. After arriving near the harbor, he found his pickup truck. He sat in the driver's seat, staring out into that ocean.

Woodward Harbor was located two miles south of the stretch of beaches. The docks were busy with trawlers coming back from their voyages. Workers attached processing pumps to the boats to extract thousands of pounds of tuna, removing the fish from the holds and pumping them into the processors.

The white hull of the seventy-foot sword-fishing vessel *Omega Thunder* caught his eye. He watched the ship come in and begin the process of unloading her catch. Crew hauled the processed bodies of swordfish onto the dock, where they were weighed, measured, and put on ice.

He watched Captain Cathy Wilson as she directed her crew. They worked tirelessly, unloading the catch with electric operated cranes. But he wasn't focused on the activity. Instead, he watched the boat. He envisioned himself on the deck, with a shotgun in hand, watching a trail of chum. In that vision, he saw the grey mass coming for a piece of bait. He could almost feel the shotgun's recoil and the wetness of blood splashing over from the shotgun blast to the mouth. The shark was big, but it had to be mortal. Anything could be killed, even a giant shark.

First, he needed a boat. He knew Cathy well. She was a compassionate type of person who would help another fisherman, though he wasn't sure she'd believe his story of a giant shark. He wasn't sure how'd he'd make the proposition: he didn't have money, and by the looks of it, Cathy was doing well for herself. He would have to play into her ego. She was the type to brag about bringing home the largest bounty of all the fishermen in the area. That bragging was always done in a restaurant downtown called *The Whitefin Bar.* Cathy always went there after docking. That's where she would be in another half-hour.

"For Nathan," he said aloud to himself.

****

From the outside, *The Whitefin Bar* sounded like it was jam-packed with unruly patrons. In reality, it only contained a third of its capacity, all of them fishermen. Located away from the high-class bar-and-grills where the tourists often gathered, it served as a place for local workers to get away from the madness.

Cathy raised a toast, whisky swirling along the rims of her shot glass.

"Seventy-five tons," she announced. Claps followed from surrounding fishermen and they all took a shot in honor of her personal record. She slammed the glass down, much to the displeasure of the bartender.

"Save some for the rest of us," said Bruno. Another fishman stood up and shouted to the hefty trawl Captain.

"She runs a swordboat, dufus. Not that it matters. You can't catch shit anyway!" Sam Merdi's unlit cigarette dangled from his lips as he spoke. His scrawny figure was the polar opposite from Bruno's. An obnoxious troublemaker, he often picked on either the largest, or most successful people in the room. Two broken bottom teeth reflected the results of antagonizing those with little humor.

Luckily, Bruno was the type to laugh at himself and relish in other people's success. He cracked open another beer, chugged it down, then turned on his barstool to look at Sam. His three-fifty-pound mass jiggled with each movement. He was practically a walking, or in this case, sitting meat stack, and his skeleton was the hanger.

"By the way, Sam, how much did those sardines you brought in yesterday weigh?"

"Just for the record," Sam stood up, his face wrinkling, "I brought in a blue marlin a week ago. Full grown, measuring fourteen feet! Weighed half as much as you!" His serious expression transformed into a comical one as he started to laugh. Soon the whole bar joined in, including Bruno.

"I know you weren't the one to bring that thing in."

"What makes you say that?" Sam said. Bruno scoffed, spitting suds.

"Really? Look at yourself. You'd be swallowed whole!"

Sam made a guilty look. The crowd then focused on the twenty-three-year-old muscular kid sitting at the table next to him. The kid looked as though he was containing a laugh. There was a proud look in his eyes, like that of a man who could barely contain his ego. He was in the right room.

"Let me guess," Bruno said, "it was the kid who hooked it."

"No…" Sam muttered, drawing chuckles from the group.

"Holy shit, kid, that was you?!" another fisherman, Jake, called out from the bar counter. Sam's second mate, Santor, raised a muscular arm, deliberately flexing his bicep when giving a thumbs-up.

"Damn, I saw that beauty! Too bad we can't bring in more of them," Bruno said, deliberately bruising Sam's ego with his words.

"How much did it go for?"

"Eighteen bucks per pound," Santor said. "I was nice enough to split it with the Cap."

"My boat, kid," Sam said.

"Hey!" Cathy said, tapping her glass to the counter, "No stealing my thunder allowed in this joint!" By the time the laughter settled, they noticed a familiar face enter the bar. The tone of the place shifted from lively to solemn.

"Redway?" Bruno said. Nobody moved. Some of them had caught wind of a boat that had sunk near Banana Reef. Some monitored the transmissions, as they often did when out at sea. Through the Coast Guard's radio traffic, they learned that the ship was the *Grand Reef*, and had gone down with all hands except its Captain.

Redway looked like a statue, staring at the many faces. Silence consumed the bar. Even the bartender was shocked to see him. Finally, Cathy stood up.

"Richard?" she said. "The hell are you doing here? You should be—" she was going to suggest he be with family, but she remembered Nathan *was* his family. Their parents were long dead, and their cousins were so distant, he didn't even know how to reach them.

"Uh…" Sam struggled for something to say. "We heard about the crash." That last word triggered something in Redway. He slammed the door shut behind him.

"That's what they're saying?"

Sam swallowed. "Um, I saw a news report on my phone."

"Bastards act quick." Redway approached the counter and took a seat near Cathy. He snapped his fingers at the bartender. "Get me a Jack Daniels." The bartender nodded awkwardly then placed a bottle and glass, which he slid down the counter. He took the bottle and chugged from the pipe. Large drops of alcohol slid down his chin. "Who here has ever hunted sharks?" He watched Cathy in the corner of his eye, already knowing she had hunted blues and even once hooked a Great White. She slowly raised her hand, while looking at him strangely.

"Sharks?" Bruno asked. Everyone in the room glanced at each other, confused. Most figured Redway was in shock and was just talking at random.

"Rich, buddy," Jake said compassionately, "if you need anything, we're here for you."

"I appreciate that. That's what I'm here for," Redway said.

"What do you need buddy?" Sam said. "Need another Jack? Bartender! Next round's on me! See, buddy? I'll help you out!"

"Just this one will do," Redway said, stopping the bartender. "I need something else, actually."

"Anything, buddy. Just name it. Is it food? Need a woman? That's what I go to whenever I'm feeling blue!" Murmurs of 'blech' sounds traveled through the bar. The mental image even managed to creep its way into Redway's disturbed mind, drawing a repulsed look.

"No! Jesus," he said. "I just asked, you idiots, who here's ever hunted sharks?" A few hands raised nervously, including Cathy.

"Rich, I don't understand," she said. "What do sharks have to do with anything?"

"It wasn't a sailing yacht that took my boat down," he said. "It was a shark. A big shark. Came up right behind us. Grabbed Nathan and chased after us."

"Dude," Sam said, knocking over the no-smoking sign on the table, "that's quite a story." Redway looked back at him.

"You don't believe me?"

"No." Sam spoke candidly, shrugging his shoulders. He felt bad, sure, but he wasn't going to let himself be taken for a fool.

Jake moved a couple of stools closer to Redway. "Maybe I can put it more tactfully: someone called in to the Coast Guard and reported they witnessed the crash…"

"That's not what happened!" Redway shouted, knocking the bottle across the counter. The room went silent, save for rattling ice in whiskey glasses held in nervous hands. They all knew Richard Redway. He was always a laid back kind of guy, rarely raised his voice except to get someone's attention. Sure, he didn't have the best judgement when it came to fishing, and could occasionally be impulsive, but he wasn't crazy. Until now.

He took a breath, regained control of his demeanor. "It was a shark. A demon. A leviathan. It was bigger than my boat. It swallowed Jacob whole. It got Ted. That kid, Pepper. It would've got me but…there was this chopper. I'm not sure what kind it was. I thought I heard gunshots, but I was just so focused on getting out of dodge. Whatever happened, they lured it away. By then, I was taking on too much water."

"This story just got WAY more interesting. Choppers. Machine guns. Shark probably belonged to a theme park and escaped!" Sam said. He lit the cigarette. Finally, the bartender came out of his frozen state and pointed a finger at him.

"Hey! You know the rules, Sam!"

"Ah, fuck it," Sam said, crunching the cigarette into the floor.

"Why didn't you tell the authorities?" Bruno asked.

"I tried, but it was clear they were five seconds from putting me in a straitjacket. They weren't gonna believe me, so I thought I'd take the matter into my own hands."

"With what boat?" Sam said.

Redway resisted the urge to reply. Why the hell was he appealing to an idiot like Sam Berman anyway? He turned to face Cathy.

"You've hooked a Great White before," he said.

"I have, but there was a bounty on it," she reminded him. Generally, fishing for Great Whites was considered illegal. However, in 2017, she was fishing along the Delaware coast near Bethany Beach when a seventeen-foot Great White attacked a nineteen-year old college student paddle boating in twelve feet of water. Though the victim survived, he had lost a leg in the attack. Shark attacks were rare, and even so, warning signs were always placed on the beach. The problem was that the victim was the son of a wealthy bank owner with many connections, and because of those connections, he was able to manipulate the local government into putting out a significant reward for the shark. Being close by, and not the type to turn down a hundred thousand bucks, Cathy set out to catch the fish. A day later, she hooked it, dragged it close to the boat, and fired a shotgun into its mouth.

With the memory came a sense of triumph. Cathy couldn't help but grin a little.

"I'm putting a bounty on this one," he said. Cathy let a laugh slip, which she quickly stopped.

"Please don't take this as an insult, but…with what money do you plan to pay me with?" It was no secret that Redway was on hard times. He didn't have a significant sum in his savings, and the year had been particularly rough so far. However, the story regarding the sailing boat, while false, might actually serve him in a sense…

"The insurance money I'll be receiving," he said. "I don't have a sum yet, but I insured my boat for as much as it was worth. Considering the circumstances of its sinking, plus the inheritance I'll probably get from Nathan's estate, I'll be able to pay whoever kills the shark…" he did some rough math in his head, "eighty grand." He wasn't sure, but it seemed like a reasonable enough number. Still, Cathy didn't look entirely convinced.

"It's illegal to hunt for Great Whites," she said. "Besides, you said a chopper was shooting at it. In that case, it's probably dead."

"If it even exists," Sam added.

"No chance," Redway replied. "I watched it chase them off. I don't know who those people are, if they were even military, but I know they didn't kill the shark."

"How do you know that?"

"Didn't see any blood."

"Doesn't mean anything. You said just a second ago that you couldn't see much because you were busy running away," Sam chuckled.

"Hell, how would you kill a shark that big—if it did exist?" Bruno said. He leaned his head against his palm, trying to contemplate the fact that he and his colleagues were actually discussing the existence of a giant shark.

"A few rifle rounds to the brain oughta do the job. Sam, I know you like to use depth charges…don't look innocent." Redway looked back at Cathy, "I think a couple shotgun blasts in its mouth will do the job."

It was silent again. It was clear to Redway that these people weren't yet sold. He needed something to entice them.

"Five grand. To anyone who goes out with me to kill it today. Whether we catch it or not. Five grand. Eighty to whoever kills it."

Now, there was a different look in their eyes. Five grand was five grand, whether it was a waste of time or not. Hell, some of them could try catching a few extra fish while they were out.

"Well, shit," Santor said. He stood up and kicked Sam's chair. "If you're not up for going, I'll take my shotgun and head out there myself." Sam should've known he'd be enticed by the offer. The kid was so eager to make a name for himself, he was probably considering the offer before the five-grand was added. Well, if he was gonna go, then…

"Pack a ton of bait. We're gonna need chum."

"See ya, suckers," Santor said, then marched out the door. Several of the fishermen exchanged glances. Some shook their heads, not just out of disbelief of Redway's story, but out of the decency of not taking advantage of a man grieving the loss of his brother and crew. Others, however, stood up. Jake was the next one out the door.

Bruno shrugged his shoulders, then stood up. "I suppose I could use the exercise."

Redway leaned in toward Cathy, burning her with his stare. Of all these fishermen, she was the one most capable of killing the thing.

Her first instinct was to say no. However, something about seeing those other fishermen going out the door sparked a jealousy in her. What if Redway's story was true, even just partly deluded. Maybe he didn't see a giant shark the size of a trawler; perhaps it was a record length Great White. It would be a shame to see someone else catch it while she sat on the sidelines and did nothing.

Whatever the case, Redway's manipulation worked.

"This better not be a waste of time," she said.

"You'll get five-grand either way," Redway replied.

"My crew won't be available. They're off with their families and friends, getting drunk and laid. That leaves you as my crewman," she said. That was no concern, as Redway was already planning on tagging along.

"Let's stop wasting time," he said. Cathy grabbed her ballcap and stood up. First, she'd have to stop at home and grab a couple of shotguns… and some supplies to rig depth charges.

CHAPTER 15

The *Armstrong's* bow sliced the ocean, sending blue-white sprays misting over the deck. The crew pushed the engines, maintaining a speed of twenty-five knots. There was a constant breeze sweeping over the deck, decreasing the temperature by almost twenty degrees.

Gina Hutson was glad she was smart enough to pack a jacket. She spent most of the trip inside of the bridge, listening to Captain Seabolt's tales of his past. To her relief, they weren't sleep-inducing stories. She learned of his upbringing in India and his experience in the Indian Navy, where he was a second-lieutenant on a Kora Class Corvette. He spoke about a rescue-response operation his ship was involved in, when a cargo ship was being attacked by armed pirates.

"Yeah, they saw us coming and tried to run. Luckily, a few of them tried firing at us." He chuckled. "Dumb idiots. Gave us the excuse we needed. We turned our AK-176 on them, and watched their little boat fall apart." He proceeded to talk about drug operations and illegal immigration, and how sometimes the Indian Navy would provide assistance to the Coast Guard during task force operations.

It had been over three hours since they departed. Since then, her eyes had been glued to the tracking monitor. The shark continued to approach Hamilton Bay, with intermittent stops every fifteen minutes or so. Her heart jumped each time, believing it had stopped to feed. If so, on what?

Her anxiety worsened when the radio broadcasted the news of the fishing vessel and sailing yacht that the megalodon had sunk. Only, it was broadcasted as a boating accident. According to the report, 'eye witnesses' alerted the Coast Guard.

I'm sure that mercenary had nothing to do with that.

It was perfect manipulation. Conceal any evidence of the shark, while also diverting Coast Guard resources away from its projected location.

A shuddering from below shattered her concentration. The snake moved again. It shuffled repeatedly throughout the voyage, bumping hard against the bulkheads. After witnessing the way it had burst from the tunnel door, the entire crew was on edge, fearing that the snake would learn it could bust through the bulkheads.

Gina noticed Seabolt looking nervous and irritated all at once.

"What the hell was I thinking, accepting this job?" he said to himself.

"Money," Gina said. "There's two things people are stupid for. Money and sex, and I doubt Gundrum used the latter to attract you to the job."

"So what if he did?" Seabolt joked.

"Then I'd question your sanity," she replied. Seabolt nodded and smiled. He studied the chart then went over a few inspection reports.

"There's a third reason you didn't consider," he said.

"And that is?"

"Ego. Or pride. Whichever makes you feel better," he said. "A pretty scientist like you could've made this kind of money anywhere. Hell, you could've gotten your own TV show. You've got the looks, the degrees, and the personality. But instead, you've decided to take on a responsibility of raising a fish that would swallow you without a second's hesitation. In the back of your mind, you had to expect ulterior motives regarding its creation."

Gina slumped in her seat.

"The worst part was that I didn't. The story Gundrum presented seemed sound enough. It made sense that putting a megalodon on exhibit would bring in boatloads of cash. The aggression, the appetite, accelerated metabolism considering its size…I figured that was a side effect from the genetic process. Or maybe I thought it was too crazy of an idea to use it as a weapon."

"Yeah, what use would a killer shark be against foreign enemies?" Seabolt said. "Or a snake, for that matter? As long as you can point it in the right direction." He was starting to sound like Miguel Lucero.

"So, I'm naïve," she admitted. "Doesn't mean I won't try and make it right."

"By catching it for Gundrum?"

"Just to solve the current situation," she said. "But I won't work for him beyond this. And I'll do whatever I can to spoil his plans." She tensed. What the hell was she doing declaring her intentions to a man, working for Gundrum, whom she had only known for a few hours? For all she knew, he would report this conversation to him.

Son of a bitch, I AM naïve.

They felt another reverberation. Again, both of them tensed.

"I'm no scientist, but I've been around enough animals," Seabolt said. "I don't care how smart Dr. Lucero thinks that thing is; it's a damn, instinctual killing machine. And it's not meant to be in our world.

Creatures from different eras were not intended by nature to share the world. Sooner or later, regardless of how successful this mission is, that monster…and that's what it is—a monster, will kill someone. A lot of someones."

"You remember that…" Gina stood up, "when you deliver it to Gundrum's buyers."

"Gotta pay my alimony somehow, Doc," he replied. Rather than engage in a debate on the morality of working for Gundrum Industries, Gina decided to get up and move around. She was not the type to sit in one place for long anyway unless she was reading a book. She left the bridge and wandered the passageways, feeling an urge to jog. She briefly considered it, but settled for a fast walk through the ship's interior instead. Eventually, she ended up near the cargo hold.

She could hear the giant snake slithering in tight circles behind the bulkhead. Footsteps tapped the catwalk. Miguel was near the door. Gina knocked gently, not wanting to startle him, and especially not the snake, with any sudden vibrations. The door opened and Miguel peeked into the passageway.

"Dr. Hutson?"

"Hi. Just Gina, please," she replied.

"Gina. Can I help you?"

"You've been in here almost the entire time," she said. "I was just checking on things. There's too much of a breeze outside to enjoy the weather, and I can't stand sitting in that bridge any longer."

Miguel opened the door wider and stepped out. Gina could see the snake. In the light, its black stripes were more pronounced. Its midbody was in the pool, while the rest of it was coiled. Its head tilted up, stimulated by the presence of another human.

"I'll be back," Miguel said to it, then shut the door.

Gina couldn't help but laugh. "You think it understands?" She hoped she didn't come off as insulting.

"I don't know," Miguel answered. "We humans tend to apply humanistic personalities to animals. We changed its environment, so I can't blame Eleven for feeling a little on-edge."

"How do you think it'll do in the open water?"

"Hard to tell," he answered. "It had no qualms about leaving the exhibit, I know that much. I suspect once I activate the chem-beacon on the shark, it'll go after it without a second thought. By the way, how far are we?"

"We're getting close," Gina answered. "Really close. Probably why I'm getting so nervous. The meg has slowed down a bit, which has enabled us to close the distance. If we close within another twenty miles, we can initiate the luring process."

"How do we do that?"

"We lower a low frequency speaker into the water to draw its attention, while dropping chum. That'll make it think a wounded animal's in the area. When it gets near, that's when you'll put your snake to work."

"Sounds simple enough," he said. "You still think you want to be in that submersible… in the water…with those two giants?"

"No. However, I might not have to get close," she said. Miguel stared questionably.

"What are you up to now?"

"Listen, Eleven will constrict the shark until it's dead," she explained.
"I already told you, I'm not getting involved with your scheme," he said.
"If we go around Gundrum's back, despite what we think of him, he'll destroy us. I'm not putting this snake in another person's hands as long as I can help it."

Gina glanced around the passageway, making sure nobody was close enough to hear them. "That'll only happen if he knows you were part of it," she said.

"How would he not know? This operation is time-sensitive. Eleven will crush that shark in three minutes, that is, if it doesn't drown it first," Miguel said. "Before that happens, I'll have to use the electro-shock in the collar to force him to detach, and lure it into the cargo hold. If I fail to do that, Gundrum will suspect my involvement. Sorry, but I've made my position plain and clear."

"You can only allow that snake to release the shark once I have it tranquilized," Gina said. "What if I *fail*?" She paused to gauge his facial reaction. It displayed a mixture of suspicion and intrigue.

"Fail?"

"Say…I miss with the tranquilizer? Or it fails to penetrate the flesh? We won't get a second chance at this. As much as Gundrum can't afford to have the megalodon killed, he also can't afford to have it loose to rampage along the coast. Potential buyers would learn of the incident and turn away, thinking these things are too uncontrollable and aren't worth the investment. Thus, that creates a chance they won't bother to purchase the snake."

Miguel bit his lip, thinking about it.

"That's…possible. It's a thin assumption."

"You know Gundrum, and you're more knowledgeable on what's going on behind the scenes," Gina said. "What do you think he would do?" Miguel felt slightly optimistic.

"IF it all plays out like that, he would probably save face in any way he can," Miguel said. "He wouldn't have Eleven put down; he's got too much invested into it. So, to turn a profit wherever he can, he'd probably expand the exhibit and put it on display, *Jurassic Park* style. Literally, his cover story would become his backup plan."

"And you would continue to study it and watch over it," she added. Her words struck like lightning, and she knew it by the way his eyes briefly lit up. Though he tried not to show it, there was an energy in his body language.

It was possible. They couldn't know for sure, but it was definitely possible.

"You're still gonna have to get in that sub," he said.

"So, you're on board?" she asked. Miguel looked away for a moment, then back at her. He was, just didn't want to say it out loud.

"For it to work, we need everything to play out like we've planned," he said. "Unfortunately, you're the only variable that can go awry, without looking like we're deliberately sabotaging the operation. We'll have to have the cables on standby, the ramp door open, pumps ready, everything. And maybe…*maybe,* he won't see through it, and won't seek retribution toward you."

Gina nodded.

"I figured I'd convince you somehow," she said. "At least, this way, we can have the best of both worlds: Nobody else will get killed, and you can keep your snake."

"Doctor—*Gina*, I only met you this morning," Miguel said. "Before you walked into my lab, I didn't even know you existed. Forgive me if I don't feel obligated to listen to moral lectures from you."

Gina opened her mouth to speak, but didn't know what to say. She didn't intend to sound so judgmental. But she did, and Miguel's reaction was justified. Somewhat. He was still more concerned with the snake's well-being than anything else. He was right, though. Who was she to be nagging him about human virtues? If the tables were turned, she'd probably respond the same way.

Before she could salvage the conversation, something up above drew their attention. Crew were running about on the main deck. There was a flapping sound. Chopper blades.

Oh, no. Is it the Coast Guard? Are they inspecting the ship? Did Gundrum register the ship?

They hurried up to the main deck. Upon stepping out, they were immediately struck by two gusts of wind, one sweeping from the bow, the other overhead. There was a black chopper descending to fifty feet, keeping pace with the ship's speed and direction.

"The mercenary," Miguel said. The fuselage door opened and a figure in black tactical gear descended by fast rope, landing on the deck.

Jason Nace let go of the rope, which was reeled back into the chopper. He listened to something in his earpiece, then flipped the bird to the pilot.

"You uncomfortable with this line of work? I know of some flower shops that'll take pussies like you in," he said. The chopper elevated and flew inland. Jason turned and saw Miguel and Gina looking at him. He tipped his ballcap like a cowboy. "Gentleman. Ma'am."

"What the hell was that about?" Miguel asked.

"Oh, he's just pissed off," Jason said.

"Something go wrong?"

"Yeah. Your fish killed most of my crew," Jason answered, stringently. "You didn't tell me it could jump out of the water like a goddamn largemouth." Gina put a hand to her mouth. She was turning pale. She had heard they had placed the chem-beacon, and of the boats sunk in the process, but she wasn't aware most of the team had perished in the mission as well.

"You've been flying around all this time?" she asked.

"We've been keeping tabs on your fish," Jason answered. "We used our available weapons to slow it down as best we could to allow you all to catch up. Unfortunately, we were running low on fuel, so Brenton had to run the chopper back to the mainland."

"Why are you here?" Miguel asked.

"Boss' orders," Jason replied.

"Orders?"

Jason tilted forward, focusing his gaze on the herpetologist. "You take issue with that?"

"I guess it's none of my concern," Miguel said. *What use would he be on this mission?*

"You know what is your concern? Catching that damn shark," Jason said. "And you better catch it, because I lost four good men trying to plant that stupid chem-thing. By the way, if that thing doesn't work, I'll feed you to your snake."

"Good luck with that," Miguel retorted.

"Yeah? If you think I'm joking…" Jason said.

"How 'bout we get ready, instead of bickering?" Gina said. "Mr. Nace? If you need something to do, you can work the speaker."

"What speaker?"

"The one we're gonna lower into the water to draw the shark in," she said. "You can listen through the headset and keep track of the soundwaves. The crew is gonna hook up the cables to the submersible so it's ready to go into the water."

"I hope you've been keeping up with that tracking monitor, because in thirty minutes, we'll be ten miles from the bay area. If that shark gets any closer than that, it won't matter what you do. Everyone's gonna get an up-close view of your precious fish."

"Then, I guess I better get into my wetsuit." Gina looked to some crewmembers standing nearby. "Do we have chum units on standby?"

"Ready whenever you are, miss," the first mate answered.

"Go ahead and get them set up. I'm gonna get below. In the meantime, bring the submersible out on deck with the lift. I'll need crew to bring up the harpoons. Don't load them; I still need to load the cannisters with tranquilizer."

"Yes, ma'am."

She turned and walked toward the structure. Miguel quickly followed her, ignoring a remark from Jason.

"Gonna watch?"

He ignored the mercenary and followed her into the passageway.

"You sure you want to do this?" he asked.

"We don't have a choice," Gina whispered. She continued going below, until she found a supply room storing her gear. "Don't worry about Nace. His job is complete. He's just pissed that he lost his crew, which is understandable."

"Then why is he here?" Miguel said. "More specifically: why would Gundrum want him here?"

"Probably to report back to him," Gina said. She opened a long silver case and pulled out a black thermal wetsuit and unzipped the back.

"Can't Seabolt do that?"

"I suppose so," she answered. "I can't really focus on that right now."

"Start focusing," Miguel hissed. "Instead of studying fish, start studying people and their actions. Their *motivations*. That guy has 'agenda' written all over him. Gundrum has him here to supervise us."

"There's not much he can do," she said. "Just keep to the plan we talked about. He won't be in the submersible with me. Once the snake is loose, there won't be anything he can really do anyway. Nothing changes. Now…" she ran her fingers under her tank top, ready to lift it off. She noticed Miguel's eyebrows raise into his forehead. "You mind?"

Miguel backed out and closed the door. For a second, he stared at the door, allowing his imagination to carry on what he couldn't witness. With all the craziness, he hardly allowed himself to take in Dr. Hutson's gorgeous appearance. It was a nice moment of levity in the middle of a very stressful circumstance. Unfortunately, a moment was all he could allow himself.

He forced his mind off of Gina and started marching back to the cargo hold.

The time had come. His chest ached like that of an out-of-shape marathon runner. In less than an hour, two prehistoric giants, with unmatched aggression, would face off before his very eyes.

CHAPTER 16

Sunny afternoon skies gleamed over the busy, white beaches of Hamilton Bay. As daytime workers left their jobs and collected their families to take advantage of the clear summer weather, the beach population ballooned to over four thousand. Far out, jet skiers, paddleboaters, sailing boats fought for space. Kids built sandcastles on the beach, while athletic fit college students suntanned themselves on the beach. Lonely onlookers sat in wicker chairs, gazing at members of the opposite sex, indulging in hookup fantasies that would likely not play out.

There was not a square foot of water in the five mile stretch that was undisturbed. People of all ages splashed, kicked, and twirled. Some remained in the shallows, while others ventured far out, supported by inflatables. Lifeguards patrolled the outer edges in small motorboats, supported by the Hamilton Police Department's Maritime Patrol. Piloting thirty-foot vessels painted in red and blue, featuring the familiar flashers over the cockpit, some of the police stayed along the drop-off area, guarding the shark nets and making sure people didn't climb over them to venture into extremely deep waters. Others kept an eye on the overly competitive boaters fighting for space in the open ocean.

Seven miles out, beneath the waves, a hungry beast approached. Vibrations from the many engines and threshing swimmers traveled far and wide, drawing it closer. It had spent a great deal of energy, traveling nearly a hundred miles within a matter of hours. Its previous victims had been successfully digested, filtered, and expelled in a cloudy mass. With its system cleared out, its body fired signals into its brain, declaring the need for replenishing lost energy. It needed to feed.

The shark gradually closed in, keeping a steady pace to preserve energy. From above, it could not be seen, as it was fifty feet below the waves, following the many signals of potential prey. The signals were distant; so distant that a normal shark without genetically enhanced senses would not be able to pick up on them. It had a while to go before it would reach its destination.

Then, like a cloud passing over sunlight, a new vibration eclipsed those that it was tracing. A vibration, like fluttering movements, more enhanced and pronounced than those from the west. The shark slowed and turned north. The source of this signal was much closer. Minutes later, the smell of blood entered its nostrils. Blood was a guaranteed sign of injured prey. Not only that, but the scent of blood was strong, meaning there was lots of it, which nearly overloaded its brain. This much blood indicated prey that was large in size, and also easy to overpower. The megalodon fired energy into its caudal fin, propelling its huge mass in the direction of this new meal.

Its gradual stride escalated into an assault velocity. As its ancestors had hunted in millennia past, it would race to the target, not only to sustain its needs, but to beat other predators to the catch, and feed before any showed up. Should any appear, there would be no other outcome but a magnification of the bloodbath that drew them together.

****

"We have your fish on sonar," Seabolt announced, lowering his radio from his ear after receiving word from the bridge. Standing on deck, he looked up at Crane 1, which towered high over the Triton submersible. Crew members lowered the low-frequency speaker over the port railing, while Jason Nace monitored the vibrations. The water was brown and oily as entire tubs of chum mixture were tossed over the transom, trailing out for nearly a mile.

Gina inhaled deeply for the fifth time in a row. Her wetsuit hugged her figure, providing warmth. Almost too much warmth. Without the heavy breeze on deck, the sun's heat was back in its full fury.

A sixth breath. It felt like her heartbeat was rocking her body. Miguel stood by the hatch, device in hand, ready to set the snake into action.

"You ready?" she asked.

"Doesn't matter now," he answered.

No, it doesn't. She climbed into the submersible and sealed the hatch. She sat inside the glass sphere, felt the controls, then initiated the startup procedure. She looked to Seabolt and gave a thumbs up. The Captain gave the order to lift the sub by holding his hand up to the operator, finger pointed, and twirling. The operator hoisted the sub, then slowly swung it out over the ocean.

Gina watched the water engulf the sphere. In the following moment, she was looking at the *Armstrong's* keel. She had to wait before engaging the engines, as the vibration would possibly attract the shark, which in turn, would cause it to attack her before she was ready to launch the assault. Bobbing in the water, the sub would simply appear as an artificial extension of the ship, as long as the shark didn't get close enough to see her through the glass. Her harpoon launchers were fully loaded, armed with enough ccs of sedative to put down a dozen elephants. Should the operation go wrong, she would always tranq the shark and drown it.

Up above, the crew hustled to get below deck.

"Go. Move it along!" Seabolt called to them.

"Don't have to tell me twice," Jason Nace said. He took off the headset and found the nearest hatch, passing Miguel along the way. "This better work."

"It will," Miguel assured him. Jason didn't look convinced. Nor did Seabolt, though he wasn't going to waste time voicing his concern.

"I thought I didn't have to tell you twice, merc," he said. Jason walked off and disappeared into the ship. The Captain waited on deck until he and Miguel were the only ones on it. "You sure you don't want to wait inside?"

"I'll be fine," Miguel said.

Seabolt's radio buzzed. *"Captain. Shark's at one-point-five miles."*

"Copy that. I want our crane operator ready. You'll have to move fast when it comes time." Located on the portside aft was Crane 2. Secured on the end of its cable was a stainless steel bar containing two razor sharp hooks. "I'll go over it once more. Once Dr. Hutson drugs that shark, and Dr. Lucero has that snake back in the hold, lower that hook down to the submersible. Once it is secured, swing the shark along the stern. At that point, we'll give the signal to open the ramp. All you in the holding tank, have that winch on standby. When the shark is in place, Dr. Hutson will detach Crane 2's cable and attach yours. Once it's ready, you'll haul the fish in, and shut that door behind it. And for the love of God, get those restraints on it. We only have one shot at this, gentlemen, and as you can imagine, it requires almost precise timing."

A series of "Aye-aye, Captain" responses came through the radio. Seabolt lowered the radio and gave one last look at Miguel.

"We'll monitor the shark's position," he said. "Are you sure you want it to get up close before unleashing the snake?"

"If I unleash it too soon, the shark may sense a threat and flee. Also, if I release it too soon, Eleven might rush out to engage. It can travel a mile much faster than this boat, and for this to work, we need them as close to the ship as possible."

Seabolt shook as a chill crept down his spine. He looked up at the crane, then the cargo hatch behind him.

"If this works, the beer is on me," he said.

"We'll need it after this day is over," Miguel said.

"No doubt about that. Well, good luck, Doc." Seabolt shook his hand then hurried back to the bridge.

A moment later, the speaker sounded off.

"One-point-three miles! Gaining speed."

Miguel could feel his hands trembling against the tablet screen. He connected the device to the chem-beacon attached to the megalodon's dorsal. A gust of wind swept over him. He closed his eyes, looked up, silently making his wish for everything to play out as planned.

"One mile!" It was Seabolt's voice this time. Miguel's eyes flashed open. He looked south over the port railing. The stretch of brown chum gave the ocean a sickly look. It gradually spread and broke apart. There was one last drum of chum waiting to be dumped.

"Point seven."

Miguel hurried to the drum, ripped the cap off, then knelt down to lift. His knees shook as he lifted the hundred-pound drum over the side. It tilted over, spilling a waterfall of blood, guts, and fish oil.

"Pace increasing rapidly."

"Good. Let him come," Miguel said. He grabbed the tablet back up, took another nervous breath. Sweat dripped down his face. The smell of death filled his nose. "Come on. Get your fat ass over here."

As if it heard him, a large swell bulged from the ocean's flat surface. In that same moment, a huge grey dorsal fin speared its way skyward. A second fin appeared several yards behind it, crescent shaped, swaying back and forth.

For the first time, Miguel saw the megalodon. Having worked with another giant animal, he didn't think he'd be overwhelmed by its immense presence. He was wrong. His hands trembled, smearing sweat over the tablet's screen.

"Open the hatch."

Seabolt must've already had his thumb on the button, because the words had barely left his mouth before Miguel heard the turning of gears. The hatch doors yawned wide. Sunlight streamed into its interior, stirring the creature within.

The Colossal Snake lifted its head toward the opening, flicking its tongue. There were no scents above aside from that of its human caretaker. It raised slowly, cautiously, ready to engage any threat that waited outside of its entrapment.

Miguel looked over his shoulder as the resurrected serpent emerged. Its head ascended twenty feet, the neck arching back into a sub-striking position. It panned across, searching the deck for anything to strike.

"Feeling cranky, huh? Hungry? Hangry? Good, I hope you're in the mood for fish," Miguel said to it. He had timed everything perfectly so far.

Now, it was the moment of truth. He swiped his finger over the screen, and lowered it to the chem-beacon icon.

"Increased speed! Brace for impact! Miguel, GET DOWN!"

Miguel's eyes turned back to the meg. Like a fighter jet firing up afterburners, the megalodon tripled its speed. In the following moment, it sliced through the trail of chum, and torpedoed the *Armstrong* with its snout. The ship shook as though rocked by an explosion. It lurched forward, the stern rising several feet high, throwing the herpetologist to the deck. His chin hit the steel panels, clanking his teeth together. The ship rocked again, this time pitching to starboard.

The snake hissed furiously, the earthquake throwing it into a frenzy. It rose another twenty feet, thrashing its head like a loose garden hose. It swung back, striking the mast. A sharp crack traveled across the ship. Meanwhile, the megalodon struck again, creating a twelve-inch cavity in the hull. The ship rocked again, distressing the snake further. A highly volatile beast in an unfamiliar environment, the beast believed the ship itself to be the threat. It twisted its body back toward the structure and lashed again, striking the crows next and splintering it into a hundred pieces.

Slithering out of the enclosure, it slithered up to the bridge, its massive eye slits peering through the glass panel at the many humans inside.

"Clear the deck." Captain Seabolt kept his voice calm but strict. There was only an inch-thick windshield between him and the serpentine head staring fifteen feet away. The bridge crew had already left their seats and backed from the instrument panels. The snake stared, studying the movement inside.

The shark struck again, rocking the boat.

Its anger pronounced in an ear-piecing hiss, followed by a devastating lash at the structure. Its open jaws smashed the bridge window, sending shards of glass hailing into the room. Personnel dove on the deck, hiding behind the control panels, while others jam-packed themselves against the door like crowded sheep.

"The hell's going on up there?" Gina yelled into her radio. She started the sub's engines and banked to starboard, distancing herself from the rocking ship. She had witnessed the first impact, then saw the ship rock heavily to starboard. So far, there was no snake in the water.

Had the device malfunctioned again?

She saw the shark coming around the stern. It was twenty yards from the ship, swimming in a semi-circle path. In the blink of an eye, it turned toward the ship, eyes rolled back, and with a stroke of its caudal fin, it closed the distance and struck a fifth time.

"Jeez!" Gina stuttered. She could see the ship swaying heavily. The shark didn't care about its superior size or the density of its hull. It was determined to bring the ship down at any cost. Perhaps it was memories of its previous entrapment, or a natural urge to kill, or genetic programming. Whatever the case, the only thing that could stop it from eventually sinking the ship was herself.

She disengaged the safety systems for the harpoon launchers, then blasted soundwaves, while continuing to distance herself from the *Armstrong.* She was five hundred feet from it now, more than enough to line up a shot, as long as she could get the shark to charge straight at her. She could see the whole six-hundred-foot length of the ship, the much smaller shark traveling alongside of it.

Gina sent off another soundwave, then fluttered the sub's arms to generate distressed vibrations. She noticed a change in the shark's movements. It had picked up on her signal and was now attempting to pinpoint her location, which only took a moment.

That angular snout was now pointed at her. Already, it was charging. As hoped, it was coming straight at her. Only, she overestimated her ability to aim a precise shot at an oncoming object coming at such a vast speed, and underestimated the disruption from the water displacement caused by its advance. Like a shockwave, the ocean rippled around the sub, shifting it upward just a few inches. Those inches made all the difference in the world. She discharged the first harpoon, which skidded uselessly over the shark's snout.

She screamed and banked to port. The shark closed in, its jaws snapping shut to her right. There was no moment of levity. As it shot past, its tail swung hard, striking the caudal fin against the starboard ballast tank. Next thing Gina knew, she was rolling to port like a soccer ball. She pulled on the controls, trying to regain control. Gradually, she slowed the roll to a stop. She was upside down and sinking now.

After a quick breath, she regained her wits. She pulled up on the control stick, rotating the Triton upward. The dark view of the ocean's depths went down like a film strip, replaced by the white light of the surface above her. She started to ascend, then gasped. The megalodon swam into view, its mass gliding effortlessly under the water's surface. It angled downward and fluttered its tail. In one instant, she was looking at its huge grey snout, marred with scrapes and bruises from its repeated collisions. The following instant, she saw rows of white teeth separating. Next came the darkness of its throat.

Gina rocked forward, nearly hitting her head on the instrument panel. She reversed engines and accelerated. The Triton vibrated, unable to free itself from the shark's jaws. Brief glimmers of light seeped in from the corners of its mouth. It was traveling up near the surface, carrying her along the way. Its jaws loosened, only to bite down again. Its teeth chipped at the sphere repeatedly. It shook its head to wedge the sub further into its throat. The little bit of light was quickly dwindling.

Gina flashed the searchlights and saw pinkish-white flesh of the shark's mouth. Gill slits, looking black from the inside, flapped open and shut like window blinds.

Perfect! She couldn't get much closer than this. She reached for the firing system. The starboard launcher was still armed, with one harpoon remaining, three shots left together in total. She squeezed the trigger and listened to the frothing sound of the harpoon shooting beneath her. Except, she never saw it enter its mouth.

"Damn it!" she yelled. The way the shark held the sub, the ballast and launchers were just below its jaw. She just fired a harpoon under its belly. Helpless, and stuck in its jaws, she was shaken in her seat again as the jaws chomped down on the sub. The teeth chipped away at the glass like triangular ice picks. Tiny cracks started to form. Warning signs flashed along the instrument panels.

Breach imminent.

Gina's throat tightened. Never was she oblivious to the danger of raising this megalodon. Still, she never thought she, of all people, would end up inside its gullet.

The snake uncoiled its mass, lifting it meter by meter out of the cargo hold. Pieces of the superstructure rained down on the deck. The more it came free, the more it thrashed. A section of its body slid across the deck, forcing Miguel to dive to his left.

Metal deck sections split apart, forming vast cavities all over the ship. A fragment of decking uprooted, launching Miguel's tablet. He watched it skid another several meters out of reach.

"Damn it. GodDAMN it!" he said, crawling on his hands and knees after it. With each added inch, his mind screamed at him for his stupidity.

Stupid. So stupid! You knew that thing was a weapon. Not just a shark—a weapon! It was designed to sink ships! LIKE THIS ONE! And you waited until the last moment. Yeah, you justified it by saying 'we can't have the fight too far away from the ship.' But face the truth, you twerp! You stupid, eco-loving moron! You just couldn't bring yourself to set it loose. And now look at what you've done!

A crashing sound above caused him to look up. The snake struck the bridge again, pulling out a huge section of decking in his huge jaws. No crew were dead—not yet.

It retracted, its neck moving to the side, crushing anything below with its weight. Miguel watched as it continued to the left, crunching equipment, debris, and decking…heading right for the tablet. Miguel gasped, then shot to his feet. That tablet would be crushed into tiny shards of plastic, and without it, there would be no controlling the snake. The thought of being crushed to death vanished from his mind. He ran as fast as he could. Pieces of structure flew past him as though carried by high winds. The creature was closing fast. Like an MLB player sliding into second, he grabbed the tablet, then went back to his feet and ran toward the bow.

He reactivated the screen, and with a touch of his finger, he activated the chem-beacon.

Signal commencing.

Miguel looked back at the snake. Its rapid movements came to a sudden stop. Frozen into a coiled position, it waited, the only motion done by its tongue. Slowly, its head turned, searching for the source of the new scent.

The water breached, drawing its attention as well as Miguel's. The megalodon raced along the surface, spraying water as it went. Miguel noticed something odd about the swells near its head. Leaning over the railing, he saw the yellow hull protruding from its mouth.

"Oh, Jesus!"

The snake stared, intrigued by the monstrous foe. It slid across the deck, studying the fish. Too slow. Miguel tensed, then amplified the signal. Implants flooded the snake's vomeronasal organ. Hissing frantically, it sprang into the water, its whole hundred-and-fifty-foot length disappearing under a tremendous splash that swept the deck.

The megalodon immediately felt the presence of another large organism. Its sudden appearance was as troubling as its size and rapid approach. Whatever it was, it was hostile.

Its need to hunt gave way to the instinct of self-preservation. The megalodon spat the submersible out, sending it spiraling several meters into the depths. It fluttered its tail, gaining distance to circle around. But it had gained no distance. Whatever was in the water, it was keeping pace. The megalodon dove. Still, the pursuer followed.

The megalodon retreated for several more yards, still unable to outpace the new foe. Rather than outmatch it in speed, it would have to do so in ferocity. It arched its body to the left, stopping all tail motion, and using its momentum to swing it around entirely until it was facing the new visitor.

The Colossal Snake did not slow. The overwhelming urge to kill this foe subdued any sense of self-preservation or attack strategy. It didn't search for bite placement. It would just attack, constrict, and tighten, like its ancestors did to ancient reptiles eons ago.

Several meters below, Gina caught her breath and rotated her sub, quickly pointing it upward. She saw a glistening white surface above her, and further down in the distance, were two enormous shapes closing in like fighter planes in World War 2. But unlike planes, there were no evasive maneuvers taken between these foes.

The resulting collision resulted in a shockwave rivaled by that of small meteor impacts. Gina, still recovering from the shock of nearly getting swallowed, was once again rattled in her seat. She sucked in a breath, fighting down any nausea, and watched the violent clash from afar.

CHAPTER 17

It was as if an invisible storm had struck the Atlantic. The tranquil swells became thirty-foot crests, rolling in different directions. Mountains of water crashed together and exploded into thousands of smaller droplets, only to accumulate into new swells.

Beneath the waves was a blur of thrashing tails, twisting bodies, and snapping jaws. The two beasts locked together, the shark biting the snake's midsection, while it retaliated with a bite above the left pectoral. The snake wound its body, looping it around the shark to initiate its constriction. The megalodon, sensing the danger, released its grip and shot like a bullet through the loop before it could compress. The snake's head jolted forward, its fangs losing their hold.

The snake lashed out for its caudal fin, but missed. Its body flapped in the water like a flag in high winds, propelling itself after the fish. The megalodon was already gaining significant distance. However, it was not retreating. It dove deep, swimming straight down, revealing its underbelly. Spiraling to keep itself from turning upside down, the shark angled its trajectory again, now completely underneath the snake. Like a surface-to-air missile, it shot skyward, aiming its jaws right for the snake.

The snake took a curling position, ready to strike. Its strike, however, was too slow. Its snapping jaws skidded over the meg's snout like a ricochet bullet. In that same instant, nerves along its midsection lit up as razor sharp teeth punched through the skin. With the snake in its jaws, the megalodon continued upward toward the glassy blue ocean surface.

Walls of water peeled out, making way for the two eighty-ton leviathans. They soared upward, both bodies twisting, tails lashing.

Two hundred feet behind them, an astounded Miguel Lucero clung to the railing. His blood streamed in rapid currents while his body stiffened from a combination of fear and astonishment. For a moment, time seemed to stand still, freezing the perfect image of the monsters suspended in midair.

Time continued on, and in the following moment, both creatures crashed down into the ocean, resulting in a rolling wave that towered over the *Armstrong*. Miguel tucked the tablet under his shirt and turned his back. The wave struck the ship, knocking it heavily to starboard. Like teetering on a swivel, the ship rocked back, throwing Miguel against the railing.

He held as it rocked again, with one hand still wrapped over the tablet. As he steadied himself, his eyes went back to the water, and the two colossal silhouettes wrestling underneath.

The megalodon swam forward, allowing the current to sweep its enemy's blood into its mouth. The snake squirmed, its body curling like a nightcrawler embedded on a fishing hook. The shark had a hold directly at its center, making it impossible to constrict. It tried corkscrewing its upper body, but stopped as the motion only served to rip its flesh further. The teeth were serrated, and every movement from the snake allowed them to act like sawblades. It needed to get the shark to let go.

The titans breached the surface, traveling up only a few meters before crashing down. The megalodon swam along the surface and began jerking its head back and forth. The snake snapped its jaws at the shark's underbelly, but only succeeded in scraping the skin. An ear-piercing hiss ripped through the air as it felt another tear in its flesh. The beast struggled, both ends flailing up and down. Large swells rippled out from the combined mass, rocking the ship further.

Still, Miguel clung on to the railing, his eyes never wavering from the fight. A sense of helplessness swept over him. The sight of the snake's blood caused a stirring in his stomach. The damn fish was killing it, and there was nothing he could do.

"Come on, Eleven! Get loose!"

The snake bit again, chipping away at the shark's chin. Its enemy continued carrying it, not even feeling the needle-like teeth picking at its flesh. The snake retracted its head, and poised for another shot. This time, it went for the megalodon's gills. Nerves shot through the shark, causing it to jolt. The intelligent snake struck again, producing the same reaction. As it bit the gills on the shark's left side, it struck its tail like a crop on the shark's right gill lines.

Sensitive nerves in the gills flared, causing the megalodon to release the snake. With a flick of its tail, it darted off. The snake sank, taking a moment to regain its energy before continuing the fight. Sinking several meters down, it coiled into a striking position, watching the fish.

The megalodon swam another hundred feet, the pain already subsided. With no intention of letting its new prey recuperate, it circled and, gaining more speed, made another run at the snake. Once again, the snake was unprepared for the megalodon's intense speed.

Jaws snapped shut around its neck, and suddenly, the snake's coiled body unraveled as it was viciously dragged backward. Its tail thrashed like a whip, fighting against the current to tangle itself around the megalodon. Its speed and maneuverability had already proved greater than that of itself. The hold on its neck gradually tightened, the tips of the teeth beginning to prod their way through the skin.

The Colossal Snake writhed. Like the tentacle of a mythical kraken, its tail arched forward and made its way to the megalodon's body. It curled behind the dorsal fin and under its belly, then back up the other side to repeat the process.

Sensing the danger, the shark released its grip and fluttered its tail to dart out of the constriction. It raced forward, but it was still dragging the snake's weight, despite letting it free. There was pressure all over its body, unlike anything it had ever experienced before. As the snake proceeded to constrict around its caudal fin, the megalodon found itself suddenly unable to move. It twisted and turned, trying desperately to get out of the predicament.

In a few moments, the snake had its entire body wrapped around the shark. With each writhing movement, the snake tightened. Unable to swim, the megalodon began to sink. Breathing was no concern for the Colossal Snake, as it could hold its breath for over an hour. Its head hovered above that of the shark's, staring down into the huge black marble eyes, waiting for the life to slip from its enemy.

"It's done it," Gina said. "Miguel! It's actually working! Eleven's got the shark in a constriction!" She waited for a response. "Miguel?"

"What are you waiting for? Get after it!"

That wasn't Miguel's voice. Nor was it Seabolt's. The process of elimination was a fast one: Jason Nace.

"Is everyone alright on board the ship?" Gina asked.

"Quit wasting time and get after the damn shark!" Jason replied.

What's his deal? she wondered. What investment did he have in the shark's capture? Miguel was right; it was obvious now that the mercenary was ordered aboard this ship by Marc Gundrum, who likely didn't trust her and Miguel to capture the shark alive.

Best course of action is to proceed as planned, she thought. *What's he gonna do from deck, anyway? The important thing is to stop the megalodon from killing anyone else. However, for my own sake, let's try and make it look like I'm attempting to line up a shot.*

She jetted the sub closer to the monsters, though she remained cautious. Though the snake was fixated on the shark, there was no guarantee that it wouldn't strike at her without a moment's hesitation.

The creatures had sunk nearly two hundred feet. The megalodon twisted a few more times before going stiff. The snake maintained its hold, its head still hovering over the meg's. Several more seconds passed, none of which contained movement from the shark.

The snake lowered its head and opened its mouth. Its jaws extended, its throat widening as though inflated by an air pump. It bit down on the shark's nose and began the process of swallowing it...

...when suddenly, the *dead* megalodon sprang back to life. It thrashed its head, unlatching it from the snake's teeth, then with all of its remaining energy, it managed a single thrust of its tail, jutting itself forward a few feet. Its jaws closed like a slab, the teeth piercing the snake's flesh right behind its head.

Sudden pain surged through the snake's body like an electric current. Both creatures were now locked in a death grip, which would soon result in both of their demises. Recognizing the danger it was in, the snake loosened its grip on the shark's body.

Desperate for air, and feeling the constriction loosening, the shark let go and darted out to the left, taking in thousands of gallons of water through its gills. The snake held back for several seconds. Blood seeped from its wounds, which weren't deep. The snake flickered its tongue, then moved up to the surface for a breath. The pain in its neck subsided and the urge to pursue the shark returned.

The megalodon continued west at a gradual pace, allowing its strength to return. With the substantial amount of energy spent, it had to refuel itself with food. Its blood oxygenated, its senses returned. It detected movement several meters behind. Its foe had started pursuit again. The megalodon, even in its tired state, would still outpace the snake until it was ready to engage. First, it needed to find easier prey to satisfy its hunger and provide an energy boost. It fixated on the distortion coming from several hundred yards ahead. The movement and vibrations indicated a smaller target, which would take less effort to consume.

Miguel stood on the ravaged deck and watched the dorsal fin soar along the ocean. It was two hundred feet out, moving in a straight line. Nearly four hundred feet behind it, the snake continued its pursuit, its body appearing like a green wiggly line under the surface.

A few crewmembers burst from the structure, some hyperventilating, others heaving over the side, while a few adrenaline junkie types cheered to the heavens, having survived an assault from a giant snake and shark.

Miguel looked up to the bridge. The whole front side of the structure was gone, broken to shreds. Reinforced steel beams had been bent effortlessly. Broken instrument panels littered the deck along with various other wreckage. On the deck itself, there was hardly a square foot of flat even space. Either the metal plating was uprooted, or caved downward by the snake's thrashing assault.

Jason Nace was one of the first on the deck. He chuckled as he examined the aftermath.

"That's a hell of a pet you've got there!" he said. He walked to the railing and watched the shark swimming off. "What the hell are we waiting for?"

"Eleven's going after it. We almost had it, but we lost it," Miguel said.

"Yeah? Where's your girlfriend?" Jason said. Miguel didn't have a radio. Jason pulled his from his belt and raised it to his chin. "Hey shark lady? What's going on down there?"

"I didn't get close enough in time. We're off for take two."

"Yeah? I was watching from the monitors. Looked to me like you were holding back?"

"Excuse me, jackass, but in case you didn't notice, I almost got swallowed by the damn thing! While trying to keep it off your ass, no less."

Miguel took the radio. "You alright? Any injuries?"

"Sub's been knocked around. Can't take another hit like that. But I'm alright."

"Then hold back," Miguel said.

"Oh no you don't," Jason said. "We're not letting that shark get away."

"You wanna take a go at it? Be my guest," Gina replied.

"Maybe I should have," he growled.

"Relax, man," Miguel said. Jason grabbed him by the shirt and pulled him close. "Let go!"

"You know what I think?" Jason snarled, his chin nearly touching Miguel's forehead. "I think you and the pretty shark lady are up to something." He shoved him backward. Miguel caught his balance and straightened his collar.

"Yeah. Like we hunt megalodons every day. It's a sport, really!"

"You know what I do for sport? I hunt down weasels like you and make them squirm," Jason said. "Don't think that won't happen to you if you don't catch that shark."

"Is that why Gundrum ordered you here? To keep me in line?"

"You're the one with the doctorate. Figure it out," Jason said.

"Oh CHRIST!" one of the crewmembers called out. All eyes went back to the dorsal fin. Miguel traced its trajectory, then felt warm beads of sweat roll down his face as he saw the fishing boat a quarter mile in front of it. The boat was going at high speed, going right at the shark.

"Oh, shit! Do they see it? Seabolt! Blow the horn! Get on the radio! Do something! We've got to—"

"Forget it, kid," Jason said. "That boat's not moving at a trawling speed. Those assholes are going right for your fish."

CHAPTER 18

"My God. Holy God, Mary, Joseph, Jesus, and whoever else I forgot to mention," Sam muttered. He stood at the helm of his fishing vessel, binoculars to his eyes. At first, he thought the sea swells were playing tricks on him, or that his drug taking days in the early eighties were catching up with him.

"Hot DAMN, Cap! It's real. It's fucking REAL!" Santor exclaimed. Sam smiled. It was official: Richard Redway was not pulling their leg. There was an honest-to-God giant shark swimming in this ocean.

"You're damn right, it's real," Sam said. He watched the fin grow larger. "Okay kid, get that dynamite ready."

"Jeez, Captain," Santor said. This time, he sounded more concerned than excited. The gravity of their situation had hit him, drowning his youthful ego. "It's twice as big as our boat! Three times as big!"

"It could the size of a star destroyer as far as I'm concerned," Sam said. "Nothing can withstand a dynamite stick to the face! Now, hurry the hell up!" Santor opened the barrel of dynamite. He was never too fond of his Captain's use of depth charges for fishing, but this time he was feeling the opposite. He strung a few sticks together and hurried for the cockpit. Sam handed him a cigarette lighter. "Have about five seconds worth. This guy is big, but he's fast."

"You think he'll ram the boat? Redway said it rammed his," Santor said.

"It won't get the chance," Sam said. "If the explosion doesn't kill it, it'll most certainly drive it off. However, you still make a good point." He cut the wheel ten degrees port then pushed the throttle. The shark was getting closer. Sam moved back to the main deck and waited. He shook with excitement, holding the lighter close to the fuse.

"Who the hell are they?" he said, pointing to the cargo ship. "Looks like they've sustained some kind of damage."

"Don't know," Sam answered. "Maybe they had a run-in with the fish. In which case, they can praise us as their heroes! Now quit worrying about them and FOCUS!"

Santor watched the fin, amazed to see how fast it had approached. Both he and Sam realized that the shark wasn't just swimming in their direction—it was actually speeding toward them!

"Oh shit! Kid! Light that fuse now!" Sam said. Santor flicked the lighter open and sparked a flame, then touched it to the tip of the fuse. Sparks zipped out in all directions. With a five-second fuse, there was no time to line up a shot. He took a brief aim, seeing the shark now closing within fifty yards. He tossed the dynamite. It went for twenty yards and hit the water. To his amazement, he had lined it directly with the oncoming fin.

A thunderous boom rang their ears, producing an orange flash, followed by an upsurge of water. Ocean droplets rained on their fishing boat, obscuring their view for a brief moment. When it settled, the fin had disappeared. They saw the shark's bulk beneath the waves, gradually sinking.

A triumphant cheer filled the air. Both fishermen met at the starboard side-deck and slapped hands.

"Son of a bitch, that was fucking easy!" Sam shouted. "Nice work, kid!"

"YEAH!" Santor cheered. "That was so easy, that was almost anticlimactic."

"Don't worry! There's more joy to be had!" Smiling ear-to-ear, Sam lit a cigarette and grabbed his radio. "*Threshold* to *Omega Thunder*. Come in, Cathy."

"What's the word, Sam?"

"You have Redway on board?"

"Standing right beside me."

"Hey, bud. That fish you say killed your brother, well, we're floating over its bloated carcass!" Other voices filled the radio.

"Are you serious?" It was Bruno.

"It's Sam. Take anything he says with a grain of salt," Jake replied.

"Why don't y'all group over here near the *Coast Prion* wreck site and find out for yourselves."

"We're not far from there. We're on our way," Cathy said.

"Sam, this better not be a joke," Redway added.

"No joke," Sam said. "Though, we might need diving equipment to get a cable on your fish."

"I'm close to that site too. I'll be there in a few," Bruno said.

"I guess I'd better have a look," Jake added.

"Good. See you then," Sam said. He sucked down the rest of his cigarette, then pulled another. He grinned again, looking at Santor. "Can't wait to see their faces when that shark comes back up—"

Without warning, the deck exploded into a thousand fragments, all vaulting out from their point of origin. In less than a second, the *Threshold* went from being a thirty-foot fishing vessel to an ocean-full of steel confetti. Decking, piping, mast fragments, propellers, engine fragments, all came apart and spread across the surrounding ocean.

In the middle of it all, the megalodon spiraled in midair, its snout somewhat scarred from the blast. It crashed back down, sending waves of debris rolling with the waves. Its eardrums were still throbbing from the explosion that momentarily stunned it, but were gradually returning to normal.

Through the ruins, it picked up the scent of blood and traced it to Sam's mangled corpse. He began to sink, his body twisted into an unrecognizable shape. Arms were bent behind his head, his severed legs trailing a few feet behind him. Clenched between his teeth was his final cigarette, which vanished along with its owner into the megalodon's throat.

It sensed the water displacement of another creature. Driven by hunger, the shark wasted no time honing in.

Santor was hurtled through the air for what seemed like forever. When he hit the water, he sank for several feet before his brain realized he wasn't flying anymore. The sting of ocean water snapped his mind into focus. He swam to the surface and drew a breath.

He gasped, seeing the floating fragments drifting all around him, while others rained down like tiny meteors. There was no trace of the vessel. Or Sam. His memory of the last few seconds was fuzzy. One moment he was standing on the deck. Out of nowhere, the deck exploded, and he was tossed.

Santor paddled, grabbing for anything that could hold him up. He found a board, which sank as soon as he applied weight to it. He tossed it aside and found a large piece of decking the size of a bedroom door, which held his weight. He pulled himself over it, then relaxed, staring down at the water.

A cloud took form underneath him. Santor lifted his head, seeing the crescent shape of fins extending from that 'cloud'. Then he saw teeth. Another watery explosion launched him high. This time, however, he was surrounded by jagged rows of teeth, which rapidly closed shut on him.

The megalodon's jaws carved him up like a deli meat slicer, effortlessly washing his chunks into the back of its throat. It splashed back down, its hunger still unsatisfied. Its hearing returned to it, and its lateral line picked up the intense water displacement of a rapidly approaching mass.

The Colossal Snake closed the distance, snapping its jaws at the megalodon's caudal fin. The shark whipped its tail, freeing itself before the snake could constrict. It turned and snapped its jaws, but the snake evaded by twirling downward. The shark followed, and with its superior speed, it closed in, jaws extended. It bit down, sinking teeth into the snake's tail.

The reptile lurched backward, spurred by the sudden pain. It turned its body and snapped at the megalodon's gills, lodging its fangs behind the slits. Nerves fired, and the shark released its grip and attempted to flee. But the snake maintained its grip, and now, trailing with the megalodon, it began fastening its body around the shark's. This time, it was careful to make sure it remained out of reach from those jaws.

Once again, the megalodon felt its body getting excruciatingly tight. With some range of motion left in its tail, it shot for the surface, breaching. The snake gradually wrapped its lower body around the caudal fin. The megalodon snapped its jaws, biting nothing but mouthfuls of water. Its body went taut, its caudal fin unable to sway. The snake maintained its grip, keeping the fangs lodged in the gill slits. After learning from the previous encounter, it would bide its time, and not let go until there was no doubt its prey was dead.

CHAPTER 19

"My God," Gina said. She brought the sub near the giants. They sank together amidst a shower of debris. The shark had gone after the boat without a moment's hesitation. *This* was the animal she raised; a creature born to kill indiscriminately. *This* would be the result of Marc Gundrum releasing it to any potential buyer, whether it be the government, a terrorist, or someone in-between.

Small clouds of blood billowed as the snake's fangs gashed under the gill slits. The megalodon struggled, but could not manage to gain the motion necessary to push water through its gills. Its body tightened, its cartilage skeleton compressing under pressure that would snap solid bones.

Gina steered the sub through a world of ship fragments. There was hardly a single recognizable piece in the ocean, making it hard to believe they belonged to an organized structure that carried human beings. And there were no human beings among them, either on the surface, or below the depths.

She activated her radio, "Miguel, I think Eleven's got it. It's not letting go this time. I think we've won."

The *Armstrong* moved toward the carnage at full throttle, quickly arriving at the edge of the debris field. Nobody was surprised that there were no survivors. They had witnessed the horrific breaching afterwards, and it didn't take a genius to know that the meg would only do that when going after prey.

They could see the creatures far below, though their details were nothing but dim silhouettes that would disappear from view in a matter of minutes.

"Come on," Miguel muttered under his breath. "Drown it. Crush it. Hurry up."

"Alright, let's stop wasting time. The snake has the fish. Tell Hutson to tranq it before it dies," Jason said. He looked up toward the structure, seeing Captain Seabolt standing on the ledge where the glass panel used to be. "Have your men get the cables ready!"

"You don't run this ship, Mr. Nace," Seabolt reminded him.

"I'm not gonna tell you again," Jason said. Seabolt stared him down from above, then got on his radio to direct his crew. He then disappeared to the back of the bridge and descended down the stairwell. Jason's eyes turned back to the herpetologist. "We're running out of time. The shark's dying, and we need it alive. I've noticed your lady is not making the move."

Miguel glared at him.

"How can you see what's going on down there?" he asked. "You claimed you've been watching. I've barely been able to see anything. Where's all your knowledge coming from?"

"I hacked the sub's camera," Jason said. He held up a smartphone, facing the screen outward. Miguel saw the creatures from the sub's POV, the shark's movements growing more and more stiff with each passing second. His eyes went back to the mercenary.

"Why?"

"Because you can't be trusted," Jason said.

"Trusted?" Miguel stuttered. "As you see, we've got her in the water, and Eleven's successfully got the sh—"

"Don't play dumb," Jason snapped, drawing the attention of the crewmembers on deck. Jason stepped closer. Miguel held his ground, trying hard not to look intimidated. "I know what you and the fish lady are up to. Gundrum's a greedy bastard, but he's not stupid. Not entirely, at least. He's smart enough to know when someone's out to sabotage him."

"What's it to you?" Miguel said. "Somehow, I'm not getting the impression that you're motivated by a loyalty to Gundrum."

Jason didn't answer, instead, glancing back down at the screen again, then back at Miguel.

"Tell her to get in position. Now."

Miguel pressed further. "Let me guess: a successful capture would result in a lot of money for you, right? Can't see any other reason a hired gun like you would have so much investment."

"Gundrum isn't stupid. You and the lady talk too much." Jason moved a hand toward him. Miguel flinched, thinking he was about to be struck. Instead, Jason reached around his shirt collar and tugged on something, then held it up. It resembled a shirt button, but also appeared mechanical. A radio device. Miguel's mind flashed to the lab when Jason 'jokingly' jostled him while laughing.

"You son of a—" Miguel yelped in pain as Jason grabbed his wrist and bent it behind his waist, spinning him around and thumping his head against the bulkhead. Jason kicked the back of his knees, putting Miguel face down on the deck, then pinned him with a knee to his back.

"Hey!"

Jason saw Captain Seabolt in his peripheral vision, stepping out onto the deck.

"Stop right there, Captain," Jason said. Seabolt slowed, but didn't stop.

"Let him go."

"Keep out of this, Seabolt. I'm keeping this fool in line." Nace grabbed the dropped tablet, which had powered down, requiring a password to reactivate. "Turn this back on."

"What the hell's going on?" Seabolt asked.

"You wanna know?" Nace said. Still holding Miguel down with one hand, he placed the tablet down and picked his smartphone back up. With a few swipes of his thumb, he retracted the camera feed and brought forth an audio recorder. A few moments later, he isolated the soundbite.

"Say…I miss with the tranquilizer? Or it fails to penetrate the flesh? We won't get a second chance at this. As much as Gundrum can't afford to have the megalodon killed, he also can't afford to have it loose to rampage along the coast. Potential buyers would learn of the incident and turn away, thinking these things are too uncontrollable and aren't worth the investment. Thus, that creates a chance they won't bother to purchase Eleven."

"That's…possible. It's a thin assumption."

"You know Gundrum, and you're more knowledgeable on what's going on behind the scenes. What do you think he would do?"

"IF it all plays out like that, he would probably save face in any way he can. He wouldn't have Eleven put down; he's got too much invested into it. So, to turn a profit wherever he can, he'd probably expand the exhibit and put it on display, Jurassic Park style. Literally, his cover story would become his backup plan."

"And you would continue to study it and watch over it."

"You're still gonna have to get in that sub."

Seabolt said nothing, though he was genuinely taken aback by the reveal.

"You saw what the shark did to this boat," Miguel said. "You know what it would've done had it been able to continue. It's a weapon, and we can't let it live. If we do, untold innocents will die."

"Says the guy who raised the creature who did *that*," Seabolt said, pointing up at the superstructure and the debris all over the deck. "You want the shark dead, yet, not the snake…which is clearly as much of a threat if not more. I sense a conflict of interests."

"I'm a scientist," Miguel groaned. "I've wanted to study this specimen all of my life. I've connected with it, and it with me. I can keep it from killing anyone. But the shark—"

"You haven't convinced me, Doctor," Seabolt said, kicking a piece of decking toward him.

"Alright, enough with the love story," Jason said. He released his grip and stood off Miguel. "Tell her to tranq the shark."

"Go take a dive," Miguel replied.

"Fine, I'll tell her myself." Jason pulled out his radio. "Dr. Hutson, I'm aware of what you and Dr. Lucero are up to. Let me simplify it for you: You're not going to let the shark die. You will capture it, attach a cable, and bring it into the holding tank. You've got nearly a minute to go before that snake kills the shark. You're going to tranq it, or else Miguel will have to release the snake, and we'll have to start all over again. Let's spare ourselves the headache and capture it while it's vulnerable."

Gina swallowed, hearing Jason's voice coming through her speakers. She nudged the sub toward the creatures. They were now near to the edge of the sub's reach, soon to disappear into the black.

I can't let it live. It'll kill so many...

"Miguel?" Her voice shook. "Miguel? Where are you?"

"She wants to talk to you," Jason said. He tossed Miguel his radio. Miguel stared at it, then stood to his feet. He lifted the radio to his lips.

"Gina?"

"I'm here. What's going on up there? Are you alright?"

"Gina...get the hell out of here. They're on to us. Take the sub to the coast. Anywhere! Just go. I'll handle the snake after it finishes the meg."

"Told you so!" Jason said to the Captain and crew. His smile turned into a demonic snarl. His closed fist struck Miguel below his right eye, knocking him on his back. Before Miguel could recover, he felt a crushing blow to his stomach.

"Holy shit, Nace," Seabolt said. "That's enough!"

"Mind the ship, Captain," Jason said. Seabolt's expression intensified.

"You don't tell me how to run my business. This is *my* ship." He approached, followed by several of his crewmembers. "And I told you to get off of him."

Jason drew his sidearm and pointed it at the Captain's head.

"No. This is *Gundrum's* ship," he said. "And he's placed me in command." Seabolt and his crew stopped, hands raised.

"This is getting out of hand," Seabolt said.

Jason scoffed. "No shit. These little punks were playing their own little scheme. They had no intention of capturing the shark. They planned to let that damn boa kill it in hopes of 'protecting human life' or some bullshit." He chuckled. "Like we don't bomb foreign countries every single day. Don't see these idiots complaining about that. Oh, but an oversized fish gets used instead of missiles…and suddenly the world is coming to an end." He knelt down by Miguel, piercing him with wide eyes and a sinister grin. "By the way, Lucero, your hopes of Gundrum cutting his losses and letting you keep the snake in the exhibit: BULLSHIT! He'll make a hundred more. See, I had a little bit of spare time on my hands while we were tracking the shark. I personally know of a dozen buyers who'll still be interested in it, and I gave all of them a personal call. Guess what? They're all interested, and they're eager to have a bid meeting with Mr. Gundrum. Government figures, private businessmen, others that'd rather remain unnamed, all of them are eager to meet your pet. And you know what else? They can hire snake docs much cheaper than you."

"Yeah? What's in it for you? A slice of the pie? A handler's fee for setting up the meeting?"

"Gotta make a living somehow," Jason said. "Frankly, even an adrenaline junkie like me gets tired of running in front of bullets to make a paycheck. Now…" he picked the tablet up and thrust it into Miguel's hands, "Get that snake off that shark."

"Up yours," Miguel replied.

"Do it, or I'll make sure you and your girlfriend are reduced to chum."

"Yeah?" Miguel snickered. "You can stomp the hell out of me if you like. But Hutson's all the way out there. That sub has enough power to get her to the coast."

"I'm not sweating it," Jason said. He pulled a device from his vest. At first, it just looked like a tiny green radio that fit perfectly into his hand. Jason extended a small antenna, and removed a cap revealing a small red button. Suddenly, Miguel knew what it was. He didn't need to be a military expert to know Jason was holding a detonator.

"Son of a bitch…" the words shot out. "You son of a bitch!"

A green light blinked under the Triton's ballast, its operator unaware of the plastic block strapped to her hull.

Gina hesitated, concerned for Miguel's safety. She tried radioing back, but got no response.

The creatures were almost out of view right now. The shark had seconds left before it was drowned.

Hurry up, she thought. If the snake killed the shark, then there'd be no more dilemma. The decision would be made, and all that remained would be to face the consequences.

Which, as she was quickly learning, were more dire than she realized.

"You won't," Miguel said. He immediately felt foolish. Of course, the mercenary would do it, and not lose a moment's sleep over it.

"Nace, it isn't worth it," Seabolt told him, ditching the macho display in favor of trying to sound reasonable. As it turned out, it only made him seem weak and pathetic.

"Shut up, Seabolt. And make sure nobody else comes on deck. Don't think I don't know you have rifles aboard. If I see any movement—ANY movement, I promise the next thing you'll hear are some very loud fireworks before I put a bullet in his brain...and yours." He spoke loudly enough to be heard by the crew, as well as the bridge crew watching from above.

Miguel flinched as Jason's thumb moved over the detonator.

"Don't..."

"You do your job, and maybe I won't."

"I can't!"

"Alright. Say goodbye to your precious marine biologist and her bath toy!" Jason pressed the button halfway down.

"Stop!" Miguel said. Jason eased the pressure after seeing the scientist unlock his tablet. There was a slight hesitation before connecting to the snake's collar, and another when he engaged the electroshock mechanism on its collar. He felt caught between the lives of everyone at Hamilton Bay, and Gina's.

"Do it!" Jason snapped. "Do it, and proceed as planned. We'll capture the beast and bring it back into captivity. At least it won't kill anyone else today."

The appeal to Miguel's good nature was enough to break the gridlock in his mind. His will to hold back finally broke with the press of a finger to the electroshock icon.

Air bubbles blasted from the Colossal Snake's throat as the electrified current surged through its body. Muscles tensed to the point of ripping. Its heart raced, its body tensing beyond its control. As quickly as it began, the current disappeared, leaving the snake momentarily stunned and weakened. Its body loosened.

Feeling the release around its body, the megalodon summoned the little energy it had left and propelled itself out of its enemy's grasp. Water seeped through its gills, enriching its blood with oxygen. The megalodon continued on, its body stiff from the strangulation. It took effort to swing its tail to gain the necessary propulsion needed. As the blood circulated, its heart rate returned to a healthy rhythm.

Its dorsal fin pierced the air above the ocean and sliced a path westward, several hundred feet off the *Armstrong's* starboard quarter. It moved slow, allowing its senses to return.

Its lateral line picked up numerous vibrations from approaching masses. They were coming in from multiple directions at high speeds. The soundwaves were similar to the floating bodies that carried fresh meat inside. And they were coming to it!

Water disruptions below brought its attention back to the giant creature that had nearly killed it twice.

The snake stayed behind, recovering briefly from the strange surge that completely stripped all control of its body, and allowed the shark to free itself. It had not felt such a sensation in over a year. It waited, unsure if the invisible enemy would make another 'appearance' or if the danger was clear. While it waited, it watched the shark swimming above.

Its memory of the shock faded and now all it could think about was its desire to kill the fish. Even with its enhanced metabolism, swallowing the shark would sustain its body for weeks. For a creature as large as the Colossal Snake, the meg was a rare treat that should not get away. It flicked its tongue, then slithered through the water.

Gina sucked in a breath. What was going on? Why did Eleven release the shark? What was happening on the ship? Was Miguel even alive? There were so many questions and no answers.

He had told her to leave, but it didn't feel right to leave him behind. She had to see the mission through. She had to make sure the shark was dead.

God, I miss the simple days when I was using submersibles to find fossilized teeth on the ocean floor. There were no genetic monsters, crazed businessmen, or psycho mercenaries in those days.

"Miguel?" She waited for an answer. A sense of dread tightened her throat. "Miguel, what's happening?" Still no answer. "Miguel, are you alive?"

"He's alive." It was Jason Nace's voice. *"If you want him to stay that way, you'll tranq the shark like you're supposed to."*

"I want to hear from him," she demanded. A few moments of radio silence followed.

"Gina."

"Miguel!"

"We...we don't have a choice. Capture the megalodon, or he'll kill you."

"Kill *me*?" she exclaimed. "He can't get me. It's you I'm worried about."

"No, you don't understand," Miguel said. *"He's planted an explosive on your sub. Don't run! He'll blow you up, and he's not bluffing."*

Gina felt like she'd been punched in the gut. She tried to reply, but only stammering gibberish came out. She took in a deep breath, trying hard to keep control of herself. A brief wave of nausea passed, while a few beads of sweat streamed down her face.

She watched the debris sinking all around her before looking back up to the shark gliding off in the distance.

"Do it, Doc!" It was Jason Nace again. His voice lacked the sense of humor it contained this morning. He was always a murderous fiend. Probably always had been for all she knew.

She put the sub in forward gear and went after the creatures, making sure to keep fifty meters of distance until the snake had the shark locked in another grip. They traveled along the surface at matching speeds, going due west.

The stress of the situation, knowing that Miguel had a gun on him, and that she was literally carrying a bomb on her sub, made it very difficult for Gina to focus. What guarantee did she have that Jason wouldn't kill them after he got the monsters back to Gundrum? Unfortunately, she was not a tactically minded person. She'd never been in a situation like this, and couldn't think of a fast solution to get out of it, other than to catch the shark.

The megalodon continued west, then suddenly took a sharp right. At first, she thought it was turning around to face the snake again. But it didn't. It kept going, picking up speed. Was it fleeing?

Other shapes appeared on the surface. Boats! Two of them. No, three!

"Oh no. Oh God, no!" she said. The shark had found more civilian vessels and was following its natural instinct to destroy.

On the *Armstrong*, Jason, Seabolt, and Miguel looked to the north, seeing three fishing vessels rapidly approaching. Their horns blared loudly, as though trying to get each other's attention.

"Who the hell are these people?" Jason said.

"Captain!" Miguel shouted. "Get on the radio! We gotta warn these people to stay back. They don't know what they're running into!"

"Maybe they do, kid," Jason said. He pointed at the largest boat. Standing on the forward deck was a male, holding binoculars to his eyes with one hand, and clinging to a rifle barrel with the other. “I think word of our fish has gotten out.”

CHAPTER 20

"There it is!" Richard Redway said. He stood on the *Omega Thunder's* forward deck, pointing at the fin. He held an AR-15 in his hand, fully loaded with a ten-round magazine. Three other mags were tucked in his waist, each containing .223 caliber rounds.

Cathy saw the enormous bulk from the wheelhouse. She could not manage a response. She stood there, flabbergasted. The bastard was telling the truth after all! It was a giant shark, like a Great White, but three times as big. Its dorsal fin was seven feet high at least. Forty feet behind it, the caudal fin thrashed the ocean's surface, putting the shark right toward them.

"Holy Jesus!" Jake radioed. His boat, the *St. Anthony*, trailed along her port quarter. Another hundred yards beyond it was Bruno's vessel, the *Dave Cordle.* Both ships were only two-thirds the size of the *Omega Thunder*, and despite this, they still couldn't match her speed.

There was no sign of Sam and Santor. All they could see was open ocean, and a damaged cargo ship closing in a quarter mile to the south.

"*Omega Thunder* to *Threshold.* Come in."

"I thought they said they killed it," Bruno said.

Oh God. They did say that, Cathy thought. She searched the ocean again. There was no fishing boat in sight.

"Maybe that cargo ship picked them up," Jake suggested.

"Let's stop worrying about it and kill that damn shark!" Redway shouted. He shouldered his rifle and popped off several rounds at the incoming beast. Cathy jolted, her instinct nearly forcing her to duck.

The shark was now coming straight at her bow. Whether spurred by the gunfire, or simply on a murderous rampage after sinking the *Threshold,* it was coming in at a speed that would implode the hull and destroy her engines.

She cut the wheel to starboard and put full power into the throttle. Redway continued popping off rounds until the magazine ran dry. The boat cleared the shark's path. It passed within a few feet of the port quarter, its left pectoral grazing the hull.

Sensing other boats, it took a right and swung its tail.

The Colossal Snake stopped momentarily, sensing the presence of the fishing vessels. It assessed whether these 'creatures' posed any sort of threat, while also keeping track of the fish's movements. Seeing the shark make its turn, the snake swam right, making a wide circle to intercept. While doing so, it shot for the surface, intending to meet the fish head-on.

"Oh, shit." Jake watched the *Omega Thunder* barely clear the shark's path. A moment later, that dorsal fin turned toward his vessel. Another moment passed, and it was already halfway to his vessel. His heart leapt into his throat.

"Shit! Shit! Shit!" He pushed the engines to their limits, trying to get his ship out of its path. There wasn't any time. The megalodon struck the keel and punched through the *St. Anthony* like a cannonball through plywood. The transom and bow spiraled out in opposite directions, while everything in-between was reduced to soaring bits of debris. Somewhere in the middle was Jake, who was dead upon impact, his body mashed against the broken interior of the cockpit. The megalodon continued swimming in a straight path for the next ship.

Bruno shrieked twice, first after seeing Jake's boat explode as though set off by a demolition charge, then again after realizing the shark that did it was now making a straight line for his vessel. He cut the wheel hard to port and throttled, making a sharp U-turn.

He regretted following Redway out here, though now it was for a completely different reason than before. Before, there was no way such a shark could be real. Now, it WAS real, and it was coming for him.

"Come on, come on, come on!" he repeated to his boat. It completed the turn. His bow was now facing north, with nothing but open water in front of him. "Come on, come on, come on, come—what the shit!"

As though racing over a speed bump, the boat jolted violently, the force of the impact causing it to spin slightly to starboard. Bruno fought against the helm, trying to correct course, while looking over his shoulder to see what it was he had hit.

His eyes widened.

No. Impossible. It just…I HAVE to be seeing things!

It looked like an honest-to-God sea serpent, like those he read about in ancient mythology. It was real, with green skin lined with black rings, with a body length nearly twice as long as the shark!

Its huge head rose from the sea and turned toward him. Despite the lack of emotion in those black slits, Bruno still sensed a burning hatred that instantly crossed the boiling point.

"What the hell is going on?!" he yelled.

The snake had positioned itself for an intercept course when the boat suddenly turned around. The impact to the back of its collar jolted its upper body downward. And right then, its overwhelming drive to hunt down the shark had vanished. It was still hungry, but its brain was no longer solely fixated on the fish. The snake felt a new sense of free will that it didn't previously have.

It also felt anger toward the puny vessel that dared to strike it. Already, the coward was trying to flee. The snake hissed loudly, its tongue extending several feet past its snout, then slithered through the water at its prey.

Large swells rolled in from the left. The shark was moving in rapidly, also closing in on the boat. Another angry hiss escaped the snake. This would be *its* kill, not anything else's! Like a green-and-black lightning bolt, it shot toward the shark, this time not out of anger, but out of pure hatred.

The shark felt its presence and angled itself to the right, meeting the threat head-on.

Razor-tipped jaws extended, and the ocean rippled from the collision of two giant beasts. Razor teeth clenched down on the snake's body twenty feet behind its head. The snake hissed, its anger drowned out in a mass of air bubbles. The shark spun itself into a corkscrew motion, dragging the snake across the surface. Twisting violently from the combined might of the attack and the current, the snake could not manage to get its body around the meg. It snapped its jaws at the gill slits, but missed, unable to focus its aim due to the chaotic motion.

It had one other attack; a broad and devastating technique used by its ancestors when battling with enormous sharp-toothed reptiles. It curled its tail back then whipped it at the shark's face. The tip struck near the left eye, splitting the skin and sending an electrified shock down the meg's body. Automatic reflex caused the jaws to open.

The snake glided free, allowing the megalodon to swim off. The fish continued on, moving south toward the cargo ship. The snake had not forgotten about the vessel that struck it. The snake continued on, picking up speed with each curvy motion of its body until it was within range. Then like cocking the hammer to a revolver, it cocked its head back, then shot its jaws at the keel.

Bruno fell forward and struck his forehead against the helm. The stern lifted briefly and splashed down. He felt the sensation of being pulled backward. He shouted incomprehensibly while grabbing at the helm to pull his hefty mass up. Back on his feet he looked ahead. He froze. There was no ocean on the other side of that glass; just green, leathery skin. The boat jittered. A moment later, the windshield cracked. The overhead began folding onto him. The windows cracked, then exploded inward. Suddenly, the whole ship caved in toward him, constricted by the enormous serpent.

Bruno screamed and turned to the door, only to find it crushed with the rest of the ship, watching the ceiling and walls surge toward him. He felt intense pressure, then the cracking of bones. His own ship crunched against his bloated body, crushing it like a grape, grinding the insides until there was no recognizable shape remaining.

The snake uncoiled and let the ship sink to its watery grave. It smelled blood that seeped between the cracks of the wreckage. Intrigued by the scent, the snake swam down to inspect it. As its enemy had learned that morning, the snake discovered that the boats carried live creatures. For the snake, they were merely bite-sized. But bite-sized was better than nothing, and its body needed any sustenance it could get. It no longer desired to eat the shark, for it had attempted multiple times, only to suffer injury each time. Ultimately, it was not worth the effort. The snake would be better off hunting these floating, artificial masses.

It felt the displacement from the other vessel, followed by the vibrations of impact. The snake circled and saw another vessel. It was larger than the one it had just destroyed. Larger meant more meat.

The megalodon zipped into view. It was engaged with the vessel, biting at the hull beneath the bow. The Colossal Snake felt a competitive jealousy. The shark also had learned that these vessels carried humans and was attempting to consume them for itself!

Ten-foot swells rolled across the Atlantic, pushed along from a serpentine mass that raced for the fresh meat aboard the *Omega Thunder*.

"Did you see that?" Cathy yelled out. Her eyes went from the approaching dorsal fin, to the sea serpent's curving body. It had coiled around Bruno's vessel and crumpled it into a piece of scrap. "What's going on? What have I gotten myself into?" The thought of giant sharks seemed implausible enough. But giant snakes?!

The sound of gunfire drew her attention back to the forward deck. Redway stood at the rail, firing rounds over the bow. Fifty feet beyond the tip of the boat was a rapidly approaching fin. She saw the two eyes under the clear water, black and soulless, before they disappeared behind white lids.

Richard Redway slammed a fresh magazine into his rifle and pointed the weapon at the shape as it approached the starboard bow. He watched the tiny underwater trails left by the bullets, which were immediately erased by the current pushed by the approaching shark.

He grabbed the bow rail and held tight. Its snout struck the hull, bouncing the ship upward. An impact crater formed beneath, allowing raging rapids to invade the ship.

"Shit!" Cathy cried out. "Damn it! Damn it all!"

Damn the shark, damn her foolish ego, damn Redway's vendetta—damn her own stupidity for indulging in his crusade, and not TURNING BACK when she had the chance. *Why?! Why did I circle back? The shark went after Jake and Bruno, leaving me with a clear getaway.* It wasn't Redway's demand that made her turn back, but the good nature of wanting to rescue her fellow fishermen. It seemed even her good decisions in this scenario had bad consequences. In this case, it was a battered ship engine, a hull breach, and flooding.

Within seconds, the bow was already dipping. Redway stood on the deck, unfazed in his determination for revenge. He looked back and forth for the fish, keeping his eyes fixed along the iron sights. The ocean spilled over the deck onto his ankles.

"Come on!" Cathy yelled, pulling the life vest on. Redway continued looking for the shark. Either he didn't hear her, or was ignoring her. Regardless, she had done enough for him. She grabbed the inflatable raft. It seemed pointless, considering the shark just impaled the hull of a seventy-foot boat, but then again, she'd rather take her chances with this than paddling her feet. Maybe that cargo ship could pick her up. With no time to ponder, she stepped to the main deck and inflated the vessel. It was like walking up a ramp. Fishing supplies rolled past her and crashed against the structure.

A tug on the ripcord inflated the raft. She laid it on the deck and took a seat inside. As she did, she looked back to the foredeck, hoping to see Redway racing from the structure. Water had seeped up around it, inching its way toward the middeck.

The stern was almost out of the water when something shook the boat. At first, Cathy thought the shark had struck again. Then she felt the teetering motion of the stern being pulled back down, and the reverberation of the resulting splash. Next came the crunching of the ship's hull and deck. A shadow swept over her. Cathy looked back, then up.

The Colossal Snake wrapped its body around the rear of the ship, its head towering thirty feet above its victim. It flicked its tongue, reared its neck into an S-shape, then struck. Cathy's scream lasted no longer than her last heartbeat. The jaws clamped over her body, crushing her skull and shoulders. The snake reared its head back and swallowed. Meanwhile, its body continued squeezing the stern, folding the hull together.

The shift in the vessel caused Redway to stagger backward, breaking his focus. He backed into the structure, then heard Cathy's brief scream, followed by heavy groans in the hull. He hurried around the side-deck, stopping halfway as he saw the snake's head high in the air, and the blood dripping from the edge of its jaw. It looked down at him, flicked its tongue, then reared back into striking position.

Redway ran back to the foredeck. The snake snapped, its jaws punching through the deck behind him. Pieces of debris exploded out into the water. The snake raised its head and spat out the inedible parts, then slithered over the structure for another go.

The cabin creaked under its weight. It savored the taste of its previous victim as it bore down on its next one.

Redway backed to the railing, mouth wide open. His mind raced, asking a dozen questions at once, while trying to seek an escape from his current predicament. With the water rising around his ankles for the second time, it was clear there was no way out.

"Fuck you, you oversized worm!"

He pointed his rifle and fired all ten rounds at the snake. It jolted, shocked by the little stings, though they failed to pierce its flesh. It coiled to strike, then turned its head suddenly over the port bow. Redway looked, then yelled as the megalodon closed in at frightening speed.

The side of the ship exploded into chunks. Redway was thrown several feet into the water, disappearing under a heavy splash.

The megalodon continued through the wreckage, pursuing its prey. The snake hissed and dove into the water, zigzagging its body to beat its enemy to the prize. But the shark was a full body-length ahead of it. The snake had a split second to act.

It snapped its jaws at the megalodon's caudal fin, causing it to swiftly turn away. The meg angled its body to the right and snapped its jaws at the snake, which swiftly detached and evaded, winding around the shark's body on a path toward its prey. With the meg behind it, the snake took advantage of the clear path and went for the fisherman.

Redway completed a few strokes before he felt the large swell lifting him up. Suddenly, he was high above the water, inside the mouth of a giant snake! Curved teeth were on both sides like prison bars, and a rotten stench filled his nose. The 'floor' and 'roof' started closing in to crush him.

The ocean exploded, and Redway saw another pair of jaws. Suddenly, he was airborne again.

An ear-piercing hiss filled the air as the megalodon launched itself into the snake, tackling it backward like a pro-wrestler. As it did, its snout struck the snake's jawline, launching the prey out of its grasp. The megalodon bit and swam low, driving the snake into the depths before letting go and circling back. The snake looped its body into a coiling position, gathering its bearings, then saw that the shark was going back up for the human. It shot after it, its springing motion granting a brief burst of speed. Once again, it latched its jaws on the caudal fin. The meg didn't stop. It swung its tail violently, whipping the snake's whole body as though it were an extension of itself. Despite the snake's weight slowing it down, it still ascended gradually.

It could see Redway paddling along the surface, just a few meters beyond the reach of its jaws.

Realizing its plan wasn't working, the snake reached high with its tail, wrapping it like a tentacle around the megalodon's underbelly. Recognizing the early stage of constriction, the megalodon hooked its head forward and dove, slipping out of the wrap. As it dove, the snake unclenched its jaws, then redirected its eyes to the prize above.

It closed the distance and attempted another bite, only for the megalodon to circle once again and intercept.

Redway kicked and paddled, his body beaten and tired, until finally he had found a piece of debris that could sustain his weight. The period of rest lasted a mere moment, before the clarity of the ocean below was overtaken by two enormous shapes.

All he felt was the initial rise of water and brief pressure from the head and feet before his mind dispersed into oblivion. The creatures struck at once, pancaking the human between their enormous masses.

With their nostrils filled with the scent of blood, the two beasts snapped at each other. They wrestled along the surface, sending huge streams of water sailing high. Fed up with this opponent, the snake attempted another constriction. Its body coiled around the meg and tightened, but not before those jaws closed down around a section two-thirds down its length, preventing a full constriction. Locked together, the beasts thrashed.

CHAPTER 21

The *Armstrong's* bow sliced through the ocean as the bridge crew worked frantically to get it as close to the creatures as possible. It took everything for the crewmates to keep their wits while witnessing the horrible events unfolding. The creatures were once again locked in combat, fighting maniacally along the surface. From a hundred yards out, all that could be seen from the ship was a mass of fins and teeth, wrapped in a leathery helix, barrel rolling repeatedly.

"I'm not going to tell you again, Doc," Jason said. He slapped Miguel on the back of the head for the third time, agitating him. "Get that thing working!" The herpetologist frantically reset his tablet. He felt a mix of emotions. There was fear, frustration, and guilt…guilt from the lives that were taken from by the snake. Up until now, it had never harmed a single human being. And within minutes, it was responsible for the deaths of three.

He had activated the chem-beacon in the cargo hold, but there was no response from the animal. An alert flashed over the screen. *No Signal.* Miguel completed another reset and tried again. He pinpointed the receiver on the snake's collar, trying to reset.

"It won't respond!" he said.

"The hell do you mean 'it won't respond'?" Jason said.

"When the fishing boat struck it, it must have dislodged the receiver," he said.

"So…what? What does that mean?" Jason said. Miguel, shaking with tension, looked at him.

"It means we've lost control of the snake."

Jason's eyes shot to the large fishing boat as the stern exploded from the constriction. He looked back to Miguel and pushed the tablet into his chest.

"Can't you fix it?!"

"Not without getting up next to it," Miguel said. The mercenary groaned and watched the chaos taking place. Now BOTH monsters were on the loose. His mind raced for a solution.

He watched the creatures struggling against each other.

"We might not have control of it, but the snake is still doing what we need it to do," he said. He clipped the detonator to his belt and grabbed for his radio, keeping his pistol wavering between Miguel and Seabolt to prevent them from feeling courageous. "Dr. Hutson?"

"I'm here."

"Change of plans. Thanks to the boaters, we've lost control of the snake. But as you can probably see, we still have an opportunity. You will tranq *both* creatures."

"Are you insane?"

"Yes," Miguel muttered.

"Nace, what you're recommending is suicide," Seabolt said. A twitch in the pistol made him shut up and step back.

"The snake is getting a firm hold on the shark, which'll present you an opportunity to get close and tranq it. Once you've planted the harpoon, get close to the snake's jaw, and tranq it. Then you'll attach a cable to each of them, starting with the shark."

Miguel glared at the gun muzzle. It was the only thing preventing him from rushing the merc and getting the detonator. There was no way this plan would work.

Jason waited for a reply. "Doctor? You listening?"

"That snake will go after me the minute I get near it," Gina said.

"You can risk getting eaten, or be guaranteed to be turned into chum if you don't," he said. "That's no cherry bomb you're carrying. You've got five seconds to comply."

Gina tucked her head down. Her eyes welled up. She wanted to scream. From the very moment she saw that mercenary, she knew he was bad news.

"Five...Four..."

A dozen murderous thoughts raced through Gina's mind.

"Three... Two..."

She applied full power to the engine and throttled toward the beasts. Toward certain death.

"Good," Jason said to her, watching the camera view on his phone, which was on the deck by his boot. He clipped the radio back to his belt and turned his gaze to the Captain. "Keep getting us closer. Have your men ready at the crane."

"You're going to get us ALL killed," Seabolt said.

Jason pointed the gun at his head. "I can start with you." The Captain grimaced, then directed to his crew with hand signals. They dispersed along the deck, prepping the crane and hatch. Each one had the same nervous expression.

The tension they felt, however, was nothing compared to what Gina was feeling below the water.

Gina controlled her breathing, teaching herself to absorb each jolting impact of the sub. She was within a hundred feet of the two beasts. Each frantic movement generated an underwater shockwave that shook the Triton.

Clouds of blood seeped from the snake's many bite wounds. It successfully wrapped itself around the megalodon's upper body, though it could not get a grip on the caudal fin, which allowed the shark to maneuver itself. It performed another corkscrew dive, throwing the snake's head and tail round and around like windmill sails.

Gina descended to keep up, but as soon as she closed the distance, the beasts were already ascending.

"Nace! There's no way I can keep up with them," she said.

"Quit with the excuses and keep trying."

She hammered the dashboard.

I oughta dock beside the ship and see how eager he'll be to blow me up then! She wouldn't though. Doing so would put the crew in danger, and there was no certainty that Jason Nace *wouldn't* detonate the device.

She tried again.

The creatures had burst through the surface again and were continuing their brawl up there.

The snake snapped its jaws, its fangs slashing deep behind the meg's dorsal fin. Blood trailed behind it, but the meg maintained its grip. Serrated teeth sank deeper, chipping the vertebrae. The snake lurched in pain, then bit again. Unable to free itself, it proceeded to wrap its upper body around the megalodon's head, blocking the gill slits and preventing water from seeping through. It was the equivalent of choking an air-breathing mammal.

Immediately, the fish felt the strain. Its throat closed in on itself. Water seeped in, only to overflow and be forced out through the corners of its mouth. Its muscles strained, and its brain felt the haziness from lack of airflow. With its tail still free, it swam, carrying the snake along with it. It zipped in tight circles, going left, right, up, and down, in an attempt to throw the snake off of it. Instead, all it achieved was a tighter constriction.

The snake slithered its upper body around that of the fish, completing another loop. In doing so, it wrapped itself over the megalodon's eyes, blinding it. Swimming in perspective darkness, the fish banked back and forth frantically. It zoomed up and leapt from the water, thrashing in midair, then landing on its back. The resulting tidal wave, towering over forty feet, rolled toward the *Armstrong* like a moving mountain.

"Oh shit," Miguel said. The wave struck the starboard side, rocking the ship heavily to port. Water sprayed the deck, knocking several crew members on their knees.

Jason staggered off balance, his gun arm raising high over his head. Miguel fell to his hands and knees, then noticed the mercenary standing several feet directly ahead. Like a track racer, he pressed a foot to the deck, then launched himself at the merc. With only a yard between them, Miguel made a bounding leap, throwing his body weight on the unbalanced merc.

Jason fell on his back, his gun spiraling from his hand. He felt Miguel's hands along his duty belt as the scientist yanked the detonator free. Jason grabbed for it but was too late, as Miguel chucked it blindly toward the starboard side.

Miguel gagged as strong fingers coiled around his neck, and suddenly he was flipped over onto his back. The world went hazy as a fist crashed down into his face, momentarily stunning him. As Jason reared back for another blow, his brain registered the sound of running feet behind him. He looked back and saw Seabolt going for his dropped firearm. The merc sprang to his feet and sprinted after the Captain, tackling him just as he stopped to pick up the gun.

The two men fell to the deck, the pistol skidding a few meters to the bow. Jason climbed over Seabolt's back and wrapped an arm under his jaw, then squeezed tight. Before he could complete the chokehold, he felt the crunching blow of an elbow to his ribs. Seabolt struck back a second time, then ducked low, slipping out of the headlock. Now on his feet, he engaged the merc head-on, but was met with a kick to the chest.

Seabolt reeled backward, silently cursing himself the whole way down. *Damn it! You should've seen that coming.* He rolled backward over his shoulder, quickly getting back to his feet. Already, Jason had closed the distance. A left hook struck Seabolt's jaw, followed by a right to the stomach. Seabolt stumbled backward, then saw another left hook coming for his face. He swept his right hand inward, connecting his hand to Jason's forearm, deflecting the punch inward.

Finally, his close-quarters training returned to him.

He launched a straight punch into Jason's jaw, knocking him back. The mercenary recovered and lunged for a grab. Two strong hands wrapped around Seabolt's collar. He tried to back away but couldn't escape the grasp. He grabbed Jason's right wrist with both hands, squeezed and bent down, while rotating his own both to the right. Jason felt both hands loose their grip, all while his right hand was twisted over and locked out. A millisecond later, his whole arm was locked out and twisted, doubling him over. A kick struck his stomach, followed by another to his chin.

There was another splash, this time along the portside. A solid blow struck the ship, rocking the ship to starboard. A sharp hiss traveled through the air. The megalodon, in its blind rage, had slammed into the ship, sandwiching the snake in the process. It swam along the hull, scraping the snake's body against it to pry it off.

The Colossal Snake raised its head high over the deck, looking like a mythic dragon.

"Get below!" Seabolt instructed his crew, while maintaining his grip on the merc. His men went for the structure. As they did, the megalodon circled and rammed the snake into the boat again.

The quake weakened Seabolt's balance, and thus his grip.

Spitting blood, Jason leaned up and spun to the right to free himself. He grabbed for Seabolt with his other hand, but the sailor, still holding on to his wrist, retightened and whirled it counterclockwise, bending it back beyond the range of motion. Forced to go with the motion or feel his arm break, Jason reeled over his right shoulder and hit the deck.

Seabolt looked past the mercenary and saw the detonator. Miguel had tried to toss it over the edge, but fell short. He thought of going for it before Jason could get his hands on it again. In that split-second of distraction, the mercenary thrust a kick into his shin, dropping Seabolt to his knee. Suddenly, the Captain felt his grasp on Jason's wrist disappear, and then the pressure of a firm grasp on his own forearm. Jason yanked Seabolt to the deck and threw an elbow into his nose, stunning him briefly before wrestling him to his back.

Jason, gripping Seabolt's forearm tightly, positioned his legs over his torso, then threw his body backward into an armbar position. Seabolt yelled as he felt his arm overextend, then yelled again when he felt the snap at the elbow.

Jason grinned ear to ear, dropping the limp arm while he stood up. He stomped a boot into Seabolt's stomach, then reached back for a knife to finish the job.

"Hey!"

Jason looked straight ahead and saw Miguel standing twelve feet away. In his hand was his pistol, pointed straight at him. Jason straightened himself, his smile disappearing.

"Back up," Miguel said.

"You even know how to shoot one of those things?"

A bullet whizzed past Jason's head. Whether Miguel intended to miss, Jason had no idea, but it was enough to make him take a step back. Clutching his broken arm, Seabolt stood up and backed out of the way.

"Fucking Jiu-Jitsu shit," he muttered.

"Get the detonator," Miguel muttered.

"You do that, then you'd better be willing to kill me," Jason warned. Seabolt groaned, both from pain and frustration. He took the pistol from Miguel.

"I know I am. Make a move. Please." The mercenary grimaced. Seabolt glanced at Miguel. "*You* get the detonator. Toss it over. I'll keep an eye on this fool."

The megalodon soared deep, still unable to loosen the snake's grip on its body. Its blood felt as though it was on fire. It spiraled again, then hooked up. Paddling its tail, it shot for the surface, unknowingly on a direct path toward the *Armstrong*.

The impact juddered the meg, the snake, and the vessel. The snake felt its head get pancaked between the hull and the fish. Stunned, its body uncoiled from around the meg. Now free, the megalodon embraced a new inflow of water through its gills. Fed up with the endless fighting, it proceeded west, following the distant vibrations that attracted it in the first place.

As though lifted by an invisible force, the *Armstrong's* bow was thrown several feet high, throwing the three men off balance. Seabolt stumbled forward, unwittingly for the mercenary. Jason leaned forward, balancing himself, and met the Captain head-on. Simultaneously, he grabbed Seabolt's wrist with one hand, then struck the injured arm with the other. The surge of pain, as well as sudden loss of balance, weakened the Captain's grip. Jason wrenched the pistol from him, then struck him with an elbow to the face, knocking him down.

He saw Miguel standing over the detonator.

"Ah-ah-ah," Jason said. Miguel turned, saw the merc pointing the pistol, then heard the crack. A seemingly invisible force punched through his shoulder, knocking him down.

Miguel crawled on his back, blood seeping from his right shoulder. Jason approached, gun pointed.

"Nice try," he said. He leaned down and picked up the detonator. "But you're not getting out of this that easily. On your feet!" Miguel stood up. Jason circled around to the middeck, where the control tablet had ended up. Despite being splashed with water, it remained functional and unlocked. "I suppose I no longer need you to handle this—"

The Colossal Snake sank several meters, its head throbbing from the impact. By the time its senses returned, it saw that the shark had disappeared. It focused its eyes on the huge ship floating above it. Ships contained prey. Spurred by hunger, the snake sped for the surface.

An explosion of water drew all eyes to the starboard railing. The snake raised its head high and gazed down at the humans on the ship. The snake looked down at the injured human, then leaned in. Miguel stood in place, unmoving, and looked up into the huge eyes. It flicked its tongue and took in the familiar scent of its caretaker.

Jason backed up. He stopped, realizing his movements drew the creature's gaze. Shooting it would do no good. Running would only result in the beast scooping him up in its jaws. There was only one viable option… provide easier prey.

He aimed the pistol at Miguel's leg and fired. The bullet grazed his thigh, missing the bone, but still causing him to fall to the deck. The snake raised its head and hissed loudly, infuriated, then bared its enormous teeth. Right then, Jason realized his mistake.

"Oh, shi—"

Eleven snapped, scooping Jason up in its jaws. The detonator and pistol were flung from his grip and skidded across the deck. His bones snapped like toothpicks. Blood rained down on the deck. The creature lifted its head and reared back, swallowing the mercenary whole.

"Holy savior," Seabolt whispered. The snake turned and eyed him, its flicking tongue detecting the scent of its next meal.

"No! No!" Miguel shouted. He sprinted to Seabolt and stood between him and the snake, holding his hands out as though the beast would understand what that meant. It moved its head side-to-side, hoping to get around its caretaker. But, alas, he wouldn't move. The snake would not be able to scoop up its prey without eating Miguel. It hissed rebelliously, then gave up. It slithered off the deck and splashed down into the water.

Taking in all the senses around it, it detected the faint trail of blood left by the megalodon. With no other prey in its vicinity, it raced west to pursue.

"God…" Seabolt said, amazed. For a moment, he had forgotten about the excruciating pain in his arm. That pain returned, along with the realization of where Eleven was headed. "Dr. Lucero. Our problems just got worse. WAY worse."

Miguel searched the deck until he found a radio.

"Gina?"

"Miguel! What's going on?"

"Hurry back to the ship."

"What about Jason?"

"He's dead. Ask later. Right now, we've got other problems."

"Oh God...Eleven... I saw him. He's going west. It's going for the coast!"

Miguel took a breath. "It's swimming right to a buffet. We've…we've got to stop him."

CHAPTER 22

"I'm not going to tell you again," Deputy Brown yelled to the two college-age so-called men, whose sailboats were neck and neck with each other.

"It's the wind man," one of them complained. "It keeps pulling us together."

"Shut up! You keep hogging my breeze," the other said.

"Oh, for chrissake! The wind isn't limited to one spot. PADDLE AWAY, you dumbasses!" Brown said. "You idiots have the whole ocean, yet you keep pulling this shit."

"Language, Allen," Deputy Lampkin said. Brown glanced at his partner. Lampkin was leaning on the helm, his eyes focused on their cooler more than the verbal altercation at hand. Brown had had enough. This was the second time he had to deal with these two punks, and they were just part of a long line of idiot tourists who thought they owned the entire ocean. At this point, he didn't care what verbs and nouns came out of his mouth when dealing with them.

"Get away from each other. Hurry up. Come on." The two sailors paddled their small boats in opposite directions. "Good. If I have to deal with your nonsense again, I'm towing you in. You think you're crammed out here? Wait till you're grounded back there!" He pointed way off to the beach.

From three quarters of a mile out, Hamilton Beach looked like one mass of bodies, constantly shifting in shape. The young men stared at it, and in their minds compared it to the several boats drifting about around them. Suddenly, the many dozens of yards between each sailboat and vessel didn't seem so bad.

"Sorry," one said.

"Me too," the other said. Neither sounded sincere, but it was enough for Brown.

He took a seat on the deck and leaned back as Deputy Lampkin throttled away. They passed various other boats and returned a few waves at some friendly onlookers.

"At least not all of them are idiots," Brown said.

"Careful man," Lampkin said. "All it takes is for one complaint, and the Lieutenant will review every second of body cam footage."

"Guy's never worked anywhere except a desk in his life," Brown muttered. He tilted his head down to stare upside down into his body cam. "In case you're wondering, Hayes—yes, I am talking about you." He sat straight, taking amusement from the sight of Lampkin cringing. The Deputy said nothing and continued coasting between the boaters. He watched a parasailer zipping about in the far distance, tugged behind a thirty-foot boot.

"I ought to do that someday," he said.

"You say that every time you see one of those parasailers," Brown replied. "Why don't you just go on one of your days off and do it?"

"Never seem to find the opportunity," Lampkin said.

"Bullshit. You live on the ocean," Brown said.

"I mean with all the mandated overtime," Lampkin replied. "When I am off, I'm so tired I just want to stay home." Brown nodded. At least that explanation made sense. While most people enjoyed the summer, the Hamilton Police dreaded it. They never had enough staff to patrol the popular tourist areas. To add to the stress, they needed to maintain standard patrols in the main part of town. Of course, the town budget allowed for them to buy several more patrol boats. Oh, but more personnel? Just two or three. 'Put the reserves to use' was the Chief's explanation. Had to keep that budget under control. How else was he going to receive his bonus at the end of the year?

The radio sounded off, distracting him from his mental tirade.

"This is Captain Howard Seabolt from the Freight Ship Armstrong for Gundrum Industries calling for anyone in the Hamilton Police Department. If anyone is picking up this transmission, please respond immediately."

Lampkin and Brown exchanged glances. Both waited in silence, hoping someone in dispatch would pick it up. Or better yet, the Coast Guard.

"Someone better answer me! This is an urgent matter!"

"Damn it," Brown muttered. He stepped up to the cockpit and grabbed the mic. "This is Deputy Brown with the Hamilton Police Department. Go ahead, *Armstrong*."

"Deputy, alert all units. You MUST evacuate the beaches and order all boats out of the water! There's a dangerous organism in the water and it's coming directly for your beach."

Brown stood, noticing his confused look mirrored by his partner.

"Uh, excuse me, Captain. What exactly is this *organism*?"

"A shark. A big shark."

Brown lowered the mic then rolled his eyes. "Oh, for crying out loud."

Lampkin laughed. "A shark? The ocean's full of them."

"Yeah, and apparently a ship, which has got to be a number of miles out, saw it. Meaning it's automatically a threat to the population according to this guy," Brown complained. He raised the mic back to his chin. "We'll get right on it, Captain." Lampkin laughed harder.

"Deputy, I'm dead serious!"

"He must've known you were being sarcastic," Lampkin said.

"That, or he heard your cackling in the background. He's probably excited now, thinking he has a buddy to take to the mental asylum." Brown closed his eyes, and tried to get 'in-character' to make himself sound a little more professional. "Captain…we can't evacuate the beaches just because of a shark sighting."

"You don't understand. It's already killed several people and it's headed your way. You HAVE to get everyone out of the water."

Now, Brown was slightly concerned, though still skeptical.

"*Several* people? We've received no reports from the Coast Guard or other police departments."

"It's coming in from the open sea. It's probably attracted to the vibrations coming from the tourist activities. It's almost there now."

"How big is this thing?"

"Big. Really big." Brown waited for him to elaborate. He could hear frustrated groans in the background. *"Ninety feet, big!"*

Now Lampkin was hollering with laughter. He had practically fallen on his knees. Tears were coming down his face. Brown too, was struggling to contain himself.

"Thanks for the alert, Captain. We'll take care of the situation," he said, not bothering to hide the amusement in his voice.

Now, Seabolt was frantic. *"Deputy, you fucking idiots! It's real! There's a ninety-foot megalodon headed for the coast and a fucking one-hundred-fifty-foot Snake following it!"*

Brown dropped the mic, his eyes wide with bewilderment.

"Oh…. MY—" he switched off the frequency.

Lampkin had finally fallen to his knees.

"This just keeps getting BETTER AND BETTER!" Their personal radios blared, transmitting laughter from fellow deputies.

"Better watch out for that big shark!" one said.

"Don't forget about a giant snake!" said another.

"There's only ONE giant snake in these waters, if you catch my drift."

"Your wife's boyfriend isn't out here today!"

"Alright, alright, alright," Brown chuckled. "Let's get back to work before we get in too much trouble." He sat back down and wiped his eyes with his hands. Lampkin stood himself back up, his face beet red and inflated by an endless smile. It took almost a full minute for him to overcome the laugh-attack.

"Ohhh! Oh, the pains in my stomach," he said.

"I think somebody out there has had a little too much booze on the job," Brown said.

"No shit," Lampkin said, wiping his eyes. "I'm almost tempted to notify the Coast Guard to go out and inspect his vessel. Anyone that crazy is probably smuggling something…and trying it out for himself."

"I wouldn't worry about it," Brown said. Lampkin snickered. That sounded like the Brown he knew—not wanting to go out of his way to handle anything. Then again, who could blame him in this case?

"God, that made my day," Lampkin said. "That's gonna be a tough act to beat."

"I don't know. I've had a few people claim they saw Elvis sailing out around here," Brown said.

"Nah, this beats even that," Lampkin said. He started laughing again. "You know, I can picture this Captain guy…assuming he even is a real freight Captain, thinking he sees a giant shark in the water. He probably saw a blue shark or something like that after chugging a bottle of Jack Daniels, and started pointing at it, while yelling to his crew 'SHARK! SHARK!'"

"SHARK!" someone screamed from afar. Both deputies laughed harder. Even the civilians had overheard the hilarious conversation. Then the screams continued. "SHARK!"

The sound of a crash drew their eyes toward the horizon. The yacht towing the parasailer had been thrown clear of the water. When it crashed down, it had split in two pieces, which quickly began to sink. The parasailer screamed as the sinking vessel began to drag her down.

"Jesus!" Lampkin muttered. He took to the controls and steered the vessel toward the action, activating the flashers and siren.

Brown got back on his radio. "Unit Eight to all boating units! Look alive. We've got a boat crash. A real bad one, likely collided with another one. Dispatch, alert EMS. All patrols, look for our lights. We're about a mile-point-two off Beach Three."

"Boat Two copies. En route."

"Boat Three copies."

Brown immediately saw flashers a half-mile to starboard. Dispatch acknowledged the radio call, followed by a string of mobile patrols inland.

"You saw that, right?!" Lampkin said. "If another boat hit it, it had to be the size of a freaking cruiser!"

"We'll figure it out soon enough. Just get us over there before that girl is pulled under."

Lampkin pushed the boat to twenty knots, weaving past stunned onlookers drifting in paddleboats, sailboats, and small fishing boats and yachts. The parasailer's thirty-foot cord was twenty feet under the water.

"Almost there," Lampkin said. Suddenly, the cord began to move to the left. It was as though the boat began to throttle under the water. It extended at a forty-five-degree angle and continued on, pulling the screaming parasailer along with it. "What in the name of—"

"Get after it," Brown said.

"What's doing that?" Lampkin thought back on the radio call. *No. It couldn't be.* Approaching civilians on various-sized boats, who had approached either due to curiosity or a humanitarian drive to assist, all stared in a mix of shock and confusion, as the screaming parasailer was dragged by an invisible force.

"Maybe the propellers are still going. I don't know, but one way or another, she's going down unless we get to her first."

The cord continued on, looking like a fishing line being dragged by a large trout. As it went, it zagged left and right, then finally began to turn in a tight circle. The parasailer shrieked as she was whipped to the side like a kite. The cord kept turning. All of a sudden, it was speeding right toward them.

"Allen?"

"Slow it down," Brown said. "Steer close. I'll grab the cord and pull her down." He leaned over the portside and held his hand, ready to grab the cord. That's when he realized it was picking up speed. A moment ago, it was a couple hundred feet away from them. In the blink of an eye, it was fifty and closing. The following moment, he saw the huge grey shape ascending, its cone-shaped snout pointed directly at their bow. Lampkin tried to veer but was too late.

Both deputies screamed as the megalodon shark they thought wasn't real smashed through their patrol boat. It raised its head out of the water, snapping Lampkin in midair. As it came back down, it made a sharp right turn, smacking Brown with a swing of its caudal fin. The impact popped the deputy like a grape, sending chunks of his body sailing for dozens of feet.

Screams from crowded boaters filled the air. Engines roared and propellers spiraled, sending boats zipping in various directions to get away. They sped anywhere. EVERYWHERE. Any direction that pointed away from the enormous dorsal fin behind them. Many of those paths crisscrossed, leading to high-speed crashes. Boats toppled over each other, sending their occupants tumbling into the waves.

With the parasailing cord stuck between two of its teeth, the megalodon zipped into the fray, snatching up terrified civilians. Teeth slashed torsos and limbs, leaving bloody bits trailing down into the depths.

It swung its tail, driving itself headfirst toward a ten-foot sailboat. The frantic soul let out a scream, which echoed deep into the meg's throat as he was swallowed whole.

Its appetite was insatiable. After traveling through several miles of open ocean, it had finally found prey in abundance and easy to catch. It found its next target, a jet ski, which had to zip sharply to the left to avoid colliding with a speedboat. In doing so, it had to turn left again, to avoid another jet ski, which inadvertently took it directly toward the meg's open mouth. The driver screamed before nine-inch teeth diced him into a dozen chunks. Spitting out the inedible jet ski, the megalodon continued its rampage.

The parasailer shrieked, each jolting motion yanking her side-to-side. In the corner of the shark's mouth, the cord rubbed against the serrated teeth it was stuck against, until finally it tore free. The parasailer hollered as she descended, the sail edges flapping in the wind. The wind caught hold of her and dragged her across a football field's length of fleeing boats.

A speedboat driver yelled as he saw the large sail falling twenty feet of his bow. He turned to port to avoid running over the helpless person harnessed to it, then yelled again right before that diversion sent him crashing into another speedboat. Pieces of wreckage hurled over other boaters and sailors, adding to the confusion and chaos.

The parasailer clawed at the sail, finally finding its edge, which allowed her to pull it off of her. She took a breath, and watched the madness that surrounded her. People were screaming on all sides. The smell of gas hit her nostrils. Bodies floated amidst the many wreckages.

Her eyes turned straight ahead. A large swell rolled toward her. In its center, a giant dorsal fin appeared. That swell peeled away, revealing an open mouth lined with triangular teeth. The parasailer didn't even have time to scream.

The megalodon swallowed its victim, then proceeded to bite down on a kayaker. Blue paddles struck the water hurryingly, their splashes disappearing into a huge swell that preceded the megalodon. The jaws snapped the kayak in half, its owner disappearing into the shark's gullet.

Flashing lights drew its eye.

"Move! Get out of the way!" yelled the deputy driving Boat Three. He sped through the carnage, only to steer away when he finally got a clear view of the meg's ninety-foot length. "JESUS!"

The deputy on deck pumped his twelve-gauge and fired it at the beast. The megalodon followed the boat, barely feeling the impact of pellets against its snout. It traveled in a straight line, gradually closing in on the stern. Empty shells littered the deck as the deputy unloaded into the beast. He dropped the empty shotgun and drew his Glock. He fired seven rounds in rapid succession, each one ricocheting off the beast's snout.

"It's not stopping!"

The driver was already on the radio. "There's dozens dead! We need the Coast Guard! The National Guard! Anyone!"

His transmission ended with the sound of a violent crash. The megalodon dipped slightly and breached, letting its huge bulk crash down atop the vessel, pulverizing it. It searched the wreckage, ultimately finding the crushed humans and devouring them. When it surfaced again, it saw more flashers from the south.

The minute the deputy piloting Boat Two saw the megalodon crush Boat Three, he circled back to retreat. His partner stood ready with the shotgun at his shoulder.

"Fuck me!" he squeaked. "It's coming right for us."

"I'm going for the docks!" the driver said.

"Fine with me! There's no way we'll be able to—what's that?" He pointed at a series of swells ripping in off the port quarter. A shape took form, and a giant snake's head burst from the water. The deputy reacted with a single shot before the jaws clamped down over him.

The snake swallowed him quickly, then snapped at the deck railing. Its upper body coiled around the vessel, easily crushing it to splinters, and mashing the deputy at the helm. It uncoiled and slurped up the deputy's flattened body. It needed more. MUCH more. Prey was all around it, completely at its mercy.

It searched the waters and quickly found a sailboat ridden by an overweight thirty-year-old. Fangs plunged into the soft flesh, ripping it up as the human was swallowed. It spotted a fishing vessel a couple of hundred yards to the south. The man piloting it tried desperately to haul hapless people out of the water. All five that had gathered on his main deck screamed in unison as the snake swam in wiggly motions toward them. Its body looped around the bow, then the cockpit. The whole front half of the boat imploded, the shockwave sending all hands into the water.

The snake proceeded to eat at its leisure, snapping its prey up one at a time.

CHAPTER 23

"No, no, no!" Miguel shouted. The binoculars dug circles around his eyes as he watched Eleven from afar, crushing boats and swallowing innocent people. Gina was on deck behind him, hands cupped around her mouth, unable to take her eyes off the horror.

The sub rested on the deck, still attached to the cable that hauled it up out of the water. She hadn't even winded down from the stress of being in the middle of the underwater fight and nearly getting blown up, and now here she was, witnessing the very event she tried so desperately to prevent.

Miguel grabbed his tablet, which was completing its remote diagnostic of the collar's damage.

"Come on! Come on!" he moaned. Finally, it signaled its completion. He read the analysis. "Just as I thought. The receiver's out of alignment."

"What does that mean?" Gina asked.

"It means that, unless it gets realigned, it won't receive transmissions from the chem-beacons. Thus, it won't pump signals into Eleven's brain and lure it to the desired location."

"Can it be realigned?"

"By the looks of it, yes," Miguel answered. "That's the problem I need to solve. If I can get it realigned, I can redirect the snake and get it back in the holding tank."

"Miguel…"

"It has to be done, Gina," he said. "I can get it back in the tank so we can get it away from here."

"Miguel?!" Gina's voice was hard. She pointed toward the beach, while keeping her eyes on him. "You see what it's doing? It's not following a chem-beacon. That's the way that thing functions! The megalodon too. They are not meant to share the world with us. We're ants to them. You can try and hide this thing anywhere in the world, and it won't matter. It will eventually kill again. No amount of technology…or passion, will prevent that!"

As though magically forced by her hand, Miguel's eyes were directed back to the devastation. Even without the binoculars, he could see the snake slashing its tail at an escaping speedboat. Screams and sirens echoed across the beach area. Police boats were speeding from the harbor, while ground units were racing to the beach to get people out of the water.

Already, the death toll had to have exceeded fifty…at the luckiest. And it would continue to climb for each passing second. Miguel clenched his eyes shut and faced the reality.

"It *has* to be destroyed," he said. The words were so painful, he was shocked he was admitting them even under these circumstances. And that brought forth another realization: that Dr. Miguel Lucero had gotten so caught up in his research, ambitions, and discoveries, that he had forgotten the basic value of human life. The greatest value on this planet, and it was being destroyed because of his research.

They hurried into the structure and joined Captain Seabolt in the bridge. His arm was resting in a sling. By the look on his face, it hurt like hell, and the stress wasn't helping.

"Anything on the radio?" Gina asked.

"The Coast Guard's been notified, but even at full speed, it'll take time for any of their ships to get here," Seabolt answered. "Chopper units are being dispatched, though they won't be any good. Can't fire on these creatures in a populated area."

"And bullets don't do any good on these things anyway," Gina said.

"So, it's up to us," Miguel said.

"Yeah, how?" Seabolt said.

"I can realign the collar's receiver. If I'm successful, I can get it to attack the shark again. This time, there won't be a psycho mercenary here to sabotage the attack."

"You're gonna need to get close in order to do it," Seabolt warned.

"That's suicide," Gina said.

"Not for me," Miguel said. "It won't kill me."

"Yeah, but I doubt it'll hold still for you," Seabolt said.

"Unless I sedate it," Miguel said.

"How? The harpoons can't pierce its skin. And I doubt it'll open its mouth wide and let you stick a needle in it," Gina said.

"No…but we do have the aerosol sedative," he said. Gina's mind went back to the lab.

The black dart looking thing!

"You packed it?" Miguel nodded, though he didn't look optimistic. Gina remembered what he said in the lab.

"Because of Eleven's thick skin, we're unable to use a regular tranquilizer. So, we tried applying an aerosol version similar to

chloroform that it would inhale through its nostrils. The problem is that it requires a high dose, which would be lethal for a human. Simply put, it could stop your heart. Contained in this room, it would've been lights out for all of us."

"It's shaped like a dart. Can't you fire it out of a gun?"

"Yes, but the problem is Eleven can move away from the aerosol cloud," Miguel said. "Believe it or not, even something as big as that can be hard to hit. My team and I always had him in a controlled environment whenever we used the sedative. Out here in the open, the aerosol can only do so much, unless I manage to hit it square in the nose. To do that, I'll need its attention *directly* on me."

"How easy is it to realign the receiver?" Seabolt asked.

"You have tools?" Miguel asked.

"Of course," Seabolt answered.

"I'll need to borrow them."

"Fine. But what about the shark?" Seabolt asked. "Is there any way we can drive it away from the beach? Somehow, I don't think it'll respond to low frequency signals when it has a buffet already in front of it."

Gina thought for a moment.

"It's gonna go where there's food—and the food is at the beach. Until it's completely evacuated, there's no way we can draw it off. Our only option will be to regain control of Eleven."

"And have them fight, right in the middle of all that?" Seabolt said.

"There's no other way," Gina said.

"Would it respond to a threat?" Seabolt asked. "Specifically, would it abandon its buffet if it felt threatened by, say, a six-hundred-foot vessel with crew shooting at it?"

In the moment that followed, Gina considered the risk to the crew, then remembered there was no time to think about it.

"That might work."

"Alright," Seabolt said, looking at Miguel, "to stop the snake, you said you'll need to get close?"

"Yes."

"I have a motorboat on board," he said. "You can use that."

Miguel nodded with appreciation. "Thank you, Captain."

"I'll go with you," Gina said.

"No, it's too dangerous," Miguel said. "You need to stay here and track the fish. If that snake sees you, it won't hesitate to kill you."

"I know," she said. "That's why I'm coming. You'll need bait to line up a shot. It won't pay much attention to you."

"Gina…"

"Miguel, I'm fucking coming along. It doesn't take a PhD to monitor the shark. The Captain can do it. Fact is, you're gonna need help, and since I'm partly responsible for this, it's right that I put myself down there along with you."

Miguel looked at Seabolt, hoping he would help talk her out of it. Instead, he simply shrugged his shoulders and bit his lip.

"*I'm* not gonna argue with her."

Miguel sighed. "Come on. We're running out of time." The two scientists disappeared into the passageways to collect their gear, while Seabolt got on the radio to his crew.

"All available hands, report to the armory. Lock and load, we're about to piss off an oversized fish."

CHAPTER 24

It only took a few minutes for Hamilton Beach to go from one of the most tranquil vacation sites ever, to a scene of pure turmoil. Police patrols stormed the beach, guiding the civilians away from the shore. There were too many to account for. Waves of people flooded the shore, many confused, looking for friends and loved ones, often crowding the already overwhelmed officers. Shouts of "Get back!" and "Get out of the water" were the only discernable words heard through the madness. Beyond that was a mixture of names being called, screams of terror, cries for help, all obscured by sounds of carnage.

Both creatures converged on the shallows, taking mouthfuls of people as they went along. Local and State police vehicles raced to the beach areas, unloading dozens of officers armed with M4 carbines, Remington shotguns, and nine-millimeter pistols. Chopper units took to the sky, each containing a trained sniper. Local news reporters, already on site for local interviews, quickly turned their cameras on the carnage. At the same time, major news sources sent out their own choppers, which arrived within minutes to broadcast the event.

Meanwhile, the state Governor got on the hotline to the President to authorize deployment of the National Guard, which was approved as soon as live footage of the unbelievable event hit the TV screens. The 165th Air Support Operations Squadron launched four Sikorsky HH-60G Pave Hawks from the Savannah-Hilton Head International Airport, which converged on the location at over two-hundred miles per hour.

Until then, the police and Coast Guard were on their own.

The four remaining Hamilton Police vessels took to the seas and sped toward the beach area. By the time they arrived, State helicopters hovered over the creatures, struggling to get a clean shot with the many civilians grouped nearby.

The megalodon was only fifty feet out from the shore, in twenty feet of water. Its stomach stirred up soot from the seafloor, the swells it created acting as a shockwave that traveled wherever it went. An unlucky man in an inflatable donut became its next target. Both the man and the inflatable ruptured simultaneously and were washed into the megalodon's throat.

A swing of its tail slapped three people out of the water, who all smashed onto the shore. It went out toward the open water, attracted by the sirens of the approaching police vessels. All four of them spread out, while EMS boats hurried to pull people from the water.

Boat Six led the charge. Two deputies were on the deck with rifles in hand. The driver steered to starboard, allowing the riflemen a clear view of the oncoming fish. Rifle shots rang their ears. Bullets bombarded the fish's snout and back. The ship steered out of the way, but the shark adjusted its path. The deputies yelled obscenities at it, furious at the lack of injury their weapons caused. Boat Five circled the shark from behind, its two deputies landing shots along its tail and back.

The megalodon changed course, turning sharply, choosing to go after Boat Five instead. It raised its head out of the water, jaws wide. The whole bow of the boat crashed into its mouth, the cabin smashing inward. Teeth and glass twirled out along the deck. The impact knocked the two riflemen to their stomachs. Both watched in horror as the jaws chomped down on the cabin, crushing their partner inside. Next was the sensation of going backward. The megalodon pushed the ship, ignoring the stings of rifle shots along its sides. Unable to swallow the boat, it raised its head high, lifting the boat entirely out of the water, then flung it to the left.

All hands aboard Boat Seven yelled in horror before Boat Five crashed on their bow, flinging the stern and the two deputies aboard. Those who survived the crash quickly surfaced…only to see the jaws closing in on them. The megalodon gulped two of them whole at once, feeling their panicked kicking in its gullet as they were digested alive. It found the broken corpses of the other officers, swallowed them, then closed in on one remaining survivor.

Boat Four sped alongside him. Its deputies reached for him, their fingers just out of reach of his.

"Come on! Grab him!" the driver shouted. The megalodon's snout broke the surface, on a collision course that would split their vessel in half. Another attempt to grab the swimming deputy failed. There was no time left. The driver applied full throttle, speeding out of the shark's path. The two riflemen cursed then looked away. The megalodon passed twenty feet behind them. Its jaws clamped down on the deputy, splitting him in half.

The driver continued steering away, eager to put some more distance between them and the shark. He heard another splash to starboard. A shadow overtook the ship. All three men looked up in time to see the serpentine body arching over their vessel.

It only took a few brief moments for the snake to wrap its body repeatedly around the boat. Like pulling the ends of a knot, its body tightened, imploding the whole vessel. It uncoiled and searched the wreckage for sinking bodies.

Chopper blades swept down over the snake as the State Bell 206 twin-engine helicopter positioned over the Colossal Snake. A gunner, secured by a lifeline attached to his harness, aimed his sniper rifle over the fuselage door. He placed his crosshairs over the creature's head and fired. The snake jolted, the impact nothing more than a needle prick to it. He fired several more times.

"Jesus, what the hell is this thing?!" he said.

"Just keep pumping lead into it! If you hit it enough, you'll oughta kill it!" the co-pilot replied. The sniper reloaded and continued popping off rounds. Finally, the snake looked up. Another rifle crack sounded off, the projectile striking its snout. The snake hissed, coiled, and sprang. From afar, it looked as though the snake was standing on end, as over a hundred feet of its body stretched for the chopper.

Though already out of range, the pilot reacted by pulling up and banking to starboard.

"Shit! Mother of a son of a bitch!"

"Lookout!" the co-pilot shouted. They had circled right into the path of a speeding news helicopter. The pilot turned left, only to realize that the news chopper had banked the same direction. In their intent to avoid a crash, they only set a new collision course. There was only a split second to react. They angled the blades for rapid descension, successfully passing underneath the news helicopter. At seventy feet, he began pulling up, sighing with relief.

"Holy mother of ass, that was clo—"

With its foe within reach, the snake raised its head high and snapped its immense jaws over the chopper's nose. Its snout punched through the windshield, sending glass raining in on the pilots. Alarms blared, signaling rotor and engine failure. With a lashing motion, the snake slammed the chopper down into the water. Rotor fragments whipped in all directions.

The beast hammered its head down on the chopper, breaking the tail off entirely. Another blow cracked the fuselage in half. The sniper inside tried to swim, but never completed the first stroke before getting snatched up.

Rifle bullets struck the back of its neck. The snake turned its head, slurping the legs of its victims. The last police vessel was retreating to the shoreline. The deputies on deck blasted away at it, desperate to land a lucky kill shot. Several stings landed along its chin, angering the beast. It coiled its upper body back, then lashed its tail like a bullwhip. With the boat just about out of range, the tip of the tail slashed over the transom, across the waist of one of the deputies. Like a bug struck by a swatter, the deputy was flung off the boat, his legs and arms flailing as his body broke in two.

The other deputy sat up and gasped for breath. She never saw her partner launched from the deck—all she knew was that he was gone. The tail had retracted, and the snake was coursing right for them.

"Go faster!" she shouted to the helmsman. She shouldered the rifle and fired several rounds at the beast, rocking back and forth as the helmsman avoided fleeing civilians. It entered shallow waters, scraping the seabed with its hull. As it reached the shore, its pursuer closed the distance. In one strike, its mouth raked across the deck, scooping the riflewoman, while pancaking the helmsman against the control console.

The panic on shore escalated. The snake, seeing the multitude of prey running about, slithered on shore. The belief that the land was their safe haven was swiftly destroyed. Anywhere the snake moved, there were people to bite. It snapped its jaws, its teeth impaling the trunk of a news reporter. It hadn't even begun to swallow before it scooped up the cameraman.

Flashing lights caught its eye. The creature reflected on its experience with the police boats, remembering the red-and-blue strobes on their structures that matched those on the cars. Additionally, it noticed several people dressed in the same colors and carrying the same loud weapons.

Police blasted rifles and shotguns. The snake shook its head, annoyed by the countless stings. High above, another police helicopter hovered, with two snipers shooting it from above. The snake screeched in anger, then set its wrath on those on the ground. Its jaws found a state trooper and mashed his body into pulp, then set down on a deputy. As it tore him in half, it lashed its tail, striking three officers at once and sending them whirling through the assortment of businesses.

The snake tore across the beach, knocking people away left and right. Finally, the band of cops disbanded, realizing they had no chance against the beast. Many of them dove into their Interceptors and burned rubber. Seeing the flashing lights now moving, the snake struck one of the vehicles. Both ends of the vehicle pointed skyward, its center crushed into scrape, forming a V-shape.

SWAT arrived in armored vehicles, deploying ten men armed with MP5 submachine guns and M4 Carbines. Even these individuals, many of them combat veterans, nearly froze at the sight of the creature. They took firing positions, hitting the beast with armor-piercing rounds.

Some of these bullets managed to pierce its skin, sending the snake to go into a frenzy. The team broke formation to avoid its snapping jaws.

With its prey running in separate directions, the snake glanced back and forth, choosing which to bite first. It settled on the tallest member, a six-foot-seven rifleman built like a wrestler. He managed to squeeze off a few bursts before it grabbed him. Like a piece of jerky wrapped in Kevlar, the officer was swallowed whole. Bullets struck its right side, drawing its attention to two SWAT members that took cover behind a tiki bar. A slash of its tail ripped through the building, driving a hail of debris at them. The SWAT officers fell backward, their weapons still blasting away. Bullets sprayed the air.

Up above, the chopper pilot sucked in a nervous breath after nearing the metallic clunks of bullets striking the hull. The next sound was the whine of a damaged main rotor.

"Oh hell! Hang on!" he told his crew. The aircraft dipped thirty feet, wobbling side-to-side as the pilot fought for control. They descended another fifteen feet. He watched the beach for a place to set down. Many of the civilians had evacuated by now, though there were several still in the water being picked off by the megalodon. However, there was room on the sand.

A green-skinned tail with black rings raised across his windshield.

"Oh fu—"

The tail slashed the cockpit, folding it in on itself. The chopper spun like a maple leaf, smashing into a gift shop. Its fuselage ruptured, exposing the fuel inside to the several sparks that ignited from the crash, resulting in a fiery explosion.

Smoke twirled high in the sky, causing a new wave of screams to fill the air.

The snake watched, its head poised in a striking position. The blast had startled it momentarily, but it quickly eased up and resumed its rampage. Several SWAT officers were retreating back into town, taking position near other shops and buildings. Other cops and firefighters rushed into the buildings, successfully evacuating the people inside.

The snake saw the river of people fleeing inland. It flicked its tongue, sensing a world of fresh meat. It slithered toward the buildings, jolting at the stings of bullet strikes. The officers fled as it neared the building, except for one who fired from the corner. The snake struck with lightning speed, its head punching through the side of the building as it scooped him up. Rubble rained down, and after a few moments, the whole side of the building crumbled from loss of support.

More police cars approached, only to turn and flee as the snake snapped its jaws. It caught one by the trunk, flipping it forward like a hamster wheel. It hit the pavement and skidded for several yards. Another vehicle sped by, the passenger pointing a shotgun out of the window. A barrage of pellets hit the snake's neck. The stings, combined with those from the remaining SWAT officers, spurred the beast into another frenzy. It lashed its whole body, striking a spa building. Chunks of brick flew into the air like shrapnel. The snake continued inland, its body crushing vehicles and pavement along the way. It followed the flashing lights of numerous police vehicles, increasing speed after seeing the bite-sized humans running between the roadblock they'd created.

Rifle rounds pelted its skin as it raced toward them. In seconds, it closed in. The line of cops dispersed, with two of them getting snatched up immediately. It lashed its tail at a fleeing vehicle, popping both tires on the left side. The car swerved, avoiding fleeing traffic along an intersection, which caused another truck to swerve…right into an abandoned fuel tanker, which had parked near a gas station.

The resulting explosion could be seen for two miles out. The ball of flame looked like an exploding stare, with flares like tentacles streaking far into the town. The snake hissed, eager to feed on more humans. It slithered further out, continuing northwest as more flashing strobes approached.

Coast Guard helicopters whizzed into the area. By now, the word had gotten around that bullets had little-to-no effect on the beasts. The pilots and crew received orders to focus on assisting EMS on getting civilians out of the water.

Amidst the flood of radio transmissions were alerts of a cargo ship approaching the beach at top speed. Pilot sightings confirmed the deck was full of crewmen, each armed with semi-automatic rifles.

Between the ship and the beach was a twelve-foot lifeboat, racing to the shore. On board this vessel was a man and woman, carrying tools and an electronic device.

CHAPTER 25

The speedboat's bow bounced upward after hitting a swell, nearly knocking Gina and Miguel backward. They held tight until it settled, only to brace for another swell. Helicopters buzzed overhead, fishing people out. A thousand feet to their right, the megalodon continued its rampage. Through the heavy splashes and whirring rotors, the two scientists could hear the panicked screams of hundreds of people still fleeing for their lives.

The sky had turned black from the burning chopper. The explosion had splashed burning fuel onto the adjacent buildings and cars. Fuel tanks ruptured, creating a domino effect of flames. Meanwhile, the snake continued its battle with the brave police that stood toe-to-toe. Body parts littered the beach, the sand now red from their blood.

Miguel looked back at the *Armstrong,* which was rapidly approaching the beach. The speaker was blasting under the water, though as Gina predicted, it failed to attract the shark. Men were running along the deck with rifles and Molotov cocktails made from the spare fuel. They still had another half-mile to go before closing the distance with the megalodon.

"Focus," Gina said. "Don't worry about them. Seabolt knows what he's doing."

Miguel faced forward again, forcing himself to witness the mayhem caused by the very creature he cared for. The creature made from the DNA taken from the skeleton he himself discovered. His mind flashed back to the day he searched that enormous cave. If only he knew what would become of that beast.

They sped past a piece of battered hull.

"My God," Miguel said. Gina glanced back and saw the face of a defeated man whose life's work had been perverted into something he never intended it to be. "This is my fault. I always suspected Gundrum's intentions. And I went along with it anyway. I should've destroyed it long ago. Burned the lab. Leaked his intentions to the news. Everything."

"You still can," she replied.

"What good will it do to these people?" Miguel said, waving a hand out to the world of carnage around them.

"To them? Nothing. To everyone else, though?"

Miguel realized her point. More than likely, Gundrum was already working on a press release and coming up with ways to distance himself and the company from the situation at hand. Jason Nace's statements on other governments and entities on other parts of the world wanting to purchase specimens had weight to it. If anything, seeing the news broadcasts of these things battling armed police, crashing through boats, and swatting down helicopters—this would probably spark a high demand. Miguel glanced at the news choppers again. The bastards—they had no idea they were practically advertising for Marc Gundrum.

He would eventually fund new projects on another facility. It would probably be on an island somewhere, far from the jurisdiction of the U.S. government. Wherever it was, it'd be a place Dr. Trish Voltz could work in isolation with her perverted science.

If anything was to be learned from this day, it was that creatures from the past were meant to stay dead. They could not be controlled. They were never intended to share the world with humanity. If Gundrum continued producing monstrosities, whether they were made from prehistoric DNA or present day creatures, there would be a thousand beaches like this one.

It had to stop here.

Seven hundred feet to go. News choppers were now buzzing around like flies. Loudspeakers sounded off as the Coast Guard tried to get them to divert from the airspace. But like dogs rushing to the sound of food, the camera choppers flooded the area, absorbing the event through their cameras. A couple of them were decent enough to lower their aircraft to the water and fish out a struggling swimmer or two. The others, however, made no such attempt.

Gina looked up to the sound of rotors directly above them. A news chopper was pursuing them specifically, their cameraman half out of the fuselage with a camera pointed at them. She felt the urge to give the finger, but focused on the situation at hand.

Four hundred feet to go.

She trembled at the sound of rifle shots. She heard a scream, followed by a smashing sound, and the gunfire immediately ceased.

The snake had moved further inland, its bulk partly obscured by the wall of flames. Other State Troopers quickly arrived, but maintained their distance. Most of them didn't even leave their vehicles. Passengers riding shotgun fired from the window.

Finally, the boat hit the sandbank. Miguel grabbed up his launcher and tools, then stormed the beach. Running through the trail of carnage, hearing the mayhem in the water behind him, the gunfire ahead of him, and the fire out to the side, he felt like a soldier storming Normandy Beach.

The scientists cleared the sand into the business area. Cars were overturned, buildings flattened, with a few stragglers running about. Most of the population had evacuated inland. The snake was a quarter-mile to the north. They could see its head rising high over the edge of the town. It was hissing, probably hurt from gunfire. It snapped down at something, and they heard a crash. Wreckage flew overhead. Pieces of a house or other small building maybe. The snake raised its head again. It continued slithering northwest, meeting new resistance as it went.

Miguel was already running out of breath.

"Damn it. It keeps moving away, and it goes faster than we can run. I don't know if we'll be able to catch up to it in time," he said.

"We don't have a choice," Gina replied.

"We need a car," Miguel said.

They found one unattended, then realized as they approached that the engine had been smashed. Most of the others around them were overturned or had other damage. Those that were functional had been driven away by their panicked owners, which resulted in numerous collisions.

They heard somebody groaning in pain.

"Over there," Gina said, pointing past a crushed bar and grill. Behind the wreckage was a State Police vehicle on its side. They ran over to it and circled around. A State Trooper was on the ground with one of his legs caught under the bumper.

"Hang on," Miguel said.

"Not going anywhere," the cop muttered. Miguel smirked. At least the Trooper had a good sense of humor. He knelt by him and examined his leg.

"Yeah, it's broken for sure. We're gonna have to get the car off of you," he said. He stood up and placed his hands on the hood. Gina took a stance next to him and pressed her hands to it. "On three. One, two, three." They pushed at once. The car teetered, then fell back onto its tires. The Trooper let out a yell, a combination of pain and relief.

They gathered by the officer to set his leg. As he was pulled away from the vehicle, he couldn't help but notice their assortment of tools, the strange tablet-looking device, and the even stranger grenade-launcher looking thing.

"Why do I get the feeling you two aren't cable-repairmen?" he joked.

"It's a long story," Gina said.

"I figured as much. What the hell are these things? Or is that a long story too?"

"It is, actually," Gina said.

The officer groaned. “Gosh, I feel like I’m in a Japanese movie.”

“I wish it was only that,” Gina said. She positioned herself near his foot. “Brace yourself, this is gonna hurt.” The Trooper yelled out as she set the bone. He took in several deep breaths, then sat up. Miguel was standing up, searching the distance for the snake. It had gained further distance.

“Officer, I hope you don’t mind, but we’re gonna have to borrow your vehicle,” he said. The Trooper nodded. Clearly, these people weren’t simple tourists or residents.

“Keys are in it,” he said. “Whatever you’re gonna do, do it fast. The Air National Guard are flying in, and when they do, this place literally will be a warzone.”

“Shit,” Miguel said. “You have an ETA?” The cop looked at his watch.

“By now, probably around eight-to-ten minutes,” he said. “Considering what’s happened already, they’ll probably be authorized to use explosives.”

“In a populated area?” Gina asked.

“Ma’am, look at what’s happening,” the officer said. “The way they’re looking at it, the damage and death toll is gonna happen regardless. And by the looks of it, it’ll continue until these things are stopped.”

Gina looked at Miguel. “You think missiles will stop them?”

“Maybe,” Miguel said. “And a hell of a lot of other people too. And if the megalodon swims out to sea, there’s no telling what other mayhem it’ll cause. It’s even more imperative now that our plan works.”

“Will you be alright, sir?” Gina asked the Trooper.

“I’ll live,” he answered. “Be careful. I’ve been around animals and know how they think. I believe that snake you’re chasing now associates our flashers with danger.”

Gina and Miguel shared a glance. An idea formed in their minds.

“I think we’ve got our bait,” Gina said.

“Let’s go,” Miguel replied. Gina took the driver’s seat. The engine rumbled to life. The exhaust and muffler were loose and the windshield was heavily cracked, but it would do. Miguel got in the passenger seat, tossed the tool bag and tablet at his feet, and punched a hole in the cracked windshield with the barrel of his launcher.

Gina floored the pedal, taking them toward the sound of chaos.

CHAPTER 26

"Dr. Hutson was right, Captain. The speakers aren't drawing in the beast," the watch stander radioed to Seabolt. The Captain was on the deck with the crew. He held Jason Nace's pistol in his hand. His broken arm throbbed, resting limp in its sling.

Crew members took position with AR-15s and Molotov cocktails.

The bridge crew steered the *Armstrong* toward the beach area. The horizon had turned black from the smoke. Air Force Reconnaissance flew overhead, detailing the situation to the approaching attack force.

Far in the distance, the Colossal Snake was ravaging the edge of the town. He could only catch brief glimpses of it through the wall of flames. The fire from the gas station had quickly spread, causing a few adjacent businesses to catch fire. For several seconds, he lost sight of the snake behind the plumes. He focused his vision on the sound of sirens coming in from the north. As he suspected, the snake was pursuing the cops. When he finally spotted it again, it was using its body as a whip, knocking over cars and trucks. Seabolt thought of Gina and Miguel and wondered if they could even get close to the beast at this point.

Damn, I hope those kids know what they're doing.

He focused his attention on the shark.

The megalodon breached the water in an attempt to grab one of the Coast Guard choppers. Its pilot pulled it up out of reach, causing the fish to crash back down into the water empty handed. There were still a couple of hundred people in the water, spread out over the length of the beach. Wreckage thumped against the *Armstrong's* hull. The crew watched for any stragglers in the water, but saw none nearby. Seabolt wasn't sure how he felt about that, as it either meant that anyone this far out was either rescued…or eaten.

"I'll remind you all that this is strictly voluntary," he said to the crew. "If anyone doesn't feel safe on deck while we engage this thing, there'll be no judgement against you if you choose to take shelter below."

"Are you done with the speech, or can we finally shoot the shark?" one tenacious crewmember said. Seabolt smiled.

"Do we have any chum left?"

"We do, Captain," another crew member answered.

"Dump it. Dump it all. Let's create such a strong scent that the fish won't be able to turn down."

"You sure it'll work, Captain? It might not abandon the available food."

"It might think it has a buffet, but if it thinks there's a much bigger animal bleeding profusely into the water, it'll come to us. If you were at a dinner party and had a choice of a bowl of cocktail weenies and a big rare steak, you're gonna choose the steak."

The crew retrieved the drums full of chum mixture and rolled them to the portside, near the firing line. Men with Molotov cocktails stood ready with cigarette lighters, while the riflemen fought to keep their itchy fingers off the triggers.

A foul smell overcame the diesel odor as they removed the cap. The brown chunky mixture splashed into the water, looking like old chili being washed into a drain.

"Dump it all. And intensify those speakers," Seabolt said. "Come on! Let's go! Let's go! Let's go!" Another drum emptied into the ocean, forming a thick cloud that swirled all the way down into the seabed.

The megalodon's stomach raked against the sandbank, stirring up another cloud of soot. It managed to intercept an unlucky skier making an attempt to race to shore. Its nose toppled the vehicle, knocking him loose. The jaws found the skier and clamped down, cleaving him down the middle. The megalodon proceeded into deeper water and felt the vibrations from a descending helicopter. It increased speed, ready to breach in hopes of snatching it out of the air.

A powerful scent filled its nostrils. Blood. The scent came suddenly. The shark slowed, ignoring the chopper in favor of studying this strong aroma. It came from the same source as the distressed vibrations it had been ignoring. As it swam further out, it detected the water displacement from a large 'creature'. The same one it had fought with before the snake interfered.

At first, the megalodon wasn't sure if it wanted to attack. The hull proved thick and inedible. It couldn't ram the vessel too many times without injuring itself in the process. However, the smell was just too intriguing.

The megalodon approached with caution.

"It's coming!" the bridge informed Seabolt.

"Full turn to starboard. Be ready to lead it out into deeper water," Seabolt ordered. The ship swiftly turned until its bow pointed out to the distant blue.

The crew adjusted firing position to meet the shark. Its dorsal fin was rapidly approaching. It was fast, though not quite at the assault speed they experienced prior. The shark seemed to be interested in studying its opponent this time, rather than biting blindly.

"Wait for it to get closer," Seabolt said. "Let it surface, then hit it with the cocktails. Once we piss it off, then it's game-on."

Several men jittered as they watched the beast near the portside. Some started regretting their decision to stay on deck. The adrenaline at least dulled the pain in Seabolt's arm, making it easier to focus. Those with the cocktails lit the rags, then reared their throwing arms back like baseball pitchers.

"Come on, you big guppy," he muttered. The megalodon arrived, brushing the side of the boat as it studied the blood cloud. The top of its head broke the water. "Now! Throw the cocktails!"

All at once, the men launched the flaming bottles at the fish with all of their might. Glass shattered, erupting flames along the shark's head. Simultaneously, the riflemen unleashed their weapons on the beast, stinging it along its back and head.

"Pull power to the engines. Lead it out to sea," Seabolt ordered. The *Armstrong* lurched forward as the propellers kicked into high-gear.

The megalodon jolted to the right, the flames quickly put out by ocean water as it dove. It swam a hundred feet out, then circled back. Riflemen continued blasting away at it, then backed away from the railing. Seabolt ordered the men to brace themselves for the upcoming impact, only to be surprised when the fish dove.

A huge spray of water preceded its leap. The fish arched over the railing and smashed down on the deck, crushing a couple of sailors.

"Sweet Christ!" Seabolt yelled. The fish writhed on its stomach, snapping its jaws left and right at the men around it. It found one and clamped its jaws around his torso, severing everything from the head and right shoulder. It tried to turn, swinging its tail in the process. One of the riflemen found himself in the path of the caudal fin. The impact sent him flying like a football, splattering across the side of the structure.

"Get more bottles!" the Captain ordered. He fired his pistol into the beast's gill slits. Its motions increased, slithering its body like an eel toward the opposite side. More Molotov cocktails were lit and tossed at the creature. Now, its whole side was on fire. "Keep hitting it. Throw some fuel on it! Someone, get the barbeque seasoning. I wanna smell this bastard cooking!"

More bottles splattered over its side and head. The shark rolled, facing its stomach toward the sky. It was a literal fish out of water…a one-hundred-and forty-ton fish. Its body arched on its tail and head, and again, it twisted. Steel plates bent under its weight, and more railing snapped as it found the edge. It hit the water, sending a wave washing over the deck. The flames disappeared instantly, and the shark proceeded to circle the bow.

"Didn't expect that," one crewmember said. Others hurried to the side and hurled after seeing the mashed bodies of sailors crushed under the shark.

"Look alive, men," Seabolt said. "We're not done yet. Let's honor our fallen by finishing this bastard off."

The *Armstrong* raced out to sea at twenty-five knots. The megalodon kept pace with it, not allowing its enemy to escape. Seabolt's eyes never wavered from the fish. He knew its next attack was inevitable. It was probably just recovering from its injuries at the moment.

Its next approach came without warning. One moment, it was moving parallel with the ship, then in the blink of an eye, it was on a collision course.

The shark turned its head and rammed its bulk against the ship, knocking it to starboard. The ship teetered for a moment, knocking everyone off balance. Seabolt held on to the crane platform, watching the water. It was getting deeper. The shark struck again, this time near the starboard quarter.

"*Captain, we have rudder damage,*" the bridge crew informed him.

"Great," Seabolt groaned. He glanced back to Hamilton Beach. Somewhere behind that wall of smoke was that snake and the two scientists. "Now's the time, guys."

CHAPTER 27

"Never thought I'd ever be doing this," Gina said. She kept the pedal floored, speeding the Interceptor past dozens of fleeing vehicles. A few civilians moved to the side, while others zipped past her to get away from the chaos ahead.

"We spent the whole day chasing after a genetically engineered megalodon, using a genetically engineered snake, both resurrected by fossilized DNA. Both are wreaking havoc. And stealing a police car is the thing that surprises you the most?"

Gina swerved, taking the Interceptor onto the curb to avoid crashing into a crowd in the street. She veered back, narrowly dodging a wreckage. They entered the business section of town. There was smoke and fire everywhere. Ambulances and firetrucks raced through intersections, barely slowing for crossing traffic. Twice, Gina nearly collided with first responders.

Three times! As they approached an intersection, Gina caught the glimpse of red lights strobing from the left.

"Damn!" she said, slamming her foot to the brakes. She let a line of firetrucks go by. As she did, she stuck her head out of the window to look for Eleven. "Miguel, I don't see it."

"How the hell did we lose it?" Miguel said.

"Hey, it's big, but it's not freaking *Godzilla*. It doesn't stand fifty meters over the buildings. It slithers close to the road. With all of these market buildings around us, it's easy to lose."

With the trucks out of the way, she continued forward.

"Wait, hang on," Miguel said. Gina scoffed, and braked again. Miguel stood out of the car and listened. Somewhere beyond the endless sirens and screaming was the sound of gunfire. He got back in the car and pointed at eleven o'clock. "That way."

Gina sped the Interceptor for another four blocks, then took a left turn. After passing two more blocks, she saw police lights passing through an intersection up ahead. She arrived at the intersection and took a right.

They stared at a world of devastation. Cars had been tossed aside like bean bags. Some had smashed directly into buildings. Cops and Fire Department personnel were pulling injured people out of cars. Others screamed from window, trapped inside three-story buildings. Behind the densely populated area was Eleven.

Miguel felt sick from seeing the devastation. He readied the launcher, sticking the barrel out through the hole in the windshield.

"Go slow," he told Gina. She steered the Interceptor through the devastation, passing rubble and overturned vehicles along the way. As their view cleared, they saw other police vehicles around the snake. The creature slashed its tail at them, weaving back and forth. Its lower body was constricted around a police van, which had been crushed like a soda can.

"I don't know if we can get its attention," Gina said. Miguel watched several officers blasting at the creature, then glanced down at the police radio. He snatched up the microphone and pressed the transmitter.

"All units, pull back immediately. Everyone fall back. Do not engage the biologic. A Navy Destroyer is a quarter mile off the coast. They've pinpointed the creature's position and are launching cruise missiles as I speak. In thirty seconds, this block is gonna go up in smoke. Move now!"

To their surprise, his lie worked. The police cars sped off in various directions. Even those that questioned the validity of whether a Navy Destroyer would actually violate the twelve-mile rule weren't going to take the chance.

"Wow, nice lie," Gina said.

"Not a total lie," he said. "If we don't divert this thing, the National Guard will be the ones leveling this place."

"Then let's get to it," Gina said. She floored the accelerator and honked the horn. The snake turned to face them and hissed. It uncoiled from the van and slithered to meet them head-on.

"Hit the brakes. Let it come to us," Miguel said. Gina stomped on the brake pedal, bringing the vehicle to a screeching stop. The beast closed in then took a striking position.

Miguel had two or three seconds at best.

And one shot.

He stuck the barrel through the windshield, aimed down the sights, and lined it up with the creature's snout. It stared back at him, unable to recognize its caretaker through the heavily cracked glass. It moved to strike.

Miguel fired. The dart crashed against Eleven's nose and exploded into a huge cloud. The snake reared back, startled, unwittingly taking in a huge breath of the sedative.

Gina put the Interceptor in reverse and backed away from the cloud. She stopped a couple hundred feet back, and watched the huge creature writhing. Its jaw was slack, its movements sluggish. It tried to pursue them, passing through the cloud. In doing so, it took in more of the sedative before it dissipated. Its head scraped along the pavement and clumsily slithered headfirst into a truck. It tried to correct course, but instead coiled into a ball.

The scientists waited a few moments. The snake remained in place, unconscious.

"Damn! Nice shot!" Gina said.

"Party's not over yet. We've got a couple of minutes at best, and no spare dart," Miguel said. They hopped out of the Interceptor and ran toward the beast, tools in hand.

The snake's tongue stuck out of its mouth as it slumbered. Hot air drifted from its nostrils, carrying with it a horrid stench. Standing next to it, Gina felt as small as an insect. Its head was the size of a Buick, and standing next to it made her throat tighten.

Miguel handed her the tool bag and examined the collar. The receiver was further up along the right side. It was a cone-shaped device, usually with green LEDs circling its base. But they were blank, as the receiver was leaning hard to the side due to the boat impact. Miguel would have to climb in order to reconnect it. He found a small alcove in the collar and hoisted himself up. He climbed as fast as he could, the reinforced steel plating of the collar feeling hot against his fingertips from exposure to the sun and surrounding fire. Finally up top, he knelt at the receiver. The square platform that attached it to the collar was folded backward. Each side contained three slots for four-inch screws. All three on the forward side had been knocked loose, as well as a couple on the left and right. The ones in the back seemed fully secure. First, Miguel needed to examine the internal components. He found a panel, which had been crumpled inward from the collision. He managed to get it open. Inside was an assortment of wires, connecting the receiving device to the collar's chemical transmitters. Luckily, none seemed to be too badly damaged. They simply needed to be re-attached.

"Pliers," he said. Gina tossed them up. He quickly reattached a few wires that had been knocked loose. The green LEDs flashed on. Miguel breathed a sigh of relief.

He shook, feeling the snake quiver. Already, the sedative was beginning to wear off. As nervous as he was, it was nothing compared to Gina, who was already half-turned to make a break for it. Miguel couldn't blame her; if Eleven awoke now, she'd be nothing more than an hors d'oeuvre.

"I hate to rush you, Miguel…"

"Toss up the drill," he replied. She tossed it up to him, then followed it up with some large screws. Miguel pushed the receiver's platform into place. He struggled, realizing the back end had been bent where it was struck. He was barely able to line up the slots. Even then, the side of the platform hovered an inch over the intended spot. "Shit." He pushed harder, trying to flatten the thing. But he might as well have been trying to push a twenty-ton bulldozer.

The snake trembled again. Its tail was beginning to nudge. Time was almost out.

"Get back," he told Gina.

"Fine with me," she said, returning to the Interceptor. Miguel placed the screws through the slots and fastened the platform to the collar. The first screw snapped due to the angle. The middle slot was a little lower, so he was able to get the screw in about three-quarters of the way. The right corner was folded back so bad he wasn't even going to waste the little time he had. He replaced a screw on the right side's center slot, then looked at the receiver. It was still teetering back, only loosely secured. The most important thing was that the wiring was complete.

"That'll have to do," he said. As he climbed down, Eleven started shifting its head. Miguel jumped and ran for the Interceptor. Gina was already waiting with the tablet extended out to him. He got in the passenger seat and took it. He swiped his finger, only to see that annoying *unlock* feature. "Fuck! Come on!" he complained. He typed in the code, watching the snake lifting its head and flicking its tongue. It raised its head and straightened its body, before looking down at the Interceptor.

"Sometime this year, Miguel," Gina complained.

"Will you knock it off! I'm doing it," he said.

"Not fast enough," she replied. Miguel punched in the unlock code, bringing up the main screen. He patched in the signal for the megalodon's chem-beacon and pressed *activate.*

The snake continued moving in, then proceeded to angle its head back to a striking pose.

"Come on! Come on!" Miguel said. He amplified the signal, causing the implants to fire intense signals into the creature's brain. It hissed, shaking its head. It raised the first half of its body high, flicking its tongue to help itself pinpoint the new signal. It faced the east, then shot off like a bullet, tearing through the roads at high speed.

Miguel and Gina caught their breaths. Gina steered the vehicle to the next intersection where the snake disappeared, just in time to see it slithering rapidly for the beach area.

"He's not wasting any time," Gina said.

"We can't either," Miguel said. "Get us to back to the shore. Let's take our boat back to the *Armstrong* and see this thing through."

CHAPTER 28

Now, more than ever, Seabolt longed for the glory days of being aboard a Frigate or a Destroyer. Hell, a simple Navy patrol boat would suffice at this point. At least they'd have fifty-cal. on board.

The *Armstrong* splashed water as another impact knocked it to starboard. The impact knocked the Captain to his knees. He heard radio traffic blasting from his receiver. The bridge was panicking. He heard reports of a hull breach and engine failure.

Crew members continued firing rifles at the fish. It was swimming a few hundred feet off the port bow. Its dorsal fin showed traces of burn marks. It continued swimming ahead, lining itself for another run.

"Come on. Is that all you've got?" Seabolt taunted it. He reloaded his revolver and made his way to the railing. Ego would not permit him to take shelter, not even in the face of certain death. The shark turned and accelerated. Seabolt and a few of his crewmen unloaded into the beast as it soared through the water. It struck the bow, pushing the ship backward.

"Is this thing a shark or freaking *Moby Dick*?" one of the crewmembers said. A tidal wave swept over the deck, followed by the megalodon. It cleared the water in a bounding leap, crashing its body against the superstructure. Its body raked the front of the bridge, peeling down exterior walls until it landed on the deck.

A large crack formed under its body and traveled along the port and starboard side. The megalodon was cracking the *Armstrong* like a toothpick. Its body floundered, wigging itself off the deck. As it did, its tail swiped the length of the deck, knocking another crewmember thirty yards into the water. The beast fell face-first off the starboard side and plunged into the ocean, then tracked down the broken body and devoured it.

"Damn you, Marc Gundrum. Goddamn you to hell," Seabolt said through gritted teeth. Ocean water began seeping in through the cracks in the ship, causing internal pressure in the passageways. He glanced around the deck and found his radio, which had fallen off his belt. "All hands, prepare to abandon ship."

In the time he had taken his eyes off the shark, it had circled back and charged the ship again. It struck its nose along the crackling starboard side, wedging the crack wider by several feet. Water was now flooding the ship in huge rivers. Crew rushed through the passageways and climbed ladders to the hatches. Life vests were passed around, while other crew worked on lowering the life boats. Radio crew connected with the Coast Guard's frequency and provided coordinates.

"Captain, we have Coast Guard ships inbound, but their choppers are busy along the beach areas. ETA on rescue is eleven minutes," a bridge member informed him.

Seabolt radioed back. "We've got no choice then but to wait. Get your life vests on and prepare to get wet. If anyone of you ever wondered what it was like to ride on the *Titanic,* today's your lucky day."

"We're just gonna get swallowed if we go down there!" a nervous crewmember said.

"Unfortunately, we're going down whether we like it or not, son," Seabolt said. "We have to ride this out for as long as we can, and hope the scientists didn't get swallowed by the snake." He glanced at the shore. From this distance, it was a blur of sand and moving bodies, with choppers looking like tiny gnats dancing over a piece of garbage.

Then, all at once, the choppers elevated, as though avoiding something. Something moved below them, splashing into the water. He wondered if his eyes were playing tricks on him. The desperate mind could be a torturous one; sometimes, one would imagine what they hoped to see.

In the following minutes, the swells grew larger and nearer. Whatever caused them was traveling along the surface, going directly towards them at incredible speed.

"Son of a bitch, they did it," Seabolt said.

****

By the time Gina and Miguel arrived at the beach, the snake was already in the water and swimming out toward the ship. They sped the Interceptor to their speedboat and stopped near the water's edge.

"Maybe we should wait here. If we follow it, we'll just put ourselves in the middle of their brawl," Gina said, watching the snake swim off into the distance.

"Hang on," Miguel said. He leaned down the radio, after hearing something regarding a cargo ship. He turned the volume up to listen, but the conversation had switched to rescue measures along the beach. "Say again, repeat transmission on cargo ship. Did they state status? Over?"

"Who is this?"

"Car thirty-nine," Gina whispered.

"Car thirty-nine," Miguel repeated.

"It seems the shark and the snake have diverted their attention to a cargo ship, about a mile offshore. They've sustained heavy damage and are taking on water. They've sent a distress signal and are about to abandon ship, but the Coast Guard is overwhelmed, and all of our boats are destroyed."

"Oh, no. Miguel, we need to get out there!"

Miguel ran a hand over his sweaty brow as he quickly thought of a solution. The cargo ship would be in the water by the time they arrived, and their little speedboat wouldn't have enough room for all the crew anyway.

He stepped out of the vehicle and looked around him, looking at all the boats and choppers moving about. His eyes traced the length of the beach, seeing abandoned paddleboats, sailboats, and other equipment. Finally, he saw what he hoped to see.

An abandoned four-motor Seven Marine drifted twenty feet out offshore, its hull covered in sand where its owner beached it and ran.

"There!" he said. He and Gina hopped into their motor-boat and steered it to the larger craft. It would be cramped, but the deck was large enough to sustain all hands aboard the *Armstrong*. "Hold tight."

All four motors kicked blue streams as he applied full-throttle, racing the boat at seventy-miles per-hour.

****

The Atlantic Ocean invaded the *Armstrong* with its legions. The water flooded the lower decks, weighing down the stern. As the back half of the ship began to dip, it widened the breach in the center, allowing the water to seep in faster. In minutes, the transom was merely inches above the water. The bow, still connected by the lower compartments, began to drag backward.

The entire crew was now on the main deck. Most grouped near the bow rail, while a few others proceeded to lower the lifeboats. The first one had just touched the water when the megalodon breached again, smashing the boat against the hull of the ship.

The terrified sailors shrieked. They piled over each other as the superstructure started to sink, dragging the rest of the ship along with it.

Some of them clung to the submersible, forgetting that it would sink with the rest of the ship.

"Shit!" someone yelled out.

"Calm yourselves," Seabolt said. He kept his eyes on the incoming swells. He could see the Colossal Snake's ringed body below the waves. "Help's here. Just hold on!"

The megalodon spat out a stale-tasting piece of hull. It lined itself up for another run at the ship, then felt the electrical impulses of a large organism rapidly approaching from the west. The smell of open wounds traveled up its nose. The familiar scent and the pattern of movement sparked the recent memory of its violent encounter with the serpentine beast. It was closing in fast, on a collision course. Like a military computer, the megalodon's defensive instinct kicked in. It turned to meet the threat, jaws partly agape, ready to extend for a massive bite.

The Colossal Snake glided into view, its whole body acting like one enormous fin. It locked eyes with the shark and bared its curved fangs. The meg kept its distance, swimming in a wide arch around the snake.

The two creatures circled each other, maintaining a precise distance of a hundred feet between them. It was as if each creature was daring the other to strike first. They completed a full pass, then a second. Eventually, they reached their fifth pass.

The megalodon dove deep, gaining momentum, pointed itself up toward the snake, then ascended at rapid speed. It passed within fifty-feet of its enemy and broke the surface, traveling high and mighty in the air.

Terrified sailors shouted as they watched the enormous shark arching back to the ocean. Open jaws led the way, descending directly atop the snake. The meg struck down and clamped its jaws over the snake's back. Both creatures rolled, their tails flailing high over the waves. They barrel rolled along the surface like two enormous wrestlers. The tail lashed like a bullwhip, striking the megalodon's underbelly and pectoral fins.

The megalodon could feel the snake slithering its lower body for a constriction. Using its superior speed to its advantage, it released its grip and darted away. The snake's coiling body closed in on nothing but water. It hissed, air bubbles streaking from its mouth. It attempted pursuit, but could not outpace the fish. Already, the megalodon had a hundred yards on it.

It stopped and rotated its body. The mighty dorsal fin cut through the water, dipping only to pass under the sinking *Armstrong*, as the megalodon made another run at the snake.

The collision sent both creatures airborne, their bodies thrashing, jaws snapping. Their bodies twisted, blood trailing behind them as they arched back to the Atlantic. A tidal splash curtained their plunge, creating thirty-foot swells that battered the vessel.

The snake screeched as nine-inch teeth ripped into its midsection. Clouds of blood burst from the slits. A heavy current assaulted the back of its head. The megalodon was propelling it backward. That current concluded abruptly with the subsequent crash of a steel hull against its body.

The whole front half of the *Armstrong* lurched upward, throwing all hands to the deck.

The snake snapped its jaws, lacerating the meg's chin with its teeth. Still, the fish wouldn't let go. It began slithering its tail back over the shark's midsection. Again, recognizing the initial pressure of constriction, the megalodon released its grip and attempted to swim off. However, this time, the snake had a decent hold.

It proceeded to wrap its body around the fish's, while biting near its snout. With its caudal fin still free, the megalodon made another run at the ship. It plowed headfirst into the bow, banging its head, and the snake's against the starboard bow. The shockwave rippled through the snake's skeleton, stunning it.

The *Armstrong* rocked to port. Crewmen fell over the broken railing into the waves. Seabolt crouched near the edge and reached with his functioning arm, but the crew hands were out of reach. The megalodon broke free of the grip and swam free, passing underneath them in its retreat. Men thrashed in the water, some caught in the swells created by the fish.

"No, no, no," Seabolt muttered. "Get the other lifeboat in the water!"

"We can't. The deck's smashed, sir. We can't get to it now!" a crewman shouted.

Water surged around the superstructure as it sank into the ocean, pulling the rest of their ship with it. The *Armstrong's* bow lifted forty-five degrees. Next came the deep, dull echoes of straining metal, and the vibrations of the rest of the decks breaking away. The ship's own weight snapped the remaining structure that remained attached to the stern. The keel cracked, sending bits of hull twirling down below with the stern. The bow crashed down like a tree.

Seabolt watched the water level continue to climb. The bow was starting to sink too. The tip pulled up a few feet, then slowly slid backward as the water filled the lower compartments.

It had been many years since the Captain felt defeated. The last time was his divorce, which was completed in '09 after twelve years. He hated the crushing feeling that came with it, and this time it was worse than ever.

He had done the right thing, righted his wrong of taking part in Gundrum's scheme, but it didn't mask the guilt of sending his crew to their deaths.

He looked to the air. There were no choppers in sight. In a few moments, they would be chest deep in the ocean, where two violent beasts lurked.

He heard something in the distance. Rotors. He searched the skies again for Coast Guard choppers. No, not chopper rotors. Motors. Boat motors!

All hands looked to the east and cheered at the sight of Miguel and Gina riding the speedboat up to their hull.

Miguel remained at the helm, keeping a watchful eye on the dorsal fin, while Gina helped pull the crewmen up onto the craft. The herpetologist turned his eyes to the Captain and waved.

"You're missing half your ship, Captain," he remarked.

"Hope Gundrum had insurance," Seabolt replied. He started guiding his men to form an orderly line to be lowered to the speedboat, while Gina continued fishing out those who had already fallen overboard. The deck was only seven feet above the water and descending fast.

Fifty feet directly off the bow, the snake emerged, its head pointed to the west. Miguel glanced behind him and saw the dorsal fin. The megalodon detected the boat and was racing.

Frightened sailors pointed and shouted, while others helped Gina haul the last man up. She glanced back and saw the shark.

"Go!"

The thrust of the boat nearly sent several crewmembers falling back into the waves. The meg's jaws bit down behind them, snapping nothing but air and saltwater. It turned to pursue, only to find itself on another collision course with the snake.

Its head was cocked back and ready to strike. The megalodon closed the distance, then dove suddenly at the last second. Its tail vaulted in a catapult motion, smacking its caudal fin against the snake's head with the force of a piledriver. The snake reeled backward, surprised and stunned from the maneuver. It sank several feet, its senses hazed.

The megalodon closed in for another attack, this time rocketing upward at the stationary opponent. It bit down directly on its throat, sinking dozens of teeth into the jugular veins. Sudden pain and loss of blood sent the snake into a frenzy. All combat instinct disappeared, leaving a twirling, thrashing creature that resembled a worm on a hook.

Miguel had circled the speedboat back to the *Armstrong*, which was now less than three feet from going beneath the waves. He lined the boats up, allowing the crew to simply cross over.

"Slow. Take it easy. It's gonna be crowded," he reminded them.

"Can't be too slow," one of the crew said, glancing back to see the deck slip down to the waves. The men piled on, only to tremble in unison as the monsters' battle returned to the surface.

Miguel's blood boiled as he saw Eleven struggling in clear agony, its throat latched in the jaws of the meg. It let out a howling screech, its tail curling back and forth. The creature looked as though it was being electrified.

"Good God," Seabolt said in awe. "I think your pet's in trouble, Lucero." Miguel's hands strangled the helm. The sight of blood filling the ocean furthered his rage. The image of those evil jaws burying their teeth into Eleven's throat was burned into his brain. The snake was now on borrowed time, of which was dwindling faster as long as it stayed latched in those jaws.

Seabolt crossed over to his boat and put a hand on the young scientist's shoulder.

"Nothing you can do for him, son," he said.

"There's one thing!" Gina said. "Captain, do you still have Jason Nace's detonator?" The Captain swallowed hard.

"Yes…"

"Is the explosive still on the sub?"

"Yes?"

Gina could hear the unspoken question in his reply: *What are you thinking?* She hopped over the railing onto the *Armstrong*. The whole crew yelled at her.

"Hey! What are you doing?" one shouted.

"Miss! That boat's sinking in case you haven't noticed," another said.

"Gina!" Miguel's voice carried over the rest. He watched her sprint to the sub and open its hatch. "The hell are you doing?!"

"We've got to give your snake another chance," she called back. "If that shark gets away, it'll kill dozens, maybe hundreds more, before anyone can stop it! I'll radio you when I get close. I'll get out through the hatch, and you can detonate the charge."

Miguel started to reply, but the marine biologist had already slipped into the sub and sealed the hatch. She grasped the controls and watched the water spill over the bow. She rode the ship down into the ocean. The surface line swept the sphere, finally engulfing it completely.

Fully underwater, she saw the beasts wrestling fifteen degrees off her portside, three-hundred yards out. Eleven was still locked in the meg's jaws, its movements starting to slow. Gina breathed shakily. She worried she might be too late.

"Keep going," she told herself. *I can't give up now.* She applied thrust and followed the two beasts along their descent.

The megalodon yanked its head left and right, ripping its teeth along the snake's neck like sawblades. Gina watched its entire body spasm from the pain. The snake was still clinging to life, nor was it willing to accept defeat. It overcame its pain and constricted its tail around the megalodon's caudal fin.

Gina felt her blood rushing. The snake managed to slow the shark. But it was obvious it wouldn't be able to hold on for long. She accelerated to full speed. Two hundred feet to go.

The megalodon rolled, trying to free its tail. It dragged the snake, which was now spewing clouds of blood from its open mouth.

"Hang on. I'm almost there," she said. One-hundred feet. She grabbed her radio. "Captain, stand by with that detonator. I'm bailing out. Count to ten, and blow the charge."

"Gina..."

"If you don't do it, more people will die. Over and out." She dropped the radio and stood up on her seat. She sucked in a breath, closed her eyes, then opened the hatch. The ocean raced into the cockpit, soaking the controls.

Gina pulled herself over the edge then lifted her feet up, planting them over the reinforced glass. From there she leapt for the surface and paddled with every last ounce of energy. She opened her eyes, squinting from the initial sting, then glanced back. The sub's momentum carried it the remaining distance. It swirled underneath the shark, its lights flickering as power faded.

More than ten seconds passed. She was actually grateful...as she was still in the blast zone. She kicked and stroked, then emerged at the surface. She raised her hands to signal for the boat, wherever it was. She could hear its motors growing louder. To the right! She turned and saw the bow, its deck packed full of sailors. On the starboard side was Captain Seabolt, device in hand. He squeezed the trigger and watched the orange flash, followed immediately by a deafening *BOOM!*

Hit by an invisible force, the megalodon spiraled repeatedly to the right. The blast had opened up numerous gaping wounds along its left side. The concussion caused its jaws to open, releasing its equally dazed opponent.

Both creatures sank for several meters. For a few moments, the ocean was still. The only movement came from the speedboat that raced along the surface to rescue a lone swimmer.

Violent instinct kicked in like electricity from a backup generator. Its caudal fin swayed back and forth, and the megalodon was moving again. It swam out, getting some much needed water circulating through its gills. With its blood sufficiently oxygenated, the fish angled its body to make its run at the small prey above.

Miguel slowed the Seven Marine alongside Gina.

"Did it work?" she asked.

"Don't worry about it. Get in the boat," Miguel replied. Seabolt and another crewmember reached down for her. She reached up, her hand falling short. She tried again, nearly latched fingers, but slipped again. She tried propping on the hull for another go, then froze after her eyes went to the stern. Miguel glanced back and saw the seven-foot dorsal fin speeding their way.

"Go!" Gina shouted.

"Get her up," Miguel told Seabolt, ignoring her request. Seabolt reached again, this time managing to lock hands. Two other crewmen grabbed hold of her, getting her halfway up.

Miguel glanced back. The dorsal fin was less than a hundred yards away and closing rapidly.

"Shit," he muttered.

A blast of water struck his face. Like a dragon from ancient legend, Eleven raised its head from the water. It looked down at its caretaker, its neck horridly lacerated and spilling blood. Its jaw was partly slack, with rivers of blood spilling between its teeth. Miguel locked eyes with the creature for what he knew was the last time.

The Colossal Snake swiftly turned, its slack jaw now hyperextended into a frightful biting pose. Startled by its presence, the megalodon had circled back. It gained distance, ready to line itself for a final run to finish off the dying snake. Its caudal fin struck the water, launching it at incredible speed. The snake reared back and waited.

Water surged through its gills as the meg closed in. Its jaws extended, ready to bite.

The snake struck first, arching its long body upward to avoid the shark's mouth. It arched its neck and sank its teeth through the gill slits, getting a firm hold. Its body looped repeatedly around its midsection, and with the last of its energy, it squeezed.

The shark dove under the boat, taking the snake to the depths with it. Its stomach pressed against its cartilage skeleton. The snake put every last ounce of strength into the squeeze. It was not a constriction designed to suffocate, but to pulverize. Pressure mounted, rupturing the shark's insides. Organs compressed and split. The shark twisted into a corkscrew motion, but failed to loosen the snake's grip. It bit wildly, thrashing its head for anything to grab on to.

Dark blood streamed from its mouth, followed by bits of ruptured stomach contents. Its eyes bulged from their sockets, then popped out entirely. Blind, the megalodon struggled, swatting its tail and chomping the water.

Blood continued seeping from the snake's wounds. Its brain began to fog, its vision fading. It had lost all sense of smell. All it knew was that it had its mortal enemy in its grasp and could not let go.

With one final effort, its head and tail extended in different directions, tightening its body like a knot.

The shark's underbelly and back touched together like a tub of paste. The jaws opened wide, not to bite, but to make way for the flood of insides that ruptured out through its throat.

Still clutched over its enemy, the snake felt the brief satisfaction of victory. Its mind then faded to black, and together, the two beasts descended to the dark abyss.

CHAPTER 29

Miguel Lucero collapsed onto a bench, exhausted. He watched the cleanup crews move in and assist the injured. Reporters dashed from one victim to another, desperate to get their scoop.

The herpetologist glanced down at the tablet, its screen blank.

Gina sat down next to him, equally spent. The Seven Marine speedboat was commandeered by local authorities to assist in getting people out of the water. Most of the *Armstrong's* crewmen gathered by the bar and made a toast to their fallen companions.

The two scientists sat silently, reflecting on the consequences of their creations.

"It wasn't their fault," Gina finally said.

"Pardon," Miguel said.

"The megalodon. Eleven. They did what they were made to do," she said. "I just…hope you don't hate it for what it did."

Miguel shook his head. Hating the creature was out of the question. Regret and guilt for what it did, he would have to live with it. But hate? No. It had saved his life willingly at the expense of its own. One could argue that it was just responding to the chem-beacon. But something in Miguel's heart knew otherwise.

"Well, kids, it's been a blast," a sarcastic Seabolt said. He approached the bench and shook their hands.

"You'd better get that looked at," Gina said.

"That's on the agenda," Seabolt said. "That, and a very long job hunt."

Gina smiled. "Gotta pay that alimony, right?"

"Well, I'm sure the money Gundrum will pay to keep my mouth shut will help with that in the short-term. Plus my hazard pay." He gestured to his broken arm. "But after that, I suppose there's better companies to work for."

"You'll figure it out," Miguel said.

"No doubt. I already have a crew," Seabolt said proudly. "Maybe I'll get back in the fishing business. I feel I might have a knack for it. Nothing can be harder than hunting a ninety-foot shark, right?"

Miguel finally grinned.

"Only a hundred-foot shark."

"Don't give that asshole boss of yours any ideas," Seabolt said. He tipped his hat then rejoined his crew. Miguel sighed and watched the distant ocean. A helicopter appeared on the horizon. He watched it approach the beach and lower to the sand.

Gundrum.

Gina knew it too. She crossed her arms, dreading the bastard's inevitable approach.

"Any thoughts of keeping your job?"

Miguel snickered, a bit surprised by the question. Then again, she did know what working for Gundrum provided for him. Giving up such funding was not a simple thing.

He watched Marc Gundrum step out of the chopper. The guy was dressed in a fresh business suit, clearly intending to make a press appearance on how he would 'assist in helping those devastated by the atrocities.'

"Let me give my resignation," he replied. He stood up and walked toward his employer. Gundrum was visibly distrait, but Miguel knew it had nothing to do with the devastation and loss of life. He saw the scientists and faked a smile.

"Dr. Lucero. Dr. Hutson, I'm very glad you made it out of this alive," he said. He clutched his hands together and observed the aftermath of the attack. "Okay, obviously things didn't go as planned. I'll go ahead and set up some interviews. But all might not be lost. With your help, we might be able to pick up where we left off—"

Miguel's fist found its way to Gundrum's mouth. The businessman fell to the sand, stunned and half-conscious.

"Consider *that* as where we left off," he said. "Whether we revisit it is up to you."

Crewmen laughed as Gundrum floundered in the sand, completely dazed. Gina followed Miguel up the beach. A smile of satisfaction lined her face. The bastard deserved more, but it was still fulfilling.

"So, what are you going to do now?" she asked Miguel.

"Me?" He scrunched his shoulders. "Not sure. Perks of living at the lab, I've been able to bank almost every dime I've made. I think I'll take a little time off."

"Alone?"

"Hopefully not," he replied. Gina smiled and squeezed his hand. They gave one last glance to the ocean, then together they walked into town.

The End

CHECK OUT OTHER GREAT DEEP SEA THRILLERS

MEGA
by Jake Bible

There is something in the deep. Something large. Something hungry. Something prehistoric.
And Team Grendel must find it, fight it, and kill it.
Kinsey Thorne, the first female US Navy SEAL candidate has hit rock bottom. Having washed out of the Navy, she turned to every drink and drug she could get her hands on. Until her father and cousins, all ex-Navy SEALS themselves, offer her a way back into the life: as part of a private, elite combat Team being put together to find and hunt down an impossible monster in the Indian Ocean. Kinsey has a second chance, but can she live through it?

THE BLACK
by Paul E Cooley

Under 30,000 feet of water, the exploration rig Leaguer has discovered an oil field larger than Saudi Arabia, with oil so sweet and pure, nations would go to war for the rights to it. But as the team starts drilling exploration well after exploration well in their race to claim the sweet crude, a deep rumbling beneath the ocean floor shakes them all to their core. Something has been living in the oil and it's about to give birth to the greatest threat humanity has ever seen.

"The Black" is a techno/horror-thriller that puts the horror and action of movies such as Leviathan and The Thing right into readers' hands. Ocean exploration will never be the same."

SEVEREDPRESS

facebook.com/severedpress
twitter.com/severedpress

CHECK OUT OTHER GREAT DEEP SEA THRILLERS

PREDATOR X
by C.J Waller

When deep level oil fracking uncovers a vast subterranean sea, a crack team of cavers and scientists are sent down to investigate. Upon their arrival, they disappear without a trace. A second team, including sedimentologist Dr Megan Stoker, are ordered to seek out Alpha Team and report back their findings. But Alpha team are nowhere to be found – instead, they are faced with something unexpected in the depths. Something ancient. Something huge. Something dangerous. Predator X

DEAD BAIT
by Tim Curran

A husband hell-bent on revenge hunts a Wereshark...A Russian mail order bride with a fishy secret...Crabs with a collective consciousness...A vampire who transforms into a Candiru...Zombie piranha...Bait that will have you crawling out of your skin and more. Drawing on horror, humor with a helping of dark fantasy and a touch of deviance, these 19 contemporary stories pay homage to the monsters that lurk in the murky waters of our imaginations. If you thought it was safe to go back in the water...Think Again!

Printed in Great Britain
by Amazon

60279542R00121